FREEKS

ALSO BY AMANDA HOCKING

Switched

Torn

Ascend

Wake

Lullaby

Tidal

Elegy

Frostfire

Ice Kissed

Crystal Kingdom

FREEKS

AMANDA HOCKING

ST. MARTIN'S GRIFFIN NEW YORK

FREEKS. Copyright © 2016 by Amanda Hocking. All rights reserved. Printed in the United States of America. For information, address St. Martin's Press, 175 Fifth Avenue, New York, N.Y. 10010.

www.stmartins.com

Designed by Steven Seighman

Tarot card art by Shutterstock/Digital N

The Library of Congress Cataloging-in-Publication Data is available upon request.

ISBN 978-1-250-08477-4 (hardcover)
ISBN 978-1-250-08478-1 (e-book)

Our books may be purchased in bulk for promotional, educational, or business use. Please contact your local bookseller or the Macmillan Corporate and Premium Sales Department at 1-800-221-7945, extension 5442, or by e-mail at MacmillanSpecialMarkets@macmillan.com.

First Edition: January 2017

10 9 8 7 6 5 4 3 2 1

There is no exquisite beauty without some strangeness in the proportion.

—EDGAR ALLAN POE

FREEKS

prologue

Behind me, the branches and trees crunched and snapped as the creature tore through them.

I didn't scream—there was no one who could come to help me, nothing that could stop the monster that lurched behind me. The only thing I could do was run faster.

Then the ground gave way beneath me. Under the pale moonlight, the tall grass and thick forest made it hard for me to see where I was going, and it was already too late when I felt my foot squelching down into the dense mud of the surrounding swamp.

I fell forward and tried to climb to higher ground, but the ground had swallowed my legs up. There wasn't enough time for me to get free.

It was close enough that I could smell the sulfur on its breath. I could hear the beast behind me—it made a strange high-pitched guttural sound, like a demonic squeal of delight.

Grabbing a broken branch, I turned around to face the creature as it tore through the trees toward me. I brandished the branch like a weapon. If I was going down, I was going down swinging.

FRIDAY, MARCH 13, 1987

1. premonitions

My feet rested against the dashboard of the Winnebago as we lumbered down the road, the second vehicle in a small caravan of beat-up trailers and motorhomes.

The sun hadn't completely risen yet, but it was light enough that I could see outside. Not that there was much to see. The bridge stretched on for miles across Lake Tristeaux, and I could see nothing but the water around us, looking gray in the early morning light.

The AC had gone out sometime in Texas, and we wouldn't have the money to fix it until after this stint in Caudry, if we were lucky. I'd cracked the window, and despite the chill, the air felt thick with humidity. That's why I never liked traveling to the southeastern part of the country—too humid and too many bugs.

But we took the work that we got, and after a long dry spell waiting in Oklahoma for something to come up, I was grateful for this. We all were. If we hadn't gotten the recommendation to Caudry, I'm not sure what we would've done, but we were spending our last dimes and nickels just to make it down here.

I stared ahead at Gideon's motorhome in front of us. The whole thing had been painted black with brightly colored designs swirling around it, meant to invoke images of mystery and magic. The name "Gideon Davorin's Traveling Sideshow" was painted across the back and both the sides. Once sparkles had outlined it, but they'd long since worn off.

My eyelids began to feel heavy, but I tried to ward off sleep. The radio in the car was playing old Pink Floyd songs that my mom hummed along to, and that wasn't helping anything.

"You can go lay down in the back," Mom suggested.

She did look awake, her dark gray eyes wide and a little frantic, and both her hands gripped the wheel. Rings made of painted gold and cheap stones adorned her fingers, glinting as the sun began to rise over the lake, and black vine tattoos wrapped around her hands and down her arms.

For a while, people had mistaken us for sisters since we looked so much alike. The rich caramel skin we both shared helped keep her looking young, but the strain of recent years had begun to wear on her, causing crow's-feet to sprout around her eyes and worried creases to deepen in her brow.

I'd been slouching low in the seat but I sat up straighter. "No, I'm okay."

"We're almost there. I'll be fine," she insisted.

"You say we're almost there, but it feels like we're driving across the Gulf of Mexico," I said, and she laughed. "We've probably reached the Atlantic by now."

She'd been driving the night shift, which was why I was

hesitant to leave her. We normally would've switched spots about an hour or two ago, with me driving while she lay down. But since we were so close to our destination, she didn't see the point in it.

On the worn padded bench beside the dining table, Blossom Mandelbaum snored loudly, as if to remind us we both should be sleeping. I glanced back at her. Her head lay at a weird angle, propped up on a cushion, and her brown curls fell around her face.

Ordinarily, Blossom would be in the Airstream she shared with Carrie Lu, but since Carrie and the Strongman had started dating (and he had begun staying over in their trailer), Blossom had taken to crashing in our trailer sometimes to give them privacy.

It wasn't much of a bother when she slept here, and in fact, my mom kind of liked it. As one of the oldest members of the carnival—both in age and in the length of time she'd been working here—my mom had become a surrogate mother to many of the runaways and lost souls that found us.

Blossom was two years younger than me, on the run from a group home that didn't understand her or what she could do, and my mom had been more than happy to take her under her wing. The only downside was her snoring.

Well, that and the telekinesis.

"Mara," Mom said, her eyes on the rearview mirror. "She's doing it again."

"What?" I asked, but I'd already turned around to look back over the seat.

At first I didn't know what had caught my mom's eye, but

then I saw it—the old toaster we'd left out on the counter was now floating in the air, hovering precariously above Blossom's head.

The ability to move things with her mind served Blossom well when she worked as the Magician's Assistant in Gideon's act, but it could be real problematic sometimes. She had this awful habit of unintentionally pulling things toward her when she was dreaming. At least a dozen times, she'd woken up to books and tapes dropping on her. Once my mom's favorite coffee mug had smacked her right in the head.

"Got it," I told my mom, and I unbuckled my seat belt and went over to get it.

The toaster floated in front of me, as if suspended by a string, and when I grabbed it, Blossom made a snorting sound and shifted in her sleep. I turned around with the toaster under my arm, and I looked in front of us just in time to see Gideon's trailer skid to the side of the road and nearly smash into the guardrail.

"Mom! Look out!" I shouted.

Mom slammed on the brakes, causing most of our possessions in the trailer to go hurtling to the floor, and I slammed into the seat in front of me before also falling to the floor. The toaster slipped from my grasp and clattered into the dashboard.

Fortunately, there was no oncoming traffic, but I could hear the sound of squealing tires and honking behind us as the rest of the caravan came to an abrupt stop.

"What happened?" Blossom asked, waking up in a daze from where she'd landed beneath the dining table.

"Mara!" Mom had already leapt from her seat and crouched in front of where I still lay on the worn carpet. "Are you okay?"

"Yeah, I'm fine," I assured her.

"What about you?" Mom reached out, brushing back Blossom's frizzy curls from her face. "Are you all right?"

Blossom nodded. "I think so."

"Good." That was all the reassurance my mom needed, and then she was on her feet and jumping out of the Winnebago. "Gideon!"

"What happened?" Blossom asked again, blinking the sleep out of her dark brown eyes.

"I don't know. Gideon slammed on his brakes for some reason." I stood up, moving much slower than my mother.

We had very narrowly avoided crashing into Gideon. He'd overcorrected and jerked to the other side of the road, so his motorhome was parked at an angle across both lanes of the highway.

"Is everyone okay?" Blossom had sat up, rubbing her head, and a dark splotch of a bruise was already forming on her forehead. That explained why she seemed even foggier than normal—she'd hit her head pretty good.

"I hope so. I'll go check it out," I said. "Stay here."

By the time I'd gotten out, Seth Holden had already gotten out of the motorhome behind us. Since he was the Strongman, he was usually the first to rush into an accident. He wanted to help if he could, and he usually could.

"Lyanka, I'm fine," Gideon was saying to my mother, his British accent sounding firm and annoyed.

"You are not fine, *albi*," Mom said, using a term of affection despite the irritation in her voice.

I rounded the back of his motorhome to find Gideon leaning against it with my mom hovering at his side. Seth reached them first, his T-shirt pulled taut against his muscular torso.

"What's going on? What happened?" Seth asked.

"Nothing. I just dozed off for a second." Gideon waved it off. "Go tell everyone I'm fine. I just need a second, and we'll be on our way again."

"Do you want me to drive for you?" Seth asked. "Carrie can handle the Airstream."

Gideon shook his head and stood up straighter. "I've got it. We're almost there."

"All right." Seth looked uncertainly at my mom, and she nodded at him. "I'll leave you in Lyanka's care and get everyone settled down."

As soon as Seth disappeared back around the motorhome, loudly announcing that everything was fine to everyone else, Gideon slumped against the trailer. His black hair had fallen over his forehead. The sleeves of his shirt were rolled up, revealing the thick black tattoos that covered both his arms.

"Gideon, what's really going on?" Mom demanded with a worried tremor.

He swallowed and rubbed his forehead. "I don't know."

Even though the sun was up now, the air seemed to have gotten chillier. I pulled my sweater tighter around me and walked closer to them. Gideon leaned forward, his head bowed down, and Mom rubbed his back.

"You didn't fall asleep, did you?" I asked.

Gideon lifted his eyes, looking as though he didn't know I was there. And guessing by how pained he was allowing himself to look, he probably hadn't. Gideon was only in his early thirties, but right now, he appeared much older than that.

That wasn't what scared me, though. It was how dark his blue eyes were. Normally, they were light, almost like the sky. But whenever he'd had a vision or some kind of premonition, his eyes turned so dark they were nearly black.

"It was a headache," Gideon said finally.

"There's something off here," Mom said. "I felt it as soon as we got on the bridge. I knew we should turn back, but I hoped that maybe I was imagining things. Now that I look at you, I know."

That explained that frantic look in her eyes I'd seen earlier in the Winnebago, and how alert she'd been even though she'd been awake and driving for nearly twenty hours straight. Mom didn't see things in the way Gideon did, but she had her own senses.

"It's fine, Lyanka," Gideon insisted. He straightened up again, and his eyes had begun to lighten. "It was only a migraine, but it passed. I am capable of having pain without supernatural reasons too."

Mom crossed her arms over her chest, and her lips were pressed into a thin line. "We should go back."

"We're almost there." Gideon gestured to the end of the road, and I looked ahead for the first time and realized that we could see land. The town was nestled right up to the lake, and we couldn't be more than ten minutes outside the city limits.

"We could still turn around," Mom suggested.

"We can't." He put his hands on her arms to ease her worries. "We don't have any money, love. The only way we can go is forward."

"Gideon." She sighed and stared up at the sky, the violet fabric of her dress billowing out around her as the wind blew over us, then she looked back at him. "Are you sure you're okay to drive?"

"Yes, I'm sure. Whatever pain I had, it's passed." He smiled to reassure her. "We should go before the others get restless."

She lowered her eyes, but when he leaned in to kiss her, she let him. She turned to go back to our motorhome, and as she walked past me, she muttered, "I knew we should never travel on Friday the thirteenth. No good ever comes of it."

I'd waited until she'd gone around the corner to turn back to Gideon, who attempted to give me the same reassuring smile he'd given my mom.

"We could go back," I said. "There's always a way. We've made it on less before."

"Not this time, darling." He shook his head. "And there's no reason to. Leonid assured me there'd be a big payday here, and I've got no reason to doubt him. We can make a go of it here."

"As long as you're sure we'll be okay."

"I haven't steered you all wrong yet." Gideon winked at me then, but he was telling the truth. In the ten years that my mom and I had been following him around the country, he'd always done the best he could by us.

I went back and got into the Winnebago with my mom and Blossom. Within a couple minutes, Gideon had straightened out his motorhome, and the caravan was heading back down the road. At the end of the bridge was a large sign that read WELCOME TO CAUDRY, POPULATION 13,665.

As soon as we crossed the line into town, the air seemed even colder than before. That's when I realized the chill wasn't coming from outside—it was coming from within me.

2. caudry

Pulling my denim jacket tighter around me, I wandered down the streets of Caudry. After spending the day setting up, I'd decided to go out on my own and explore the town for myself. Despite the initial dark premonitions, setup had been rather uneventful.

Camp had been set up on the edge of town, right along a thick forest that bled into the wetlands, behind the fairgrounds. If I ventured too far from the trailers in the wrong direction, the ground gave way to sticky mud hidden in tall grass. The trees around seemed to bend forward and lean down, as if their branches were reaching out for us. Long vines and Spanish moss grew over everything, and I swore I'd never seen a place so green before.

After the sun finally set and the heat of the day began to break, everyone settled in, happy to rest after many hours on the road. All of the base camp was set up, and we'd begun getting the carnival ready to open tomorrow afternoon.

Even though I hadn't gotten much sleep, I was too restless to just stay in the motorhome. I slid out quietly, moving between the trailers to avoid someone stopping me or asking to tag along. Living in the carnival like this meant I was almost never alone, and sometimes I just needed to get out by myself and clear my head.

I didn't have to walk that far until I'd made it into Caudry town proper, and it was just as green as the outskirts of town where we were camped. Buildings seemed prone to a mossy growth on their sides, and the streetlamps had orbs of light glowing around them, thanks to the humidity.

While the center of town appeared more like any of the other hundreds of towns I'd visited before—all bright and clean and shiny and new—the peripheral parts were like ghostly reminders of a long history. I stuck to the side streets, hiding away from the glossier parts of Caudry.

On a street called Joliet Avenue, I found an area that must have been glorious in its prime. Huge houses verging on mansions lined the streets, hidden behind willows and cypresses towering above them. The streets were cobblestone, but they had begun to wear and crack, with grass and weeds growing up between them.

As I walked down the street, I heard the faint sounds of a party several houses down. It was a strange juxtaposition of the fading gothic beauty of the neighborhood with the rock music—one of Bon Jovi's latest hits, "You Give Love a Bad Name"—and new cars parked in front of it.

A wrought-iron fence separated me from the party house. Large stone posts flanked either side of an open gate, and

I paused at the end of the driveway. It curved in front of the house, and it was overflowing with parked cars, including a cherry red '86 Mustang that stood out sharply against the white mansion.

Every window in the house was on, making the house glimmer on the darkened street. At one time, it had probably been nestled on the edge of a plantation, but the town had grown up around it, burying it in suburban streets and overgrown trees.

White streamers were strung from the overhanging branches of the trees, making it seem as if the trees had extended their grasp, reaching closer to the ground to snatch anyone who got close.

The house loomed over the street, reminding me of a monster from a slasher flick, and neither the neon balloons attached to columns nor the brightly dressed partygoers could shake it.

It was a massive two-story white antebellum manor, with a balcony supported by thick columns. Some of the party guests had drifted out onto it, singing along to the music that blasted from the stereo.

Still standing on the cobblestones at the end of the driveway, I was near enough that I could see the people fairly well, dancing and laughing on the brightly lit balcony. A guy sat on the railing of the second-floor balcony, drinking from a red plastic cup.

With his back to the street, the popped collar of his silver blazer blocked his face. Slowly, he turned away from the party. His brown hair was pushed back, and he surveyed the parking lot that the front yard had become.

Then I felt his eyes settle on me. I was hidden in the shadows of the street, so he wouldn't be able to see me. Or at least he shouldn't have been able to. But there was something about his expression—the furrow of his brow, the shadow across his eyes—and I was certain that he was looking right at me.

I smiled at him and tried to quiet my heart hammering in my chest. There was nothing about this that should have my pulse racing so fast. But then he returned my smile.

A brand-new Mercedes squealed to a stop at the end of the driveway, and I took that as my cue to move on. The passengers tumbled out of their car, laughing loudly, and I stepped away from the driveway.

As the couple from the Mercedes walked toward the house, the guy stumbled, but his female companion held him up so he wouldn't fall. He wore dark sunglasses even though it was past ten at night and smiled at me as they approached.

I smiled politely, meaning to just continue on my exploration of Caudry, but as I slid by, the guy reached out and grabbed my arm.

"Where are you going?" He'd turned to face me, and he let go of me so he could push down his sunglasses.

"Logan, we don't know her," the girl said, sounding annoyed.

Her black hair was permed and fluffed into a perfect coif, and her crimson lipstick stood out against her light brown skin. She wore a skin-tight leopard-print minidress with shiny red pumps, and I'm not sure how she managed to keep her footing while steadying her friend.

"Are you sure?" He tilted his head, looking up at me.

"No, we haven't had the pleasure of meeting. I'm Mara, and I'm assuming that you're Corey Hart," I said with a wry smile.

"Funny." He glanced back at the girl in the leopard-print

dress. "She's funny." He straightened up and turned back to me. "It's a party in there, and you should go in." Then he gestured wildly to the neighborhood and shouted, "Everyone should come!"

"*Logan!*" The girl tried to hush him.

"You see her?" Logan pointed to the girl. She stumbled as she tried to hold him up, and I reached out, grabbing on to his arm to help steady them before they both fell back. "This is my beautiful girlfriend Selena, and tonight is her twenty-first birthday. So everyone should help her celebrate, even you . . . strange girl I've never seen before."

I'd only wandered out with the intention of seeing Caudry and clearing my head, and I shouldn't stay out too late since we'd have even more setting up to do in the morning. But it would be a nice change to spend time in a house instead of a stuffy old trailer.

"If I wouldn't be an intrusion," I said, looking to Selena to confirm that it was okay.

"My boyfriend is a drunken mess," Selena said with a half-smile. "But he's right. This is my big party, so if you want to join, you can. If not, I'll just drag this idiot in myself."

"Well, since it's your birthday, I should at least help you get him to the house," I said.

"Thank you." Selena offered me a grateful smile as Logan threw his other arm around my shoulders.

"The more, the merrier!" Logan laughed as Selena and I started leading him up to the house.

I glanced up at the balcony to see if the guy was still up there, but I didn't get a good look. Helping Selena with Logan required all my concentration, since he barely seemed capable of standing on his feet. I had no idea how she would've managed it on her own, even without the heels.

"Logan decided to start with birthday cocktails early tonight," Selena explained as we weaved between the cars parked in the driveway. "Even though it's *my* birthday, he thought he needed to go celebrate out at the bar while I was having a party here. And then he called me to pick him up, so I had to leave my own party to get him."

"Hey, hey." Logan held up a finger and tried to defend himself. "Happy birthday." He tried to kiss her on the cheek, and she leaned away.

"You're still gonna be in the doghouse when you sober up," Selena told him.

When we opened the front door, we had to push through people to get to the living room. The entry opened into a massive front hall, with a curved staircase and a chandelier, and even that area was filled to capacity.

As we walked farther into the house, it didn't get any less crowded. If I had to guess, I would say that Selena had invited the entire teenage population of Caudry, along with a chunk of southern Louisiana.

When we finally made it to the living room, Selena dropped Logan unceremoniously on a white leather sofa.

"There," Selena said, speaking loudly to be heard over the music and the people talking. She smoothed out her dress and stared down at her boyfriend, who appeared to be on the brink of passing out.

"At least he can't cause trouble when he's sleeping," I said.

"You would think so, but knowing him, he'll find a way." Selena turned and smiled at me. "You have to at least have a drink, for helping me."

"No, that's okay." I shook my head and smiled. "I don't really drink anyway."

"I'll get you a soda or something, then," Selena said. "Lugging that idiot around was hard work." She gestured to Logan, who had already begun to snore. "You deserve at least one drink."

I'd been to parties before, but never ones like this. Not only was it packed, but everyone here was dressed like they came off MTV or out of a teen magazine. They were all flashy and bright, while I wore a flowing skirt and a denim jacket almost as old as I was.

"Just one drink!" Selena was backing away. "Stay right here, and I'll be right back."

She disappeared into the crowd, presumably running off somewhere to get me a soda. I'd planned on waiting for her to return with it, but people kept bumping into me as they tried to get by.

From the outside, the house had looked glorious—albeit foreboding—and now that I was inside, I was thrilled at the prospect of being able to see it on my own. After spending the past decade living in a motorhome, one of my guiltiest pleasures was looking around actual houses, and I'd never been in one quite as nice as this.

It was a strange setup. The classic antebellum architecture clashed against the ultra-modern plastic furnishings, looking more like they belonged in a showroom in New York than in a two-hundred-year-old house in the Deep South.

Next to the plantation shutters was a round sofa in bright red. A giant shiny white sculpture sat in one corner, but I hadn't the faintest idea what it was supposed to be. An Andy Warhol print hung on one wall, with a Piet Mondrian on another.

Many of the pieces I recognized from the books I'd picked up in my travels. There wasn't much to do on the road, so I spent most of the time with my head in a book.

I'd edged my way out of the living room and went into what I can only guess was another sitting room—this one furnished as garishly as the last—but stopped when I caught sight of another painting.

It was an anarchist drawing of graffiti-style writing and paint smeared haphazardly across it, with a cartoon wolf in a top hat lusting after sausage. The only colors were beige, black, white, and red, and there was something abrasive yet captivating about it.

"*Wolf Sausage*," a guy said from behind.

When I turned back to see who was speaking, my heart skipped a beat. It was *him*. The guy from the balcony.

The first thing I noticed—after his eyes, which I could finally see up close were an amazing dark golden brown—was how tall he was. While I'm on the short side, he stood nearly a foot taller than me, and the way he kept his chestnut hair pushed back probably added another inch to him.

He had this imposing presence to him, even though his tone had been friendly, and part of me felt like I should be afraid. It wasn't that he was handsome—though he was. Dark arched eyebrows, high cheekbones, and a hint of something devilish playing on the smile on his lips—almost like Jim Morrison but with his short hair tamed instead of Morrison's uncontrolled mane.

I couldn't really define it—not what should've frightened me about him, and not what made me defy that fear. But it was there, quickening my pulse and heightening my senses, and I found myself smiling back at him.

"What?" I asked before I'd gone too long staring at him without speaking.

"The painting," he said, but he kept his eyes on me. "It's by Jean-Michel Basquiat, and it's called *Wolf Sausage*."

I glanced back at the picture and noticed that both the words "wolf" and "sausage" had been written on it several times. "That seems like an apt title."

"Yeah, it is." An amused smile curled up at the edge of his lips, but his eyes narrowed slightly, as if inspecting me. "I saw you outside."

"You may have," I said, pretending not to know what he was talking about. "I was enjoying the night air."

"Are you a friend of Selena's, then?" he asked.

Before I could answer, he reached out suddenly and pushed me to the side so a few people could get by. They were laughing loudly and liquid sloshed out of their plastic cups. I would've found myself covered in beer if he hadn't moved me out of the way.

To save me from getting soaked, he'd put his arm around my waist, pulling me closer to him. Our bodies weren't touching—not exactly, but when he breathed deeply, his chest pressed against mine.

I considered staying in his arms, but that would probably

seem creepy and weird since we'd just met. As soon as the people had gone by, I moved away from him, and he dropped his arm.

"So you never answered my question," he said. "Are you friends with Selena?"

"Kind of, I guess. I just met her."

"Hmm," he said, almost as if he didn't believe me, and I met his gaze evenly. "How did you get invited to this party exactly?"

"There you are!" Selena shouted, saving me from an explanation, as she hurried over to us with a can of Pepsi. "I was afraid you'd left."

"Nope. I'm still here," I said.

She handed me the can. "I wasn't sure what kind you'd like, so I hope this is fine."

I smiled. "Pepsi is great, thanks."

"So. I see you met my little brother." Selena put her elbow on his shoulder, attempting to lean on him, but since he was much taller than her too, it left her at a comically awkward angle. "I don't know what Mom and Dad fed him as a kid, but he just wouldn't stop growing."

He glanced down at his sister. "We were just talking about how you two know each other."

"Logan is completely smashed, and she helped me haul him inside," Selena explained, straightening up so she wasn't leaning on him so inelegantly.

"And yet Logan is still the best boyfriend you've had so far," he said with a thin smile.

Selena swatted him on the arm, but kept her attention on me. "I know you said your name outside, but I'm sorry, it's totally slipped my mind."

"Mara," I said.

"Mara?" her brother repeated.

I nodded. "Mara Beznik."

"Gabe Alvarado." He held his hand out for me to shake. "Nice to meet you."

"Likewise," I said as his hand enveloped mine.

"And I'm Selena Alvarado." She leaned forward, interjecting her hand, so I shook it. "Anyway. This is my party, so I should mingle. But I do hope you stay and have fun." She stepped back, then clapped Gabe on the arm. "Play nice."

"I always do," he told her.

"Well, I don't want to be a party crasher," I said after Selena had disappeared into the party. "I should probably head out."

"You're not crashing," Gabe insisted. "You promised my sister you'd stay for a drink, so you should at the very least do that."

"I guess I can." I opened the soda and sipped slowly from it. "So this is your house?"

"Well, my parents' house, but yeah, I live here with them and my sister." He looked around, as if noticing how grand the house was for the first time.

"It's a nice place," I said, admiring it. "Your parents don't mind that you're having a party?"

"Well, they're out of town for tonight," he admitted, looking around. "But they're used to there being huge parties. My uncle Beau used to have these big blowouts every spring, and people from all over the country would come."

My eyes widened. "Wow. And I thought *this* party was big."

"Yeah." He leaned closer to me then. "It's kind of noisy down here. Why don't we go someplace quieter so we can talk?"

I'd been taking a drink from my Pepsi, and I had to put my hand over my mouth when I started laughing.

"What?" Gabe straightened up, a confused expression on his face.

"I didn't know people actually used that line." I wiped at the soda from my mouth and smirked up at him. "Does it usually work?"

"Sometimes, yeah." He nodded. "So?"

"So what?" I asked.

"So I do want to talk to you." He stared down at me, a smile playing on his lips, but his eyes were hopeful. "And it is awfully loud down here. Will you go someplace quieter to talk? I promise I won't try anything else." He paused. "Not unless you want me to."

I looked up at him and considered my options. I could leave this party and walk back to my trailer, where my mother and Blossom would already be asleep, and I'd either finish my V. C. Andrews novel or go to sleep myself.

Or I could stay here at this party and talk to this guy with bedroom eyes. Maybe he'd try to kiss me, and if he was nice enough, I might even let him. Or not, but the option of a real kiss was almost always better than a night in bed with a book.

"Okay," I said finally. "Let's go someplace quiet."

"Excellent." He grinned.

3. arcana

Your bedroom?" I asked with a cocked eyebrow. "Really?"

Gabe stood in the doorway with a look of exaggerated innocence. He'd flicked on the light and gestured back to the room behind him.

"It's just quiet. That's it," he assured me. "And there's plenty of room. So you don't even have to sit anywhere near me."

I leaned forward, peering into his room, surprised by how spacious it was. It was probably bigger than my whole trailer, but I would never tell him that. His unmade bed had to be at least twice the size of the narrow twin mattress I slept on every night.

A small TV with a Nintendo hooked up to it sat on a dresser, and a beanbag chair sat in front of it. Band posters covered the walls, mostly for INXS and The Smiths, but there was one of a scantily clad Madonna. The stereo in the corner was buried underneath cassette tapes and records.

Dirty clothes were overflowing from a hamper. Otherwise,

it looked fairly clean for a teenage guy's room. Or at least compared to the guys' rooms I'd seen.

"What do you say?" Gabe asked, leaning on his door with an imploring look in his eyes. "Are you in or are you out?"

"Well, I have come this far already." I sighed dramatically, causing Gabe to laugh a little as I stepped into his room.

"You made the right call."

He shut the bedroom door behind me, instantly muffling the noise of the party. The voices were almost silent, but the thumping bass from Run-D.M.C. still made it through the walls.

"Why don't I put on music?" Gabe suggested. "But at a much more reasonable decibel."

I slipped off my jacket and tossed it on his bed, while he rummaged through his cassettes. "Sure."

"Do you like U2?" Gabe asked as he adjusted the volume.

"I don't know," I admitted. "I haven't heard that much by them."

While he played around with his stereo, I walked around, admiring his room.

The sense of permanence I felt in this room was something I would never feel in my trailer. No faux paneling. No crank-operated skylights that leaked whenever it rained. This was a home, and I couldn't help but feel a twinge of envy. Not necessarily of Gabe, but just of being able to have a life like this, of having a home that didn't change location every week.

"So," Gabe said when he finished adjusting his stereo, and music played softly.

I stood at the far wall and looked back at him over my shoulder.

His mouth was open slightly, and he stared at me with the strangest expression on his face. I waited a moment for him to say something, but when he didn't, I began to feel self-conscious and rubbed at my arms left bare from my sleeveless lace top.

"What?" I asked finally.

"Nothing." An embarrassed smile broke out on his face, and he shook his head.

I sat down on the bed, and he waited a beat before sitting beside me. "Have you lived here a long time?"

"Not really. I was actually born here, but we moved away for a while. We just came back this past summer." He motioned around us. "This is actually the family home, like, my grandparents owned it, and their parents before them, and on and on."

"I thought I hadn't detected a Southern accent," I commented.

"No, I grew up in upstate New York. My mom has a strong accent, but the rest of us don't."

"So are you glad to be back down here?" I asked.

"I don't know. If I'm being honest, I didn't really wanna come back. I was supposed to be starting college this past fall, and I had everything all planned."

"How did you end up here?"

"My mom's brother died, and he left us the house and everything. Since it's the family estate, my mom refused to sell it, and she insisted that I postpone all my plans for higher education and come back here. Selena was more than happy to drop out, but I'd been looking forward to NYU."

"That seems like a weird thing for a parent to insist," I said.

"I don't have any experience with higher education, but I thought that parents usually pushed for you to go."

"Yeah, my mom can be strange sometimes." He shook his head. "What about you?"

"I'm mostly just passing through." I evaded the question as best I could. Things always went much better when people didn't know I lived with a traveling carnival.

He leaned back, and I felt his eyes searching me again. "So, what are you, some kind of vagabond?"

"What?" I laughed to cover up how caught off-guard I felt. "Why do you ask that?"

"I don't know." He shrugged. "You implied that you're traveling soon, and you kinda look bohemian."

"How do bohemians look?" I asked.

"Like you?" he asked, then shrugged. "I don't know. I think it's the earrings."

My earrings were dangling feathers, and I touched one. "The feathers? Madonna has an earring like this."

He looked down and pointed to my arms. "What about those? Do they mean anything?"

All down my left forearm, I had tattoos of little black paw prints leaving a trail from my inner elbow down to my wrist. I touched them when Gabe leaned over to get a better look. He was so close, I could smell the mousse in his hair, clean and fresh.

"Not really. I just thought it'd be cool."

"They are pretty cool," Gabe agreed.

He reached out to touch them, and the light umber skin of his hand was nearly as dark as my own. His fingers trailed across my skin, sending small tingles down my arm everywhere he touched.

Then he stopped and leaned back to look up at me. His eyes were mesmerizing, but it was his mouth that really caught me. His lips seemed to have this permanent smile at the edges, even when he wasn't really grinning, like he knew some kind of private joke.

His eyes weren't enchanting because of the rich color, but because of the wicked glimmer to them. Somehow, even when I was outside and too far away to really see, I'd noticed that gleam—a promise of something a little sinful and dangerous—that made my heart pound loudly. As he looked at me now, I felt my pulse quicken and heat flush my skin.

That's what I'd thought I should've feared when I was downstairs, but in truth, it was that glint of something else that had actually brought me here.

"Do you have any more tattoos?" he asked.

"A couple. But they're hidden under my clothes."

He smiled crookedly. "Maybe I can see them some other time then."

I laughed but didn't disagree with him. "What about you? Do you have any tattoos?"

"None yet, but it's for the best. My parents would kill me if I got one."

The music stopped, followed by the sound of the tape clicking a few seconds later. Gabe got up and went over to the stereo so he could switch it over. While he was up, he took off his blazer and tossed it on his hamper, leaving him in just a white T-shirt that fit nicely over his toned frame.

The music started playing again, and Gabe sat down next to me again, sitting closer than he had before, but I didn't comment on the mere inches between us. He leaned back a bit so he propped himself up on his elbows.

When he did, his shirt rode up just a little bit, exposing the smooth flesh above his jeans. I saw the hint of the outlines of his muscles before he pulled his shirt back down, covering himself, and I looked away before he caught me staring at him.

"I just realized something," Gabe said. "We've been talking about me the whole time, and you've hardly said anything about yourself."

I shrugged. "There's not much to tell."

"Oh, I really doubt that. You're all dark and mysterious." He swirled his hand in front of me, as if to emphasize the mystery. "I bet you're filled with untold secrets."

I laughed. "I'm not, really."

"Prove it," he challenged me. "Tell me a secret. *Any* secret."

"Okay." I bit my lip, thinking. "What constitutes a secret?"

"Something you've never told anyone before."

"Not anyone ever?" I asked.

He shook his head resolutely. "Nope."

I leaned back and crossed my leg over my knee as I thought. Truthfully, I had plenty of secrets. But it was hard to think of something that I would want this guy to know.

"You tell me something first, then I'll tell you something."

"Okay." He nodded. "Now I'm getting a read on who you are, sneaking around the rules like that."

"It's your game, so it only seems fair that I get to name my own terms. Now, it's your turn. What's your secret?"

He absently pulled at a string on his comforter, or at least he tried to do it absently. But his hand was right next to mine, so when he tugged at the string, his long fingers brushed against my hand.

When I didn't say anything or move away, he lifted his eyes to meet mine. His smile had fallen away, and though his expression was serious, I could still see the hint of something wicked. Even now, when he was dropping his pretenses and preparing for a confession, he couldn't completely get rid of the darkness that drew me to him.

"I really want to kiss you," Gabe said finally.

"You've never told anyone that before?" I asked with a smile. "You've never wanted to kiss anyone?"

"Well, I've never told anyone that I wanted to kiss you, the mysterious Mara Beznik, before," he clarified.

I laughed lightly. "Why do I feel like you've played this game before?"

"I haven't. I swear," he insisted, but I wasn't sure that I believed him.

"So why haven't you?"

"I don't know." He shook his head, still smiling up at me. "It doesn't seem to be working, so maybe it's not such a great game."

"No, I meant, if you want to kiss me, why haven't you yet?" I asked.

"I guess because I didn't realize it was an option. I thought you might slap me or . . ."

His words died on his lips because I leaned down and kissed him. He was already so close, but to avoid an awkward angle, I had to lay down next to him.

When my lips pressed against his, there was a hesitation. Gabe was tentative at first, as if he thought this might be some kind of trick, but when he realized it wasn't, he kissed me fully. His tongue parted my lips, bold and hungry. He put his hand on my side, to pull me closer to him.

My shirt had ridden up, so his hand was pressed to the bare skin of my side, and the instant I felt his skin against mine, a cold pain jolted through me. A blast of arctic air suddenly surged over me—through me, really, piercing my heart like a jagged icicle.

I pulled away in surprise, and for a split second, I couldn't breathe.

But then it was gone. The chill, the pain, everything had disappeared almost the instant it had started.

"Are you okay?" Gabe sat up, and when I braved looking up at him, I saw the concern in his eyes, warming the burnt caramel color.

"It's nothing." I smiled, but it didn't come as easily as I liked.

"You sure?" he asked.

"Yeah. I just got a chill. That's all." I tried to play it down, not just for him but for myself. "Now. Where were we?"

Gabe looked down at me for a few moments longer, as if to decide whether he believed me or not. I must've been convincing because an easy grin returned to his face.

"Let me think. I believe you were right about here." He put his hand on my waist, and when I didn't recoil, he pulled me back down so I was lying on the bed. "And I was right about here."

His lips hovered right above mine, as close as they could be without touching, and he searched my eyes, almost daring me to kiss him again. But I'd kissed him the first time, and now I was waiting for him to make the move.

Finally, after what felt like an eternity of anticipation, he closed his eyes and his lips found mine. His hand was still on my waist from when he pulled me back down, and the instant our mouths met, his hand tightened, gripping me, and I wrapped my arms around him.

SATURDAY, MARCH 14, 1987

4. judgment

The bed felt luscious underneath me. I hated sleeping in the Winnebago when it wasn't moving, but being on a real mattress and wrapped in the downy comforters, I couldn't help but sleep well. It was how I imagined napping in a cloud would feel.

Morning sunlight streamed in through the curtains when I opened my eyes, and I stretched. The house was completely silent, so I'd guessed that the party had finally come to an end. When I'd fallen asleep late last night, the sound of the bass had still been thumping through the walls.

I sat up and peered over the edge of the bed to see Gabe lying on the floor. A pillow was smashed under his head, and his hair that had been so carefully smoothed out last night stuck out at all angles. The blanket draped over him had slipped off, revealing the bare bronze skin of his chest.

When I'd fallen asleep, he'd had his shirt on, so I'm not sure exactly when he'd ditched it. Not that I minded getting a view of it this morning. He was more toned than I'd initially thought, and now I wished that I'd taken things a bit further last night. At least to the shirtless stage, anyway.

We'd made out for a while, but I'd stopped things before they got too heated. I liked having fun, but last night just hadn't felt like the right time to take things further. Gabe hadn't seemed to mind when I put the brakes on, and we ended up just talking for a long time.

I'd told him about my mom and offered a few stories about my life, being as vague as possible when it came to the who, what, and where. I'd intentionally left out anything that might connect me to a traveling circus, dodging his questions as artfully as I could.

It'd gotten so late that I'd begun to fall asleep, and Gabe suggested I spend the night. I considered going home, but it was a bit of a walk, and honestly, every chance I had to sleep in a real house on a real bed, I took it. I'd said that I didn't mind sharing a bed with Gabe as long as it was just for sleeping, but he'd insisted on taking the floor.

I slid out of bed slowly to avoid any creaking or sound. I thought about waking Gabe up, so he could take the bed, but I didn't want to have that awkward morning-after conversation. Even though we'd both been sober last night and hadn't done that much, in the harsh light of morning, everything always felt so much more uncomfortable.

I waited until I was downstairs to slip my shoes and jean jacket back on, and then I snuck out the front door without waking anyone. The walk back to camp was a little confusing, even in a town as small as Caudry, and I nearly got lost.

I made it back just as people were waking up. Betty Bates had already done a load of laundry and was hanging it out on the line to dry. A voluptuous woman in her forties, she would've been considered a real beauty by most if it weren't for the thick beard below her lipsticked smile.

Her husband, Damon, was well over six feet tall and as pale as a ghost, but that's not why he'd joined the sideshow. It was the fully developed third leg he had, that looked particularly odd as he carried a basket of clothes over to Betty.

As I made my way in through trailers, I saw that the tiger run was being set up for Zeke Desmond's two tigers, Safēda and Mahilā. It had been six years since Zeke and his tigers had joined our little band of travelers, but I still hadn't stopped being amazed by the giant cats.

Safēda was a rare white Siberian tiger, with gray stripes so light, they were barely visible. When I approached the cage, Safēda rubbed her head up against the metal bars. The cage was on wheels, making it easier to slide on and off a trailer, and it sat a few feet off the ground, so I reached through, stroking her thick fur as she walked past.

Her sister Mahilā was much younger, and she had the light golden-and-white color of the offspring of a white tiger. Zeke had rescued her from a circus that hadn't been as kind, and her beautiful fur was broken by jagged scars from being beaten. She was much more leery of people, and stayed hidden at the back of the cage.

"Good morning, pretty girl," I said as I ran my hands through Safēda's lush fur.

"Well, well, look at what the cat dragged in," Seth snickered, and I looked away from the tiger to see him carrying a heavy metal gate over his head as he walked past me.

"Funny," I said dryly.

I quit petting Safēda, and when I stepped away from the cage to follow Seth, the tiger reached her giant paw out through the bars, trying to stop me, and I had to duck out of the way.

"So did you stay out all night again?" Seth asked me.

"It seems that way," I replied coyly.

Seth set the gate down next to the other fencing he'd been putting up for the tigers' outdoor pen next to their traveling cage. It had been built to withstand two charging 600-pound tigers, and yet he moved it with ease. He was well-muscled, but his strength surpassed that.

Like many of us in the traveling sideshow, he'd been born with something that made him different. Some were more human conditions, like Betty's beard, but others came from something supernatural. Seth possessed a strength beyond reason, and I'd seen him lift a pickup truck off the ground with his bare hands before.

"Where's Blossom?" Seth asked, glancing over at me as he walked back to the trailer to get more pieces of the fencing.

"What do you mean?" I looked around, as if expecting my occasional roommate to be standing behind me.

"She wasn't with you?" Seth paused and turned back to face me.

Sometimes Blossom went out with me to explore the town, but most of the time, I went on my own. Since we lived on the road in a traveling show with fifty other people, I enjoyed the solitude that the long walks provided.

I shook my head. "No, she wasn't with me last night. She probably crashed at my trailer."

"I don't think so." Seth's brow furrowed in concern. "Your mom was going around looking for the both of you. Gideon calmed her down by telling her that you guys must be together, so you'd be safe."

"Crap," I whispered. "Thanks for giving me the heads-up. I should go make sure my mom's fine, and see if Blossom made it back yet."

As I rushed through the campsite, I told myself that I shouldn't be worried. Blossom was sixteen and a runaway. Sometimes she went off on her own, and she could handle herself.

But I felt that strange chill growing inside me again, the one that I'd felt when we'd arrived at Caudry.

I opened the battered screen door to the Winnebago and my eyes immediately darted to the small bench where Blossom slept. It was empty, and though I wasn't really surprised, my heart sank to my stomach.

The trailer wasn't empty, though. Gideon was in our tiny galley kitchen, sipping his morning coffee. The little TV sat on the dining table across from him and played a fuzzy morning news show it picked up on its rabbit ears.

"Morning, Mara," Gideon said, and he pointed to the beaded curtain that served as a door to the back bedroom. "Your mom's been looking for you."

Despite their age difference—Gideon was over ten years

younger than my mom—he and my mother had been dating rather happily for nearly a decade, but they'd never lived in the same trailer. The spaces were so small that it made it impossible for two of them to have any privacy if they shared a motorhome with me.

Our current Winnebago had much more privacy than any of our previous ones, and that was a small bedroom with two twin beds. It used to have a pocket curtain-door, but it was broken, so we only had the beads.

"Mara?" Mom asked, and a second later she pushed through the beads, making them clatter. "Finally, you're home." Then, after assessing that I was indeed all right, her eyebrow raised, and her gray eyes hardened. "Did you and Blossom have a nice time last night?"

"I had a nice time," I replied carefully, and I tried to erase any sign of worry from my face. "But I don't know about Blossom. She wasn't with me."

"What do you mean?" My mom's eyes widened. "Didn't you go out together?"

"No, I went out on my own to get some air," I tried to explain as calmly as I could.

"What about Roxanne?" Mom asked, referring to my best friend and fellow carnie Roxie.

My mom had this strange habit where she never called anybody by shortened versions of their names. Me, she referred to with the term of affection *qamari* all the time, but everyone else got their full names.

"I don't know. I didn't see her," I admitted. "I didn't know

Blossom had left, but Caudry seems like a really great small town. I met some really nice people, and Blossom probably did too. I'm sure she's fine."

"No, no, don't give me that." Mom shook her head, causing her necklaces to clatter against each other.

First thing in the morning, and she'd already donned her jewelry. Most of it was cheap costume jewelry, except for one, the only necklace she actually slept in—a large key that hung on a thin leather strap. The head of the key was a skull with two bright red rubies for eyes, and it seemed to stare at me while my mom began her lecture.

"You can't keep doing this," she said. "Staying out all night in strange places."

I groaned in exasperation. "Everywhere we go is a strange place!"

"No, not like this." She shook her head again, more fiercely this time. "This place is different."

"Lyanka, it's a small town, and Mara came home safely," Gideon said. "I'm sure Blossom is fine too."

An amethyst bandana was holding back my mom's thick black hair. Her lips pressed into a thin line, and she rubbed the back of her neck. She cast her gaze to the floor, letting her mind run wild with worry.

Gideon put a hand on her arm, and she let her shoulders relax and leaned into him. "It will be all right, love. We'll only be staying here a week, and then we'll be moving on. Everything will be fine."

"I know you're right so often, and I hope you are this time."

She lifted her eyes imploringly to me. "Please, Mara. Can you try not to give your old mother a heart attack and stay close? At least while we're here?"

I gave her my most reassuring smile. "Sure, Mom."

She walked over to me and put her hands on my face. "I worry about you, *qamari*. I only want you to be safe and happy."

"I am, and you don't need to worry about me so much. I'm almost nineteen. I can take care of myself."

Brushing a strand of hair back from my forehead, my mom smiled sadly down at me. "I only wish that were true. But there are things in this world that no one can ever prepare for."

5. carnival

Unlike many of the other members of the sideshow, I didn't have a specific job. My mom was a fortune-teller, Gideon did a magic show, Zeke had his tigers, Brendon and his family did acrobatics, Seth was a strongman. My best friend Roxie Smith was in two acts—she helped out Zeke, and did a peep-show revue with two other girls.

I had no talent. No special ability, making me essentially a roadie. I did what was needed of me, which usually involved helping set up and take down, and various menial tasks. I cleaned the tiger cages and emptied out latrines when I had to. It wasn't a glamorous job, but it was crucial to our way of life.

Since Roxie worked with the tigers, Mahilā actually tolerated her. Roxie was helping me clean out the tiger cage they traveled in. The cage was open to a fenced-in enclosure Seth had built, so the tigers could roam as they pleased.

Safēda lounged in the grass, the sun shining brightly on her white fur. Whenever we stopped, Safēda seemed content to just lay in the sun, sleeping the entire time, but as the older tiger, it made sense.

Mahilā paced along the fence, occasionally emitting an irritated guttural noise in between casting furtive glances back toward Roxie and me. Her golden fur was mottled with scars from her past life in the abusive circus, including a nasty one that ran across her nose.

"So where *did* you go last night?" Roxie asked, her voice lilting in a singsong playful way. She was out in the run, using a hose to fill up a blue plastic kiddie pool so the tigers could play in it, while I was on my hands and knees scrubbing dung off the cage floor.

Her bleached blond hair was pulled back in a ponytail, and the sleeves of her white T-shirt were rolled up, revealing her well-toned arms. The cut-off jean shorts she wore barely covered her bum, and her old cowboy boots went up to her knees— her chosen footwear anytime she was at risk of stepping in tiger poop.

With fair skin, full lips, large blue eyes, and a dainty nose, Roxie was pretty and deceptively tough. Being a beautiful carnie was not an easy job, and dancing in the revue under the stage name "Foxy Roxie" didn't help that. But she made decent money doing it, and Roxie never put up with anybody's crap. I'd seen her deck guys much bigger than her and lay them out flat on their backs.

"I was just at a party," I said as I rinsed the brush off in a bucket of bleach and warm water.

"A party?" Roxie looked over at me with a hand on her hip. "How'd you get invited to a party so fast?"

I shrugged. "I was just exploring town, and I saw some people hanging outside of this big house party, and they invited me in."

"So what are the people like here? Are they nice?"

Safēda had gotten up and climbed into the pool, and then she flopped down in it, splashing Roxie as she did. Roxie took a step back, but kept looking at me.

"I don't know. The people I met last night seemed nice, and they were superrich, so that bodes well for the town, I guess."

"Like how rich?" Roxie asked.

"Like their house is practically a mansion." I dropped the brush in the water and sat back on my knees, taking a break to talk to her. "It was the nicest house I've ever been in, hands down."

"Is that why you spent the night there?"

Roxie understood my fascination with houses. Well, "understood" wasn't the right word. It was more like she knew of it, but didn't understand it all. She'd grown up in an upper-middle-class family, in nice houses with basements, and thought they were about as boring and lame as she could imagine.

"Partly." I nodded. "It was a really amazing house. There were pillars out front, and the front hall was bigger than my trailer."

"It's just a house, Mara." Roxie shook her head.

"I know but . . ." I trailed off, trying to think of how to explain it to her. "You know how you felt when you first joined the sideshow two years ago? How everything seemed so exciting and fun, and I was like, 'We live in cramped trailers. It kinda sucks.'"

Roxie nodded. "Yeah. But I still think this life is a million times better than my old life. I get to see everything. I get to decide things for myself. I can leave whenever I want. There's nothing to hold me back or tie me down."

She'd finished filling up the pool, so she twisted the nozzle on the hose to shut it off. Stepping carefully over an old tire and a large branch that the tigers used as toys, she went to the edge of the run and tossed the hose over the fence, before Mahilā decided to play with it and tore it up.

She walked over to the cage and scraped her boots on the edge, to be sure she didn't track any poop inside, before climbing up inside it.

"So what was the other reason?" Roxie asked.

I kept scrubbing for a moment and didn't look up at her when I said, "Gabe."

"*Gabe?*" Roxie asked. "That sounds like a boy's name."

"That's because it is."

"Did you have sex with him?"

"No." I shot her a look. "We just made out a little."

"What what what?" Luka Zajíček happened to be walking by just in time to hear that, and he changed his course to walk over to the tiger cage. "Is that what you were up to last night?"

"That's what sucks about living in a community so small. Whenever anything happens, everybody knows about it right away," I muttered.

Luka put his arms through the cage bars and leaned against it, in the area I'd cleaned already. Since he was rather short, the floor came up to his chest, and his black hair fell into his eyes.

His eyes were the same shade of gray as mine, but his olive skin was slightly lighter than mine. We first met him when he joined the carnival four years ago, and the first thing my mom said was that she was certain that we were related somehow.

Unfortunately, Mom knew next to nothing about our family tree to be able to prove it. All she could really tell me was that we were a mixture of Egyptian, Turkish, and Filipino, with a bit of German thrown in for good measure.

Luka had been born in Czechoslovakia, but he'd moved here with his family when he was young, so he'd lost his accent.

He had recently roped me into helping him with a trick. He'd stand with his back against a wall, while I fired a crossbow around him. Originally, Blossom had been the one to help him, but she kept missing and shooting him in the leg or arm, so he'd asked me to do it because I had a steadier hand.

"So you made out with some local guy last night?" Luka asked, smirking at me. "Are you gonna see him again?"

"He's a local guy. What do you think?" I asked, and gave him a hard look.

Luka shrugged. "Sometimes you bump into them again."

"And that goes so well when they find out that I work and live with a traveling sideshow," I said.

The floor was spotless, or at least as spotless as tiger cages can get, and I tossed my brush in the bucket and took off my yellow rubber gloves.

"We can't all meet our boyfriends in the sideshow," I reminded Luka as I stood up, and it only made him grin wider. He'd been dating Tim—one of the Flying Phoenixes—for the past three months.

"But you didn't see Blossom anywhere in town last night?" Roxie asked, and Luka's smile instantly fell away.

A sour feeling stirred in my stomach, and I looked out around camp through the bars of the cage, as if Blossom would suddenly appear standing beside a trailer. As I'd been doing my chores all morning, I kept scanning the campsite for her, expecting her to return at any moment with a funny story about how she'd gotten lost in town.

But so far, she hadn't. And the longer she went without coming back, the worse the feeling in my stomach got.

I shook my head. "No. I didn't see her at all last night."

"She's gotta turn up, though, right?" Luka asked. "I mean, it's not like there are really that many places she could've gone considering she has no money or car and she's in a small town."

The tigers were still down in the run, so I opened the side gate and hopped down out of the cage. Roxie got out behind me, then we closed the door.

"I should talk to Gideon," I decided as Roxie locked the cage up behind me. "It's not like Blossom to do this."

"It's not totally *unlike* her, though," Roxie pointed out. "When we were in Toledo six months ago, she disappeared for a few days with that weird commune, and came back just before we were leaving, totally baked out of her mind."

Blossom had grown up with parents who pretended to be hippies but were really just a couple of drug addicts. That— along with her unexplainable telekinesis—led to her dabbling with drugs and alcohol at a young age, before the state intervened and shipped her off to a group home.

My mom tried to keep her clean of her bad habits, but sometimes Blossom just liked to run off and do her own thing. That wasn't that unusual for people who lived in the carnival.

"But if you're worried, you should talk to Gideon," Roxie suggested. "Luka's right in that Blossom really couldn't have gone far. Maybe you can scope out Caudry."

"Since that sounds like a mission that may take a bit of time, can you help me and Hutch with the museum before you talk to Gideon?" Luka asked. "The exit door is jammed, and we can't get it open, and Seth is busy helping set up the tents."

"Sure. Between me and Mara, I'm sure the two of us can get the door unstuck," Roxie said.

I dropped off the bucket with the other tiger supplies, and then followed Roxie and Luka away from our campsite to the fairgrounds on the other side of a chain-link fence. We always stayed close to the rides, the midway, and the circus tent, but we didn't actually sleep there. It was much better for everyone if we kept our private lives separate from the crowds.

Many of the games were already set up, and the Ferris wheel was in the process of being erected as we passed. Near the end of the midway was a long black trailer painted with all kinds of frightening images of werewolves and specters, along with happier pictures of mermaids and unicorns, and the sign was written in bloodred:

TERRIFYING CURIOSITIES & ODDITIES OF PAST & PRESENT

Beneath that were several smaller signs warning "Enter at your own risk. The creatures inside can be DISTURBING and cause NIGHTMARES."

The entrance to the left was open, but the exit door at the

other end was still shut. Wearing a pair of workman's gloves, Hutch was pulling at the door with all his might. His neon green tank showed that his muscles were flexed and straining in effort. The bandana kept his dark brown hair off his face, but sweat was dripping down his brow.

"Let me have a try, Hutch," Roxie said.

"What?" He turned to look back at her. "Door's stuck."

"I can see that. That's why I said let me have a try."

"Okay." Hutch shrugged and stepped back.

Hutch's real name was Donald Hutchence, but nobody ever called him anything but Hutch. He didn't have any special powers, unless you considered being really agreeable and easygoing a super power, so, like me, he was left doing whatever else needed to be done.

Roxie grabbed the door and started pulling on it, and when it didn't budge, I joined her.

"Luka, go and push from the inside," Roxie commanded through gritted teeth.

Both Luka and Hutch went inside, pushing as Roxie and I pulled. And then all at once, the door gave way, and we all fell back on the gravel. I landed on my back, scraping my elbow on the rocks.

Roxie made it out unscathed, and Hutch fell painfully on top of me, so he'd avoided injury. Luka crashed right on the gravel, though, and the rocks tore through his jeans and ripped up his knees and the palms of his hands pretty badly.

"Do you need me to get a Band-Aid or anything?" Hutch asked as he helped me to my feet.

"No, I'll be okay." I glanced over at Luka and the blood dripping down his knees. "What about you? Do you want any-thing?"

"Nah. Just give it a few minutes." Luka waved it off and sat down on the steps leading up to the museum door.

No matter how many times I saw it, I couldn't help but watch. His knee was shredded, with bits of gravel sticking in the skin. Right before my eyes, the bleeding stopped, and the rocks started falling out, as if pushed by his flesh, and the skin grew back, reattaching itself where it had been little mangled flaps.

Within a few minutes, Luka's knee was healed completely.

6. prejudice

Gideon's old F150 groaned to a halt in the town square, and I gulped down my nerves as he turned off the engine. The cracked plastic stuck to my thighs below the hem of my dress.

As soon as Gideon agreed to go into town, I'd changed quickly out of my cleaning overalls and into a paisley sundress that had been my mother's in the seventies. He'd stayed in the grubby clothes he wore for setting up—tattered jeans and a blue work shirt stained with oil and paint.

He rested his arms on the steering wheel, leaning forward and staring ahead at the small building before us. Stone pillars flanked the doorway, and *Caudry Police Station* had been written in iron letters across the top.

Neither of us wanted to be here. Working on a traveling sideshow, we'd had more than our fair share of run-ins with cops who thought we were nothing but trouble. I'd once seen a sheriff in a small town actually spit on my mom, calling her a witch playing with voodoo.

But when I'd gone to talk to Gideon, to see if we should look for Blossom, Mom had overheard, and insisted that we do everything we could to track her down. Gideon tried to calm my mom, reminding her that Blossom hadn't even been gone for twenty-four hours yet and she'd probably still turn up.

Since we didn't really know the town or where to look, Mom suggested we go to the police station. To keep her from losing her mind, Gideon and I had reluctantly agreed.

"All right, let's get it over with," Gideon grumbled, and got out of the truck, so I followed suit.

He opened the door to go inside, and a bell jingled loudly. I meant to follow him, but I had the strangest feeling of being watched. My feet felt frozen on the sidewalk, and I looked around the town square, half expecting to see a crowd of beady eyes staring at me.

But there was nothing. No one.

"Mara?" Gideon asked, still holding the door for me.

"Sorry," I mumbled, and hurried in after him, trying to ignore the feeling.

Inside the station, avocado and off-white tiles checkered the floor, and dark wood paneling closed us in. A man sat behind a desk in a brown police uniform, pecking away at an ancient typewriter next to an overgrown fern.

He glanced up at us with small brown eyes, then immediately turned his attention to the document before him. His lips were unusually full, and as he typed, they puckered, like he'd just eaten a lemon. The shiny metal tag on the front of his uniform read DEPUTY BOB GENDRY.

"Ahem." Gideon cleared his throat and shifted his weight

from one foot to the other. I'd taken to playing with a small braid I had in my thick hair and staring at the Louisiana flag that had been pinned up on the wall behind the desk.

With great flourish, the deputy pulled the paper from the typewriter and set it aside. Then he looked up at us, managing a sickly smile as his eyes darted over the thick black tattoos that covered Gideon's forearms.

"What can I do you for today?" Deputy Bob asked, his Southern accent dripping with condescension.

"We were just wondering if you could help us find someone," Gideon said, and his words came out low and defeated. His shoulders slumped, and he fidgeted with the silver band he had on his finger.

"You're not from around here, are you?" Deputy Bob arched an eyebrow.

Gideon sighed. "No. We're with the carnival that's in town for the week."

"A girl who travels with us didn't come home last night," I added, before the deputy could comment on the fact that we were carnies.

"Maybe she's just lost her way around town," Deputy Bob suggested.

"We thought that was maybe the case," Gideon said. "But we don't really know where to look for her either."

Deputy Bob let out a heavy breath, like he was doing us some great big favor. He opened the drawer to his desk and pulled out a form. Without saying anything to us, he took a pen and jotted down a couple things on the form.

"Since she hasn't been gone long, I can't file a missing

persons report, but I can take her information in case she turns up somewhere," Deputy Bob said finally. "Describe her for me."

"Her name is Blossom Mandelbaum," Gideon began. "She has frizzy brown hair, brown eyes. Lots of freckles. She's about 5'2", maybe 5'3", I would guess. She's sixteen."

Deputy Bob looked up at us then, narrowing his already tiny eyes. "Sixteen? Is she your daughter?"

Gideon shook his head. "No."

"Are her parents traveling with you?" Bob asked.

"No," Gideon replied, swallowing hard. "She's a runaway."

The deputy set down his pen and folded his hands on the desk. "You've been harboring a runaway?"

"It's not like that," Gideon started, but Deputy Bob wasn't having any of it. He leaned back in his chair.

"Maybe she ran back home." Deputy Bob shrugged one shoulder.

"She didn't," I insisted, and he turned his harsh gaze to me.

Before he could say anything, the bell of the door chimed loudly. I glanced back over my shoulder to see a woman carrying a stack of fliers and folders in her arms.

"Hello, hello," she beamed, her lips stained bright with lipstick.

She appeared to be in her early forties. She wore a pink pencil skirt with a loose blouse, and her blond curls cascaded around her, adding a couple inches to her petite frame. Her pumps clacked on the tiles as she walked over to the desk, and her golden chandelier earrings jingled.

The sour feeling returned to my stomach, twisting it up, and

I realized that now would be a good time to make our escape, lest Deputy Bob decide to press charges against Gideon for traveling with a sixteen-year-old runaway.

"Sorry to interrupt, I just gotta get all these papers down," the woman said as she slid in past me and plunked the stack on Deputy Bob's desk. I'd taken a step back, but she turned her attention toward Gideon, alternating between speaking directly to us and the deputy.

"I've been going around collecting applications for the Summerfest in June," she went on. "It's been hard getting everything I need, since so many people went to the Equinox Festival over in Tangipahoa Parish. But you're here, Deputy, so maybe you can start filling out the form, if you're not too busy?"

Bob pushed aside our form and reached for the stack of papers the woman had set on his desk. "What did you want me to fill out?"

"Oh, just grab any old form in there as long as it's empty." She waved him off. Then she turned to face us fully. "I'm sorry, I've been rambling on and on, while you're been standing here, looking lost. Are you new in town?"

"They're with the traveling carnival," Deputy Bob told her with a sneer.

"Oh!" she exclaimed, and put her manicured hand to her chest. "I'm so excited to have you here. I'm with the mayor's office and work on planning community events, and I'm thrilled to have a fun attraction here like this to compete with all the hullabaloo going on in Tangipahoa Parish and down in New Orleans. I'm always telling the mayor, we gotta keep the excitement up if we wanna keep the kids here."

"I'm sure these people have work they need to be doing," Deputy Bob chastised her. "You should stop bothering them."

She rolled her eyes, but offered us an apologetic smile. "He's right, I'm sorry." Then she stuck her hand out at Gideon. "I'm Della Jane, by the way."

"Gideon Davorin," he said gruffly, shaking her hand.

"Mara," I replied when she took my hand. Her grip was soft but firm, and she smiled so brightly, her blue eyes twinkled. Della Jane reminded me of a less buxom Dolly Parton, and I couldn't help but warm to her despite the unease in my stomach.

"Let me know if there's anything I can do for you while you're here," she said when she released my hand. "Anything at all."

"We're actually looking for my friend," I blurted out, causing Deputy Bob to glare at me. "Her name's Blossom Mandelbaum, and she travels with us. She went out last night, and we haven't seen her since."

"She's sixteen and she's a runaway," Deputy Bob interjected. "There's not—"

"She didn't tell anyone where she was going?" Della Jane's brow furrowed with concern, and she moved so she was standing in front of Bob, blocking his view of me and Gideon. "Does she usually disappear like this?"

"Not really," I said, feeling sheepish. But something about the way Della Jane was looking at me, so hopeful and worried, made me feel as if I had to be totally honest with her. "She did hang out with a commune once for a few days, because she liked the music. But she told us before she left."

Della Jane snapped her fingers. "I got it. She probably went over to the Tangipahoa Parish music festival. They have all kinds of bands, going on for the next week to celebrate the equinox. Does that sound like something she would enjoy?"

"It does . . ." I admitted reluctantly. "But she would've told us."

"Maybe she just hitched a ride and didn't have a chance," Della Jane suggested. "But I can see that you'll be worried until she shows up again. So I'll tell you what—"

Abruptly she turned her back to us and hurriedly wrote something down on the corner of a flier. Then she tore off the corner and faced us again, handing me the paper with *Della Jane* and her phone number scrawled in beautiful loopy handwriting.

"If you haven't heard from your friend in the next day or two, give me a call," Della Jane said. "I'll look into it personally and see if we can't find her. How does that sound?"

"That sounds great. Thank you." I smiled at her, but it felt weak.

"Thank you again," Gideon told her, and when I didn't move, he put his hand on my back to gently usher me out of the police station.

As soon as we stepped outside, Gideon let out a sigh of relief. With the sun shining brightly above, it was a warm spring day, and thanks to Della Jane, things had gone better in the police station than I had hoped for. She'd given a logical explanation for where Blossom probably was—safe and sound listening to bands.

Despite all that, I couldn't shake the chill inside my chest, like my heart had been encased in ice.

7. night terror

I had no idea where I was, since I was completely surrounded by black. And in that darkness, a face began to emerge. An old woman, her face gaunt, and the folds of gray flesh wrinkled and shriveled to the point of mummification.

She began to move toward me, as if gliding through the emptiness. Her gown billowed out around her, a dark fabric making her appear larger and more threatening. Not that she needed the help. Her gray hair stuck out maniacally around her head, like a crazed halo, and her eyes were black as coal.

"What do you want?" I asked, trying to say something to stop her from coming at me.

She opened her mouth then and began to scream—her words came out rapid fire, shrill and furious. It made it impossible to understand, but what little I did pick up wasn't a language that I knew.

"I don't know what you want! I can't understand you!" I told her, but that only made her angrier.

Her wails grew louder, echoing through my skull, and then she extended her hands toward me. Her fingers were long and the nails were yellowed, and somehow I knew that if she got me, she'd never let me go.

I turned to run away from her, but the ground fell out from under me. There was nothing to grab on to, no matter how I tried to reach out, and I tumbled down into a bottomless pit of blackness.

Then, just as I felt my body slam into the hard ground, I opened my eyes and sat up.

Panting heavily, I realized with great relief that it was only a dream. I was safe in my own bed, but I couldn't seem to stop my trembling and slow the panicked racing of my heart.

The room was dark, with the only light coming in from the hall and spilling in through the narrow gaps between the strings of beads. Still, I could make out the familiar shapes of my room, and after the nightmare that felt all too vivid and intense, I took comfort in taking inventory of the normal things in my room that weren't screaming banshees.

Posters adorned my half of the room, covering the narrow bits of paneling that weren't covered by windows. I only had one full-size poster, tacked up on the side of the closet, of David Bowie. The rest were smaller ones, like a tour poster for the Cure, ticket stubs for *Aliens*, and a flier for the sideshow from a state fair last summer.

Books were stacked to the brim on my nightstand. I kept as many as I could, but eventually, Mom would make me part ways with them to make room for new ones. My stereo and cassette tapes were stacked on the small vanity at the end of my mom's bed next to the closet-size bathroom.

Across from my bed was Mom's own narrow twin bed, neatly made the way it always was. Her half of the room was much cleaner and more organized than mine, but she had extra scarves and jewelry hanging from tacks above the window, since she'd run out of room everywhere else.

After we'd gotten back from the police station and delivered what little news we had to my mom, I'd finished helping set up, and then I'd snuck back to my trailer to take a quick nap. I couldn't have gotten more than a couple hours of sleep last night at Gabe's house, since we'd stayed up so late talking.

My mom had made the curtains from dark upholstery fabric and black lace, making them almost impenetrable to light, and I peeled them back from the windows. The sun had almost completely set, which meant that I'd overslept.

I swore, then hurried to get ready. The AC had gone out in the trailer, so my mom and Gideon had put a window air conditioner in the dining room. It stayed in place with duct tape, bungee cords, and a hope and a prayer.

I'd only just turned it on when I came inside, so it had been crazy hot and I'd stripped down to a tank top and panties to sleep in. Now I hurried to pull on a light dress. The carnival would be opening soon, and though I didn't perform in any shows or run any stands, I worked hard as a gopher for everyone else.

I flicked on the vanity light and grabbed my makeup from the drawer and quickly put on eyeliner and mascara, finishing it off with scarlet lipstick that popped against the caramel tone of my skin.

Then I noticed the scrap of paper with Della Jane's number was tacked to the top of the mirror, with one of Blossom's necklaces dangling over it. Blossom kept most of her stuff in her own trailer, but since she spent so much time here, some of it ended up left behind.

But that's not what made my gaze stop short. I'd left Della Jane's number on the table in the kitchen, and Blossom's necklace hadn't been in here at all.

Mom must've come in and put it up here. Strange that I hadn't woken up when she came in, but I had been very sleepy. . . .

I tried to shrug it off, and on impulse, I grabbed Blossom's necklace and dropped it over my head. There was no time to worry about anything else, or even think about the nightmare that still left me feeling jumpy. I had to see if my mom needed any help.

As soon as I stepped out of the Winnebago, with the door creaking shut behind me, I heard the sound of the carnival. The music came from the midway—happy-go-lucky circus tunes from speakers set up along the booths—but mixed with that, I could hear laughter and talking. It was already under way, which meant I was very late.

Gathering my skirt, I dashed toward the carnival. The fairgrounds hadn't felt so far away earlier when I'd been helping out with the museum and my mother's booth, but as I dodged between trailers and nearly ran into Betty, it seemed to be miles away.

I couldn't remember where the gate was that kept our

motorhomes fenced off from the carnival. I ended up finding a gap in the chain link where it had been cut and slid through it and ran to my mom's tent.

Her tent was small—only big enough for three chairs and a tiny table. The fabric was a dark violet that shimmered, even in the fading twilight. *Fortune Teller* was painted on the sign above the door, along with several mystical-looking symbols that really meant nothing.

There was another sign, pinned to the curtain that served as a door, with the words *Mystic Lyanka—Sees All, Knows All.* It featured a fairly nice painting of my mom that Gideon had done years ago. She'd been younger then, so her skin had been smoother, her eyes brighter, her smile wider. But even in the painting, there was an air of mystery about her.

"The message in the cards is clear, though the vision is hazy," my mom was saying, and I peeled back the curtain, just enough so I could peek in.

An intricate rug of black and gold covered the expanse of the tent floor, and while it did have a rather luxurious appearance, in reality, Mom had picked it up at a garage sale for a dime two years ago. The same with the velvet throw pillows that lined the edges of the tent.

A chandelier hung from the center of the tent above the table, lit with thin white candles. The table and chairs were a matching set, and actually were antiques that my mom had inherited from her mother. From what I understood, my grandma had conned them out of a rich woman she'd met at a flea market.

Most things in here were props, set up for mood, but the tarot cards and stones were real. Mom even had a crystal ball, though she almost never used it, because she said it rarely worked. She might take money from strangers for her gift, but my mom never lied about the things she saw. Or didn't see.

Mom sat facing the door to the tent, her eyes focused on the cards in front of her. She still had a deck of cards in her hand—the images faded and worn from years of use—and she absently shuffled them.

The chairs across from her had two teenage girls sitting in them. Their backs were to me, so they didn't notice me peeking in on their reading.

"You need to trust your heart." Mom tapped a card in front of one of the girls. "That's very clear. There's going to be a change, and the outcome can be good or bad depending on how well you listen to your heart."

"So should I break up with Dean?" the girl asked.

"I can't say." Mom shook her head. "But a change is needed."

I let go of the curtain, letting it slide shut, and waited beside the tent until Mom had finished. My mom was always truthful about her visions, but what people wanted from her usually had less to do with fortunes and fates than it did therapy.

Most of the time, people just wanted someone to listen, and even when she didn't have much to help them in the way of her gift, Mom was always happy to help.

Once the girls had finished their reading, thanking my mother profusely as they exited, I slid inside to see how she was doing.

"Sorry I wasn't here before," I said as she slid the cards back into a pile. "Do you need anything?"

She shuffled the cards and stared down at the rug. "You can get me aspirin and water."

"The headaches are already starting? How many readings have you done?" I asked.

"That was my second one." She motioned to the door, where the girls had just left. "But the first one was more intense."

I frowned. "Mom."

"I'm fine." Mom looked up at me. The scarf wrapped around her head kept her dark hair out of her face, and her eyes were grave. "It's the life that chose me, and it's fine. Can you get me the water and pills before the next customer comes?"

"Yeah, sorry." I gave her a contrite smile. "I'll be back."

8. the magician

I ran back to the campsite, once again using the hole in the fence since I couldn't find the gate. I grabbed the water and aspirin from the trailer, but as I went to leave, I noticed the door to Gideon's trailer was open and warm light was spilling out.

I went over and climbed up the metal steps to his door. He stood next to his desk, going over something among stacks and stacks of paperwork. Black suspenders hung down around his waist, and his shirt was off. His muscled torso was heavily tattooed, but my eyes were always drawn to the one on his back.

It angled from the side, going from above his hip toward his spine. The letters were wobbly and barely legible, but Gideon had been fighting it the whole time he'd gotten it. It was more of a brand than a tattoo. Gideon said they'd used the sharp end of a metal pipe, heating it over fire, then dipping it in ink, before they'd written the word "freak" into his flesh.

That had been his first tattoo, and the only one he'd gotten that he hadn't wanted. He'd only been fifteen at the time, and three weeks later, he left England forever. He'd hoped it would be better in America for people like him, and when he found it wasn't, he decided to make it better. That's why he'd started this sideshow—to create a place where people who didn't belong could belong.

I leaned against the doorframe. "Gideon?"

"Are people already showing up?" he asked without looking up at me.

"Yeah, but I wanted to talk to you about my mom."

He looked up, concerned. "Is she okay?"

"Yeah . . . Well, no." I shook my head. "She says she is, but all of this is really taking a toll on her."

He grimaced, then scratched the back of his neck. "The break didn't do anything for her?"

"Not really. She's only just started, and the migraine is already setting in."

"I would like her to quit as much as you would, but she won't." He sighed. "Not right now. We need the money, and she knows it. Maybe after this, if we get a big enough of a payday, she can take a break for a while."

"I was thinking . . ." I shifted my weight from one foot to the other. "Maybe we could talk about me taking over for her."

Gideon shook his head. "Lyanka would never let you do that. You know that."

"But it's getting too hard on her," I insisted. "Nobody's meant to do a thousand readings a year for twenty years straight. She's exhausted."

"Which is why she'd never let you do it." He gave me a

knowing look. "Once you open your mind to the spirits, you can't shut it again."

"I don't even think I can open my mind to the spirits. I don't have the same gift as her. But I can still read a deck of cards."

"That's even worse," Gideon argued. "Then you'd just be a hustler, and you know how Lyanka despises frauds."

"It doesn't matter whether she likes it or not. Mom isn't going to be able to do this stuff much longer, and if I don't start stepping in to take her place, she's gonna end up destroying her mind and going insane." I paused. "Just like her mother did."

"I know, and I agree with you, Mara. But it's not up to me."

"Why not? You're the boss," I reminded him. "You have the power to hire and fire people."

"I can't exactly fire my girlfriend." He looked back down at the papers in front of him. "And it's not that simple."

"Gideon. We need to do something," I told him firmly.

He chewed the inside of his cheek, staring off for a moment, then finally relented with a heavy sigh. "All right. I'll talk to Lyanka, but in the end, she'll do what she wants to do. You know how she is." He pointed to the bottle of pills in my hand. "If her head's already hurting, you better get that aspirin out to her."

I ran back to the carnival, and when I reached my mom's tent, a client was inside with her. I ducked in, apologizing as I did, and gave Mom the water and the aspirin. Then I quickly exited and looked around to see if anybody else needed help.

Since the carnival had just started, everything was well stocked, and nobody seemed to need anything. I walked along the edge of the fairgrounds, preferring to stay in the shadows behind the tents and exhibits than mingling with the crowds.

A burst of light came from the other side of the fence, and I looked over to see Roxie playing with a small ball of fire in the palm of her hand.

"You should be careful with that," I said as I walked over to her.

She shrugged, letting the flames burn blue and yellow a second before closing her fist, extinguishing them. Whenever she was bored or anxious, Roxie resorted to playing with her pyrokinesis.

Right in front of us was a booth selling cotton candy, and another one that had a ring-toss game. We stared in between the booths at the people walking down the midway.

"Looks like a lot of people are coming already." I leaned on the fence next to her.

"Yeah, that has to be a good sign. Especially after the dry spell we've had."

"Are you doing a show tonight?" I asked.

"Yeah. Just the peep show at eight," Roxie said. "Zeke says the tigers need a rest, so we're doing that tomorrow."

Roxie apparently grew tired of people watching, so she once again made a fireball in her hand, but instead of a usual ball of fire, it was a small red spark that immediately went out.

"Dammit," Roxie muttered. "My pyro has been acting weird all day. Sometimes I can't even make any fire at all."

"Maybe you've been using it too much," I suggested, even though I'd never heard of Roxie having any issues with her fire before.

"Maybe," she agreed, sounding unconvinced, but a small fireball formed in her hand, which seemed to relax her.

I stared ahead, trying to get a count on how many people might be here. Gideon had heard from a trusted friend that we would do well here. Since it was such a small town, I'd been dubious, but based on the turnout we were already having, it looked like his friend had been right.

And then I saw him, and my stomach dropped.

I'd actually seen Selena first, her black hair pulled back in a ponytail, as she held hands with her boyfriend, Logan. Another guy walked beside them, his hair slicked back, and wore a pair of shades that matched Logan's.

That had been enough to startle me, but then Gabe had appeared at her side. They'd stopped right across from where I was hidden in the darkness behind the booth, but they were too far away for me to hear them.

"Oh shit," I whispered.

"We're far enough away," Roxie insisted, shifting her fireball from one hand to the other. "Nobody can see the fire."

"No, not that. It's Gabe. He's here."

The fireball instantly went out, and Roxie leaned forward. "Which one?"

"That one." I pointed to where Gabe stood, laughing at what Selena had said to him.

"He is hot. *Wow.*" Roxie sounded impressed. "You should totally get on that. I mean, if you hung out with him tonight, that would be like two dates, and that would fit your no-sex-on-the-first-date rule."

I didn't want to argue with her. Tall and lean, Gabe somehow looked even better than I remembered him. The sleeves of his denim jacket were pushed up to his elbows, and his smile was radiant.

"Last night wasn't a date, and bumping into him at the carnival hardly counts as a date, either," I countered Roxie's logic. "Plus, if I'm like, 'Hey, how are you? I'm a carnie,' that will probably shut down any interest he has in me."

"You say that, and you see how often me and Carrie get hit on," Roxie said, referring to the other girl who danced with her.

"That's different. You're a tiger tamer's assistant, and you dance sexy," I said. "I do grunt work and clean up poop. I don't have the same appeal."

"Don't tell him you're a carnie," Roxie suggested. "Just pretend you came to the carnival the same as him. Most of the people here don't actually work here. He won't think anything of it."

"I don't know." I debated as Gabe went up to the cotton candy stand, momentarily disappearing from my line of vision.

"Mara. Just go. Have fun," Roxie commanded.

I turned to face her. "How do I look?"

She readjusted my necklace and fixed the thin strap on my dress, then smiled approvingly at me. "You look good. Go."

"Do you wanna come with me?" I asked.

"I would love to, but I can't. I should go get ready. It's close to showtime."

"Okay." I smiled uncertainly at her. "Thanks."

"Don't do anything I wouldn't do."

"So . . . what?" I laughed. "That means I can do everything?"

"Not everything. I would never go to that guy's house and admire the architecture. So don't do that," Roxie said as I started to walk away. "In fact, try not to look at any buildings at all."

9. diversions

Since emerging from the shadows behind the booths would probably seem a little creepy, or at the very least raise questions about where I had come from, I decided to run into Gabe in the gap between two booths a little way down.

But then I glanced out and saw that Gabe was holding cotton candy as Selena picked off several pink tufts. He wasn't looking in my direction at all, so I stepped out in the bright lights of the carnival. I couldn't just stand there, staring and waiting for him to approach me, so I decided to play whatever game I happened to be closest to.

When I realized what game it was, my smile instantly fell away. It was the milk-bottle toss, where you threw a rubber ball and tried to knock down weighted bottles. I didn't mind the game so much, but the guy who ran it—Doug Bennett. Gideon was the head of the whole traveling carnival, but Doug was in charge of the midway, and sometimes he could be a jerk about it.

"You gonna try your luck again, Mara?" He had one foot on the corner as he stared down at me, chomping rather loudly on chewing tobacco.

"Pretend you don't know me," I said.

Doug's bloodshot eyes appeared confused. "What?"

"Please. Just pretend you don't know me," I begged, and out of the corner of my eye, I saw Gabe and his family walking toward me. "For one night."

Doug held out his grimy hand. "Then pay me if you wanna play."

"*Doug.*"

"You want this to look real, then give me two dollars." He opened and closed his hand, motioning for me to give him money.

"Ugh," I groaned, and quickly dug into my bra, where I had exactly three dollars. Doug winked at me as I handed the cash over to him.

"Step right up, little lady, and win yourself a prize!" Doug shouted, putting on his full carnie routine. "Or would a strapping young man care to win a prize for the lady?"

"I can win a prize for myself," I hissed with a thin smile plastered on my face. "I just wanted you to—"

"Mara?" Gabe asked.

I turned back to see him walking over to me, and I smiled at him. "Gabe. Hi."

"How about you?" Doug leaned over the counter, still shouting so everyone around would hear him. "Would you like to win the pretty lady a teddy bear?"

"As I was just telling this nice game operator, I am perfectly capable of winning a prize myself," I said.

Gabe eyed me up appreciatively and smirked. "I'm sure you are."

"Then why don't you win him a prize?" Doug turned to me. "I'm sure a young man like him would love one of our *de*-luxe teddy bears," he said, pointing to the small, cheap bears that were hanging up all over the booth.

"Pardon?" I asked.

"You know what, I would." Gabe walked up to the counter next to me and looked up at the blue teddy bear.

"What?" I asked, still not completely understanding what was happening here.

"I'd like a teddy bear." Gabe grinned at me. "Nobody ever wins one for me. I always have to give them away, and I want one. It'd look great on my bed."

"Everyone, watch as this strapping young woman wins the handsome young man a prize!" Doug shouted, speaking to the small crowd that was gathering around us. "She will prove her strength and her skill! Watch as she takes aim and proves her love—"

"Just give me the balls." I cut Doug off and held my hand out. "I'll do it."

As he dropped the three lightweight rubber balls into my hand, Doug winked at me again. He moved as far to the side of the booth as he could get, which was good, because if he got in my way, I'd probably chuck a ball at him.

I threw my first ball, and it slammed right into the top bottle. That one was easy. Unlike the ones at the bottom, it was weighed about what a milk bottle actually weighed. The bottom two were filled with sand and were much heavier.

Doug had suggested actually gluing them down, but Gideon thought that was taking things too far. Still, it was almost impossible to get all three of the bottles down. At least for people who hadn't spent hundreds of hours of their life playing this game.

With the second ball, I threw it hard, aiming for the bottom center between the two bottles, and they both went down. They actually fell so hard that one of them ricocheted off the back wall before flying into the counter.

The people who had gathered around to watch applauded, and Gabe let out an approving whistle.

"I got down all the bottles in less than three balls, so I believe I have my pick of the prizes," I said, smiling up at Doug. "And I'll take the teddy bear."

"Here you go, little lady." Doug pulled down a bear and handed it to me. "And we have another champion! Fellas, step right up, and see if you can beat a girl."

"I'm moving on now, but thank you." I stepped away from the booth and handed the bear to Gabe, who looked impressed. "Here you go."

"That was quite a feat of strength," Gabe said.

"Thank you."

"You remember my sister, Selena, and her boyfriend, Logan Montgomery." He motioned to them with the cotton candy, and Selena took that as an invitation to walk over to us. Logan followed behind her with his friend in the matching shades. "And this is Logan's friend, Troy Gendry."

The name *Gendry* flashed back to the badge of the unhelpful deputy in town. Troy barely looked at me when Gabe attempted to introduce him, and even though he and Logan were still a few feet away from me, I could smell the alcohol coming off them in waves.

"I've been trying to get Logan to win me something since we got here." Selena pointed her thumb back at him, and over the top of the shades I could see Logan give an exaggerated eye roll.

"Babe, if you want a tacky bear, I'll buy you a tacky bear," Logan said, loud enough so that everyone around us could hear, and Selena scowled at him. "I don't need to spend time and money winning you one."

"You don't have to keep the bear." I pointed to the bear that Gabe had under his arm. "You know, if you don't want to."

"Are you kidding me?" Gabe sounded offended. "I'll treasure this forever."

I laughed. "I'm sure you will."

He turned to his sister, handing her the rest of the cotton candy. "Hey, Selena, do you mind if I head out? I think I'm gonna go walk with Mara and check things out."

"Yeah, that's fine. It was nice seeing you again, Mara." She smiled at me.

"Yeah, you too." I gave her a small wave as I started walking away with Gabe.

We walked down the midway, neither of us saying anything at first. Gabe twirled the blue bear in his hands, and I tucked my hair behind my ear. I was acutely aware that all the booths around us were filled with people I knew, people who were watching us and could easily out me as a member of the side-show.

"So, you snuck out pretty early this morning," he said, giving me a sidelong look.

"Yeah, sorry." I smiled sheepishly at him. "I had some things I needed to do today, and you were sleeping soundly, so I didn't want to wake you."

"I was afraid that my snoring had frightened you off or something."

I laughed and shook my head. "No, you didn't snore."

"I didn't? Well, that's good to know." He smiled, then looked around, as if something just occurred to him. "Are you here with anyone? I'm not pulling you away from your friends, am I?"

"No. My friends, um, are watching a show," I said, since it probably would seem weird if I came to the carnival alone.

Then again, I had gone to a party last night by myself. But that was all the more reason to make up friends now. I didn't want to give him the idea that I was some kind of strange loner.

"Show?" Gabe asked.

"Yeah. There're acrobats in the tent." I pointed to the end of the midway, where a large red-and-white-striped circus tent was set up next to the rides. *The Fantastic Flying Phoenixes* was painted across the top in big letters, with a poster of Safēda and Mahilā off to the side, advertising the tiger show.

"Really? And you didn't want to check it out?" Gabe asked.

I shrugged. "I'm just not that into acrobats, I guess."

"So, you're too good for acrobats, and you're an expert at the milk bottle game. What do you wanna do next? Do you like any rides?"

"Yeah," I said. "I am kinda partial to the Ferris wheel."

I did actually love the Ferris wheel, but I was also looking for an excuse to get away from the bright lights of the midway and the prying eyes of nearly everyone I knew. My mom was busy in her tent, but if she came out, she'd spot me, and I wasn't entirely sure how she'd react if she saw me flirting with a townie, no matter how cute he was.

"How about this? Since you won me this handsome bear, I'll pay for your ticket," Gabe suggested. "Sound fair?"

I nodded. "Yeah. That sounds perfect."

10. rota fortuna

W hen we went over to the Ferris wheel, we had to wait in line, and I was surprised to see that the line was already so long since the carnival hadn't opened that long ago. It worked in my favor, though. The guy running the ride was so busy that he didn't even notice me when Gabe handed him our tickets, let alone comment on knowing me.

Gabe held the door open, letting me climb into the lavender gondola first, and he got in beside me. He put his bear on the far side of the bench, and he had to slide up next to me so his leg pressed against the thin fabric of my dress.

The ride jerked to a start when it began moving, causing me to lean against him. I laughed and moved away when it smoothed out again, as the car rose slowly into the night sky. Some of the lightbulbs that ran around the edge of the wheel had gone out, so the farther we went from the ground, the darker it became.

Each of the sixteen gondolas was painted in a different color from a pastel rainbow, but it had been a very long time since they'd been touched up, so the paint was chipped and faded from the sun. The logo for *Gideon Davorin's Traveling Sideshow* had been painted on each of the doors, but it was almost unreadable now.

The wheel came to a stop again when we reached the top, as they unloaded and loaded passengers at the bottom. The gondola jerked a bit, and Gabe moved closer to me. His arm brushed up against mine, but he didn't move it. His skin felt warm and tempting, the back of his hand resting against mine, but I didn't take it.

Above us, the moon was fat and bright. It was warmer today than it'd been yesterday, though it had begun to cool since the sun had gone down. The humidity had stayed the same, and a white halo danced around the moon.

"It's a full moon," I said, mostly just to say something.

"Almost full," Gabe corrected me. "Not quite, though."

I tilted my head, looking at it harder, and realized he was right. An almost imperceptible sliver was missing from the side. The wheel moved back again, making the gondola sway slightly, and Gabe finally took my hand, sliding his fingers loosely through mine.

"My mom always said the full moon brings out the crazies," I told him as the ride once again came to a stop.

"Yeah, my mom always said something similar," he agreed, and there was a weariness in his words that made me look over at him. He stared down at our hands, a pensive expression on his face, his thumb rubbing gently on the back of my hand.

We'd reached the highest part of the Ferris wheel, and I looked out around us. Below us, the carnival was so far away, it looked almost magical. All the lights and colors and the soft sounds of the music all mixed together, and we weren't close enough to see how faded and run-down everything had become, so it all seemed rather pretty.

"This is my favorite part," I said.

Gabe lifted his head to look at me. "What?"

"Sitting at the top of the Ferris wheel when it's paused like this. You can see everything, and the whole world seems so quiet and far away. It's peaceful."

"You spend a lot of time on Ferris wheels?" Gabe asked with an arched eyebrow.

I smiled demurely. "Not as much as I'd like."

"You have dimples when you smile," he said with a bemused grin of his own.

"Yeah, I know." I wanted to stop smiling then, but of course, I couldn't. The small indents in my cheeks whenever I smiled had been the source of teasing as a child, and now that I was older, they succeeded in making me look younger, like a darker-skinned Shirley Temple. "It's kinda the bane of my existence."

Gabe laughed. "Why? They're adorable."

"Mmm, yes, that's what every teenage girl dreams of being called—*adorable*."

"Sorry, I'll correct myself, then. They're sexy. Like crazy hot," Gabe said with exaggerated sincerity. "I can barely contain myself when you smile."

"Thanks," I said, suppressing my laughter.

His smile fell away, and so did mine. The wicked glint lingered in his eyes—a permanent reminder that there was something about him I shouldn't trust—but I could see something smoldering in them, something that I'm certain reflected in my own eyes, and my breath came out more slowly.

Gabe leaned in, kissing me on the mouth. He let go of my hand, and his arm slid around my waist. The ride jerked as it began to move again, swaying our gondola, but it didn't make us break apart. If anything, it only made us more fervent, knowing that we only had a short time left on this ride, a short time left to feel the strength of his arm around me, the heat of his lips against mine.

It was when the ride stopped again, almost halfway back down, that he pulled away. To kiss me, he'd turned sideways on the bench, facing me, and his arm rested on the back of the gondola. I leaned against the side, smiling at him and trying to catch my breath.

He licked his lips, then took my hand again. As he entwined his fingers with mine, he looked down at our hands. For a few moments, neither of us said anything, content to let our bodies cool.

"I was afraid I wouldn't see you again," Gabe said finally.

"Me too," I admitted.

I wanted to believe that I didn't care. That making out with a guy, then leaving him behind when I moved on to a different city was fine with me. And maybe it was, most of the time.

But pretending I hadn't felt a pang of regret and remorse as I'd snuck out of Gabe's room this morning would be a lie.

Gabe looked up at me. "Are you glad you did?"

"Yeah, I am." I smiled. "What about you?"

"I'm not sure yet. I'm leaning toward maybe," he said with a smirk.

I laughed but he silenced me with another kiss. It wasn't as intense as the first one, but that didn't mean it didn't taste just as sweet.

"Should we go again?" Gabe asked as we came nearer to the bottom. "We should go again. If I give the guy twenty dollars, do you think he'll let us go around again without getting in line?"

"He'll do it for ten," I said. The guy running the ride would actually probably do it for even less than that, but if Gabe was that easy to part with his money, I didn't want to stiff him on a tip.

Gabe dug in his pocket, and when he pulled out a ten-dollar bill, I was beginning to think that he might have a never-ending supply of cash in there. When we reached the end of the ride, Gabe offered him the money, and the guy gladly let us go again.

"Where were we?" Gabe asked as soon as the gondola rose higher in the night sky, and turned back to face me.

He pressed me against the side of the gondola as he kissed me. Part of me knew I should be afraid. We were nearing sixty feet off the ground, and we were leaning back over the side of a swaying car.

But I didn't care. I barely even noticed.

When he stopped kissing me, his arm was still around me, and he smiled crookedly as he stared into my eyes. Then he leaned back, putting what little space he could between us.

"You know, since I have you hostage on this ride, I should be using the time to find out more of the deep, dark secrets that you refuse to tell me," Gabe said.

I laughed. "Why are you so obsessed with me having secrets?"

"Because you have them," he insisted with an unrelenting grin.

"How do you know?"

"Am I wrong?" he countered.

"There's nothing deep or dark about me," I replied evasively. "I bet you're the one with all the secrets."

"Never." Gabe tried to look me in the eyes when he said it, but there was a subtle shift, a glimmer of something dark, and I knew he was lying.

"No, I can tell. I can see it in your eyes," I told him. "You're hiding something."

He didn't deny it this time. "So are you."

"Okay." I folded my arms over my chest and stared expectantly at him. "So tell me your deepest, darkest secret."

"I . . ." He started to say something, but his expression became pained. He turned away and leaned forward on the railing in front of us, resting his arms on it. "I would if I could."

"Why not?" I asked, surprised that he was admitting hiding anything.

"We've only . . . this is what? Our second date?"

"We're counting last night as a date?" I asked, thinking of my earlier conversation with Roxie.

"Any night that ends in kissing is a date," he assured me with a smile. "How about on our . . ." He paused, thinking. "Fifth date, we tell each other our big secrets."

"You think we'll make it to a fifth date?" I tried to make a joke of it, but my smile felt forced.

It actually stung a little thinking about future dates. The sideshow never stayed anywhere for more than a week or two, and I knew for a fact that Gideon planned on pulling out of here next Sunday. Unless we saw each other every day—and I doubted that even the clingiest of suitors would plan for that—there would be no way we'd make it to five dates.

"I'm trying to bribe you," Gabe said. "If you tolerate me for three more dates, you get to know a secret. That's a heck of a deal, really."

"But what if I don't have a secret?" I asked.

"You do."

"And what if you're lying and you don't have one either?"

The corner of his mouth was curled up slightly, but his eyes were serious. "I'm not."

"Okay. It's a deal," I said, knowing I'd just agreed to something that would never happen anyway. The carnival would have closed up, and I'd be long gone before I ever heard his secret, or he ever found out about mine.

The ride came to a stop, and Gabe got off first. He took my hand, helping me down, and then, with our hands still linked together, we walked around the rides, but we didn't go on any more. We talked, not about anything important, and he made me laugh.

It was the closest thing I'd ever had to a true date, the way I imagined dates would go. For a little while, I even forgot to worry about who might see Gabe and me together, and how they might react if they did.

That all came to an abrupt halt when we approached the shimmering tent where my mom worked. The curtain was tied open, meaning she didn't have any clients, and though she couldn't see us from where we stood, if we went any closer, she definitely would.

"Do you wanna get your fortune read?" Gabe asked, since I'd stopped short.

"Um, not tonight." I let go of his hand and stepped away from him. "What time is it?"

He checked his neon-colored Swatch. "It's nine thirty."

"I should probably get going." I offered him a rueful smile. "The acrobat show is over. I need to find my friends."

"What's the rush? Are you Cinderella?" Gabe asked. "Will you turn into a pumpkin at nine thirty-one?"

"No, it's just later than I thought. That's all." I took a step back, moving away from my mom's tent, but he stayed where he was, giving me a curious look.

"Okay. So can I call you?"

"Um, I'm kinda in between phones now." Since I'd spent so much of my life on the road, I hadn't had a real phone number in years.

He took a step toward me now. "What about our third date?"

"You still wanna do that?"

"You don't?" Gabe asked, sounding surprised.

"I do," I said. "When?"

"Tomorrow?"

"Okay," I agreed, before even trying to decide whether I'd be busy or if that worked or not. "Where?"

"How about we meet here again? Since you don't have a phone. Unless you want to give me your address—"

"Here's great," I replied quickly. "Does eight work for you?"

"Yeah. That'll be great." He nodded. "I had fun tonight."

I smiled back at him, hoping I wasn't beaming too much. "Me too."

Before he could say any more, I turned and ran back toward the circus tent. When I was certain that I was far enough away that he couldn't see me, I darted between the booths and headed back toward the campsite.

11. temperance

The midway and the rides stayed open until midnight, but the shows stopped at eleven. The carnival was really divided into two parts—the rides and games that a person would find at the fair, run by Doug, and the sideshow and acts that someone would find at a circus, run by Gideon.

Though Gideon had the final word on everything, the midway and the sideshow really worked as two separate autonomous entities. We even kept our camps separately. Those of us who worked in the sideshow kept our motorhomes parked in an oblong, and during the day, we'd often gather together for meals.

Doug had his own carnies and gophers who ran all the games and the rides, but the sideshow only had Hutch and me. Hutch technically ran the museum, but that didn't keep him too busy, so he ended up helping out with odd jobs a lot.

After Gabe left, I spent the rest of the night trying to avoid the fairgrounds, since I didn't want to bump into him or his family again. I cleaned up around the camp, helped Gideon out with some of his bookkeeping, and prepped a meal for when the carnival closed. Most people returned from work with a huge appetite, so we usually ate the biggest meal of the day around midnight.

My mom returned a little before eleven. I was outside, cooking up potatoes in tinfoil on the grill, and she walked right past me without saying a word, hurrying into our Winnebago with her shawl pulled tightly around her.

"Mom?" I called after her, but she didn't answer.

She'd finished up early, and she'd ignored me. Both of those were bad signs, so I moved the food off the grill, then went into the trailer to check on her.

"I don't need you," Mom snapped as soon as I came inside.

Hunched over the kitchen sink, the lines in her face looked more prominent than normal. Her hands gripped the end of the counter with such intensity that her knuckles had turned white.

"Why don't you go lie down?" I suggested gently. "I could put on music for you and turn it down low."

"That won't help, Mara!" Mom shouted. "Nothing will make this damn headache go away, so why don't you just go run along and do whatever the hell it was that you were doing before I came back and ruined your night?"

"Mom." I sighed.

My mother was an animated and passionate person, but she didn't usually yell at me like this. The readings did this to her, draining her energy, hurting her mind. Not all the time, but more and more, nights were ending like this.

"I was just making food outside. Did you want me to get anything for you?" I asked.

"I already told you no!"

A half-empty glass of water was sitting on the counter next to her, and she grabbed it and suddenly hurled it at me. I ducked out of the way just in time, and it smashed into the wall behind me.

"*Mom!*" I yelled. "You can't just throw a glass at me!"

"I don't know, Mara!" She waved her hands wildly as she spoke, and her eyes were frantic. "What can I do? I can't do anything! And I don't even know where Blossom is! I can't help anyone!"

"I know you're hurting, but this isn't helping," I told her as calmly and reasonably as I could. "You need to find a better way of coping. You can't keep acting like this every time you have a bad night."

The door creaked open behind me, and Gideon leaned in. "Is everything okay in here?"

"Everything's great! Nothing's fine!" Mom shouted, and then laughed, as if to punctuate her schizophrenic statement.

I could only turn back and look at him. I didn't say anything to Gideon—not just because my mom was right there, but because if I tried to speak, I'd cry. Helplessly, I shook my head and pressed my lips together to keep the tears from spilling over.

"Go on, love," Gideon said softly, his British accent warming his words. "I'll calm her down."

"Where are all my tapes, Mara?" Mom demanded.

A stack of cassette tapes had been sitting on the counter. They'd fallen out of cupboards yesterday when we'd been driving into Caudry, and I just hadn't put them all back yet. But now, in a fit of rage, Mom swung her arm out, knocking them all to the floor.

"Lyanka." Gideon pushed past me and walked toward her. "You need to stop."

"No. Why do you all think you can tell me what to do? Did Blossom hide all my tapes?" Mom asked him, her voice trembling.

"This isn't about her." He rubbed the back of his neck, then he turned back to me. "Why don't you find somewhere else to sleep, all right? I'll take care of her, but it might be a long night."

I nodded, then rushed out the door just as my mother began swearing at him. She continued shouting for a while after I left, and it traveled through the thin walls of the motorhome. But eventually Gideon put on music, and that either drowned out the sound of her yelling or calmed her.

People started arriving back at the campsite shortly after that, and we all ate together around picnic tables underneath a couple strings of white Christmas lights. When we finished, I opted to head over to the trailer that Luka, Seth, and Hutch shared, and Roxie decided to tag along.

There were other places I could've hung out if I wanted to, but Luka, Seth, and Hutch had the nicest one. It was a 1986 Winnebago Minnie Winnie 24RC, and they'd paid almost thirty grand for it last summer. Considering the sideshow was going broke, that was an exorbitant amount of money.

Luka and Seth had made all the money on their own, though. Between shows, they'd go out to bars and trick drunk guys into betting that they couldn't do something. Seth was supernaturally strong, and Luka could heal from anything, so he'd swallow glass or pound nails into his hand. It still hurt like hell, but for the right price, it'd been worth it.

They'd made most of their money before Hutch had stumbled upon us. He'd run away from a rough home life with his entire life savings in his pocket, which amounted to a couple grand. It was that final contribution that put them over the edge, so Luka and Seth had let him live with them.

He'd still added the smallest share, so he had the bunk above the cab, while Luka and Seth claimed the bunk beds in the back. It was a chic trailer, and the boys had it decked out with the latest amenities, like a TV and VCR and a tape deck with speakers built in throughout the trailer. Not to mention a top-of-the-line AC and heater, so we all spent a great deal of time hanging out in their camper.

When we went into Luka's camper, I slid into the dinette bench next to Roxie. Luka went over to the fridge to get out a couple bottles of beer, and Hutch pulled out the deck of cards before sitting down across from us.

"Where's Seth?" I asked, noticing that their third roommate hadn't followed us inside.

Luka set four beers down on the table, then sat across from me. "I think he went over to hang out with Carrie."

"And that's why I'm here." Roxie grabbed a bottle and flipped the top off. "There's only so many times I can put on headphones and pretend that I can't hear Seth and Carrie having sex over Joan Jett."

"Yeah, that makes sense," I said, and took a beer for myself.

"So, what are we playing tonight? Poker? Gin? Blackjack?" Hutch asked as he shuffled the deck of cards.

"How about gin? We haven't played that in a while," Luka said.

"Gin it is." Hutch finished shuffling and dealt the cards. When he'd finished, we all organized our hands. "Okay. So here's what I don't understand. Can you see my cards, Mara?"

I shook my head. "Not unless you show them to me."

"But your mom could see them, right? If she were playing with us?" Hutch asked.

"No." I looked at him over the top of my cards and saw the bewilderment in his brown eyes. "She's not psychic."

"But then how does she see stuff?" Hutch lowered his cards and the furrow in his brow deepened.

"She's a necromancer," I explained. "She has contact with the spirits, and she sees what they tell her. Sometimes they give her insight into the future, or into people's true motives. But that's only because spirits can see more than we can."

"And that's different than being psychic how?" Hutch asked.

Laying his cards facedown the table, Luka chuckled a little. He leaned back in the booth, content to drink his beer and watch Hutch try to sort this all out.

"Hutch," Roxie said, eyeing him severely. "You've been traveling with us for, like, nine months, and you still haven't figured this stuff out?"

"It's confusing." Hutch shrugged and lowered his eyes as he shifted his cards around in his hand. "Maybe you don't know because you grew up around it or you've been playing with fire and shoving swords down your throat most of your life. But for me, it's all a bit strange still."

"Where I grew up, there was nobody around who could do the things I did," Roxie said, her expression darkening.

"They all thought I was a freak and practically ran me out of town," Luka chimed in. "It wasn't until I joined the sideshow that things started making sense."

"Right." Hutch looked between the two of them. "Because people explained things to you."

"A psychic can see your thoughts, read minds, that kinda thing," I told him. "A necromancer talks with the dead. That's the difference."

"And Gideon's psychic," Hutch said.

I nodded. "Right."

"So he could read my cards, if he were here right now?" Hutch asked.

"He could, if he wanted to," I allowed. "But he usually works to keep out of other people's minds. He doesn't like invading their privacy."

"How does he do that?" Hutch asked.

"There's a couple different ways," I said, explaining it as I best understood it from what Gideon had told me. "One of them is practice, another way is keeping himself distracted and busy. He's always reading or talking or doing something. He never just sits alone."

"Alcohol helps," Luka added, taking another drink of his beer.

Roxie nodded, laughing in agreement. "Oh yeah, alcohol definitely dulls the extra senses."

"So then why do you guys drink?" Hutch asked.

"Sometimes, that *is* why," Luka said.

"The year before I joined the sideshow, I was on a nonstop drinking binge, trying to make it go away," Roxie said.

Hutch looked over at her. "You don't like being able to make fire?"

"Pyrokinesis is all fun and games until you accidentally burn down your family's house, destroying everything you own, including your pet goldfish, and burning your stepdad's hands," Roxie told him flatly.

In her early teens, Roxie had begun to realize that she had the power to create fire, but that wasn't the worst of her problems. Around the same time, her stepdad realized that she was blossoming into a beautiful young woman, and he decided that he should act on it.

Roxie did her best to control the fire, and for the most part, she did a good job. It was just much harder to keep under wraps when she was upset or frightened. When her stepdad snuck into her room late one night, she'd finally had enough.

Unfortunately, the fire had gotten away from her. While the firefighters were still hosing down the rubble that had once been her home, Roxie turned and walked away, and she never went back.

"But we're, like, super poor right now?" Hutch asked.

"Well, we're always kinda poor, but yeah." I sighed. "We're pretty broke."

"Then why doesn't Gideon just go to Vegas and bet it all?" Hutch asked.

I shook my head. "Gideon has played in poker games before, but only when he's desperate. He doesn't like cheating."

Luka picked up his cards and leaned forward on the table. "So, are we gonna play cards, or what? I've had a long night already."

For the first time, I noticed the weariness in Luka's face, the kind of look he'd get after a long night of working. He didn't have a show tonight, but he'd been performing for tips, wandering around the midway swallowing swords and juggling knives. But that kinda thing usually didn't affect him this badly.

"What happened?" I asked as he dealt the cards. "Why such a long night?"

"It was mostly fine until toward the end of the night," Luka explained. "There were these two rich townie assholes wearing sunglasses even though it's the middle of the night, and they were drunk as hell."

I grimaced and my heart began to race as I realized to my dismay that it sounded like Luka was describing Logan and Troy, two of Gabe's sister's friends.

"They were just being punks and asking me what would happen if they stabbed me through the stomach," Luka said. "They just wouldn't let up, even when I tried walking away. One of the guys had a girlfriend, and she kept trying to drag him off and apologizing. It was really sad, actually."

That definitely sounded like Logan, Troy, and Selena. At least it seemed like Gabe wasn't around and hadn't joined in. I lowered my eyes and tried to keep my expression blank. I didn't want to hear the lectures from Roxie or Luka about associating with them, especially not after I'd had such a nice time with Gabe earlier tonight.

"Eventually, Seth came over and chased him off," Luka finished. "But it still sucked dealing with them."

"I'm sorry," I mumbled, because there was nothing more I could say.

12. townie

We played a full game and had started the second one when Tim Phoenix came in to join us. Other than being leaner and younger than his brother, Brendon, he looked almost exactly like him. Blond hair, blue eyes, and a bright smile, it was easy to see what Luka saw in him. Not to mention how good he looked in his acrobat uniform.

"Am I interrupting?" Tim asked.

Luka shook his head. "Not at all."

Tim kissed Luka, then sat down at the swivel chair across from the dinette. "So, Mara, I didn't have a chance to talk to you earlier today. How did it go at the police station? Do they know anything about Blossom?"

"She hasn't been gone long enough for them to really investigate, but it sounds like there's a big equinox music festival going on one county over, so she might've gone there," I explained. "If she doesn't show up in a couple days, I have a number I can call for more help."

"I told you." Roxie poked me in the arm to emphasize her point. "Blossom loves chilling out, getting high, and listening to jams. That equinox shit sounds right up her alley."

"We don't know for sure that's where she is yet," I pointed out.

"Not yet, but we will when she turns up just before we roll out of town," Roxie said. She set her cards down in the center of the table and leaned back against the wall, so she was facing me. "Anyway, how did it go with that guy tonight?"

Luka set his cards on top of Roxie's. "What guy are you talking about?"

"Didn't you hear?" Roxie asked with a smirk. "Mara was doing the nasty with a townie."

"So what?" Hutch asked, sounding irritated. "Are we just done playing then?"

I rolled my eyes. "We didn't hook up."

"Oh, yeah." Tim grinned. "I heard about that."

I tensed but tried to nonchalantly take a sip of my beer. "What did you hear?"

"I heard you guys were making out on the Ferris wheel," Tim said.

"We just kissed a couple times." I tried to play it off but nobody seemed to be buying it.

"I saw him. He's cute," Roxie said.

Luka leaned forward on the table, eyes wide and excited. "So are you gonna see him again?"

"I don't know." I lowered my eyes and didn't know how to answer the question. I wanted to, and we'd made plans to, but I wasn't actually sure that I should. "Maybe."

"I always worry about dating a townie. What if you get attached?" Tim asked, expressing my sentiments.

"Well, it's not just that. I mean, he's a *townie*," Luka said. "You know how they can be to people like us."

Before Luka had gotten involved with Tim, he'd once tried to date a townie, and it had ended with the guy and a few of his friends beating the crap out of Luka when they realized he worked as a sideshow freak.

And that was only one of many similar stories I'd heard. My romantic entanglements hadn't turned out as badly as they had for some people, because I usually had the good sense to get out of there before they realized who or what I was.

I shook my head, deciding that my urge to see Gabe was overriding all of my fears. "We're just having some fun, and I'll be okay."

"Yeah, Mara's a real pro," Hutch said, making me sound like a prostitute. "She does this kinda thing all the time."

"Thanks, Hutch," I said dryly.

Roxie yawned. "Anyway, it's getting late. I probably should head back to my trailer. Seth and Carrie have to be done by now."

"Are you crashing here tonight?" Luka asked me.

"If you guys don't mind." I stood up so Roxie could slide out behind me. "My mom's kinda in a funk."

"Yeah, it's no problem. If Seth doesn't come back, you can sleep in his bunk in back," Luka offered, motioning to the back of the trailer.

I noticed a disappointed look on Tim's face and shook my head. "No, that's fine. I can sleep out here." I patted the bench cushions that were about a hundred times softer and fluffier than my own bed. "Me and Hutch can have pillow talk."

"Good. You can tell him what it's like to kiss with tongue," Roxie teased as she opened the door. "He's been dying to find out."

"I've kissed girls before!" Hutch called after her.

She waved as she stepped outside, letting the warm night air waft into the trailer. "Night, guys."

Once she was gone, we cleared off the table. The dining table and couch folded down into a nice-size bed, and Tim started getting it ready for me while I threw away the empty beer bottles. Hutch hopped up onto his bed above the driver's seat and Luka came back with blankets and a pillow from Seth's bed.

"Need anything else?" Luka asked after he handed me the bedding.

"Is it cool if I borrow, like, a pair of jamma pants, so I don't have to sleep in my dress?" I asked.

I could've gone back to my own trailer to get something to sleep in, but I didn't want to risk waking up my mom. She'd be all apologetic now, and she'd want to cry and hug me, and I was getting tired and didn't really want to deal with that.

Luka got me a pair of pajama pants out of his wardrobe, and I went back into the bedroom to change. Their plastic accordion door actually worked, unlike my own, and I pulled it closed behind me.

I slipped off my dress, leaving me in my tank top and panties, and then I pulled on the pants. They were a little loose on me, so I pulled the drawstring as tight as I could.

As I was doing that, I heard this strange hissing sound, like how I'd imagine a really giant cobra would sound if it were really pissed off.

"Do you guys hear that?" I asked, and pulled the bedroom door open.

Luka nodded. "What the hell is it?"

"I have no idea," I said, and the sound only seemed to grow louder.

Tim apparently decided that he should find out, so he opened the front door. He leaned out, looking around, and I came up behind him, standing on my tiptoes to see if I could see anything, but there was nothing. Tim stepped outside, and I followed him.

"Are you guys seriously going out there to check out a strange noise?" Hutch asked. "Didn't you see *Friday the 13th* parts one through four?"

"Quiet," Luka shushed him, but he stayed just inside the trailer.

"We'll be right back," I said as I ventured farther out into the campsite.

I could hear Hutch muttering, "So, I'll take that as a no, you did not see them."

Luka's motorhome was the only one that had lights on, so everyone else must've been asleep. A streetlamp glowed behind Gideon's trailer, and the moon shone above us, making it just bright enough where I could see.

Tim was ahead of me, and he went left, so I decided to go right. A few lawn chairs were sitting out in front of Betty and Damon's trailer, and they'd been tipped over. Other than that, I didn't really see any signs of trouble.

"Oh, shit," Tim said.

Luka left the safety of his motorhome and jogged over to where Tim stood beside Gideon's trailer, and I hurried over to join them.

"What?" I asked, but as soon as I reached him, I saw the problem. Spray painted in neon green on the side of Gideon's trailer was one word:

It wasn't even spelled right, but I'd come to learn that the people who usually defamed our trailers very often had poor spelling. No matter how many times I heard it hurled at me, it never hurt less, and it never felt any less angry or cruel.

"What a buncha dicks," Luka said, and he took his boy-friend's hand.

I sighed. "Looks like I'll have something fun to scrub off tomorrow."

Tim tilted his head, listening. "Do you still hear that?"

I hadn't heard anything, but as soon as he mentioned it, I noticed a low, guttural sound. But it had a gurgle to it too, like an overflowing soda bottle mixed with an injured animal.

"That is not a spray can," I said.

Tim pointed to Roxie's Airstreamer, shimmering like a silver bullet in the moonlight. "It's coming from Roxie's trailer."

Luka held on to Tim's hand, trying to slow him down, so I sprinted ahead. The noise grew more pained, and almost recognizable—like it was human. I raced around the back of Roxie's trailer, running toward the noise.

I nearly tripped over Seth's shoe, and then I saw him. It was dark enough where the blood looked black, and Seth was completely drenched in it. He'd been shredded—his arms, legs, everything was sliced up. His stomach had been torn open, and his entrails were spread out around him like slick sausage.

Somehow, he was still alive, but a slash across his throat made it impossible for him to talk. I crouched down next to him and took his hand. He squeezed back, but he no longer seemed to have the superior strength he should've. His eyes stared up at me, filled with terror, and blood spilled out from his lips. He opened his mouth to speak, but no words came out.

SUNDAY, MARCH 15, 1987

13. provisions

The water was cold, freezing my fingers, but I barely even noticed it, even though they were raw from how long I'd spent trying to scrub Seth's blood off my hands.

Behind me, the sun rose lovely above the treetops, promising another beautiful morning, while I used a sponge and bucket to try to wash off the graffiti from the side of Gideon's trailer. Roxie had tried to wash all the blood from beside her trailer, and from the corner of my eye, I could see a huge rust-colored puddle slowly drying.

I'd exchanged my bloodied pajamas for jean shorts and a T-shirt, and though I'd really wanted to shower and wash away everything, I'd felt like there was too much that needed to be done. I'd settled for washing the blood off my skin and pulling my thick hair back into a ponytail, then went to work.

Everyone else had gathered in the center of the camp, arguing and placing the blame squarely on Zeke Desmond and his two tigers.

Well, not everyone. Gideon and Carrie were still at the hospital with Seth.

"You know bloody well that it wasn't my tigers!" Zeke shouted. He'd been yelling so much that his face had begun to turn beet red, matching the shock of hair that sprang wildly from his head. "They're still in their pens, and if they'd gotten out, they'd still be out."

"The gate to their cage was open!" Doug shouted. He'd left his post in the midway camp to come over and give us all orders, since Gideon wasn't here.

"They were still in their cage," Zeke insisted. "They didn't go anywhere."

In the aftermath of discovering Seth, the tigers' gate had been discovered wide open, but both of them were still inside, cowering in the corner. Mahilā had been making a plaintive mewling sound all morning, which many of the people in our troupe took to be a sign of guilt.

But no one else had really taken to actually confronting Zeke. They stood in a small semicircle crowded around Doug and Zeke, watching the two of them go at it. Except for my mother, who was still in her trailer, and me, because I couldn't just stand there doing nothing.

I kept picturing Seth, and the weakness of his hand as it gripped mine. I had to keep moving so I wouldn't think about him so much.

"You heard what Mara and Tim said," Doug said through a mouthful of chewing tobacco. "It looked like Seth had been mauled by a tiger."

"No, we never said that." I stopped scrubbing the trailer and looked over at them. "Seth was attacked by something, but we never said we thought it was a tiger."

Doug scoffed. "What else could it be? There's no bears around here."

"I don't know," I admitted, and lowered my eyes.

"It was probably the same vandals that spray painted Gideon's trailer," Zeke suggested, not for the first time.

"You think a person did that?" Doug pointed over to the puddle beside Roxie's trailer.

Zeke folded his arms over his chest, standing as tall as he could. "It wouldn't be the first time that the locals had come after us like that."

Doug shook his head. "They've got no reason to. We just got here, and we haven't done anything."

"They had no reason to deface Gideon's trailer like that either, but they did," Zeke countered. "And you know how people have treated all of us."

Tim shook his head, and when he spoke, his voice sounded hollow and cold. "No, you all didn't see Seth. There's no way a human did that." He stood a few feet back, looking at the ground, and Luka had his arm around him.

Doug threw his hands up in the air. "Then it must be a tiger."

"It's not one of my tigers!" Zeke continued to protest. "Safēda wouldn't hurt a fly, and Mahilā wouldn't go anywhere without her sister."

Brendon Phoenix—Tim's older brother and the patriarch of *The Fantastic Flying Phoenixes*—had been holding back, standing in front of his trailer with his wife and three-year-old daughter. But he left now, walking over to stand in between Doug and Zeke.

He'd been with the sideshow for a long time. Whenever Gideon had business to attend to elsewhere, he usually left Brendon in charge.

"Everyone needs to just calm down," Brendon said. "Nobody knows what happened to Seth, okay? And whoever—or *whatever*—it was, it doesn't do us any good to fight amongst ourselves."

Doug spit a huge wad of gross tobacco spit on the ground, right near Zeke's feet. "We need to get rid of those damn tigers."

"Doug, we're not getting rid of anything," Brendon told him firmly. "And the carnival opens in a couple hours, so why don't you go back over and calm down your people?"

"The carnival is still on?" Doug laughed darkly. "You must be joking."

"I'm not." Brendon turned to survey the crowd around us, speaking to them. "Seth was hurt, and we're all sorry about that, but that doesn't change anything. We still have a job to do, and yesterday, we hardly made enough money to get us out of this state, let alone put food on the table. We need to go back to work."

Doug looked like he wanted to say more, but he just shook his head and started trudging back toward his camp.

"With Seth out of commission, we have to find something else to fill his strongman act," Brendon continued.

"Luka could step in," Hutch suggested. "He has his sword swallowing and fire breathing."

"I could work with Luka," Roxie offered. She'd been sitting on the steps in front of her Airstream, taking it all in, but she stood up now. "Make it a bit more elaborate and exciting."

I thought about mentioning the crossbow trick I'd been working on with Luka, but truth was, I didn't feel much like performing, and Roxie had it covered. But I still planned to get my crossbow out tonight and practice with it—if there was something attacking the camp, I wanted to be prepared.

"Why don't you two talk it over and see what you can come up with?" Brendon asked.

With Doug gone and under Brendon's direction, the carnival slowly rolled into motion. Brendon was right—there was still a lot to do if we wanted to open today, and we had to if we wanted to get out of here eventually.

Hutch came over to me, and without saying anything, he grabbed a sponge from the sudsy bucket and started scrubbing beside me. A bandana had been looped around his forehead to keep his shaggy brown hair out of his face, and it highlighted the dark circles under his eyes. None of us had gotten any sleep last night.

The campsite had started coming alive—people chatting with each other, things being moved around, breakfast being made. But then it all suddenly fell silent, eerily so, like someone had hit an off switch on a radio.

And then I saw him. Coming in between the trailers with blood staining his clothes, Gideon had returned, and he was alone.

14. divination

Everyone kept their distance, silently watching Gideon, as if he'd become contagious, and if you went near him, what happened to Seth would happen to you too.

My mom must've been watching for him from inside the Winnebago, because she ran out toward him, her shawl billowing out behind her.

"How is he?" Mom asked, her voice soft but desperate.

"It's not good." Gideon took a deep breath and spoke loud enough so everyone would be able to hear him. "Seth is alive, but . . . Carrie's staying with him, and I think she should be up there for as long as he is."

"Does that mean he doesn't have very long?" Hutch asked.

Gideon rubbed his forehead. "I don't know."

"Did Seth say what happened?" Betty asked, frowning through her beard.

"Did they rule out the tigers yet?" Zeke asked. "Doug has been insisting it's my tigers, but you know that it can't be."

Gideon held up his hand, silencing everyone. "I will be out to talk to all of you, but can you give me a few minutes to get cleaned up?"

"Back up, everyone," Brendon commanded. "We'll have a meeting before the carnival starts. Go about your business."

Mom put her hand on Gideon's back and walked with him into his trailer. I'd been cleaning the side of it, but I walked closer to the back door, where their words could travel through the screen door.

"Lyanka, love, will you get me your cards?" Gideon asked.

"You want me to do a reading?" my mom asked.

"If you can, please," Gideon said, and there was a desperation in his voice that terrified me.

"Yes, of course. I'll be right back."

I took a step back, so I was more hidden around the corner of Gideon's trailer, and watched as my mom darted out of the trailer. As she walked across the campsite to our Winnebago, she pulled her shawl more tightly around her, as if keeping out a chill only she could feel.

If I tried to talk to Gideon while my mom was there, she'd only tell me to leave him be and that he needed his rest. And I knew she was right, but I couldn't shake the image of Seth, the darkness of his blood covering him. I had to find out what happened.

Slowly, I climbed up the steps of Gideon's trailer. The only light came from the morning sun streaming in through his dusty curtains. He sat hunched over the table with one hand buried in his black hair, still in his bloodied clothes. A half-empty glass sat beside a bottle of whisky next to his hand.

I pushed open the screen door without knocking, and Gideon lifted his head to look back at me. Outside, he'd kept his eyes down, but now he was looking right at me so I could see them— how the light blue had gone so dark, they were almost black.

"What's going on?" I asked.

He looked away, but it was too late. "It's nothing."

"Gideon, I saw it in your eyes, and I saw Seth before he was taken to the hospital." I stepped closer to him. "What happened?"

"He couldn't speak," Gideon said finally. "But I read his mind."

"And?" I pressed when he didn't go on.

"It was mostly pain, blurred images. But whatever hurt him, it wasn't human."

My heart dropped, even though I'd known it all along. Having my fears confirmed didn't make me feel any better, though.

"What was it?" I asked.

"I don't know." Gideon paused to take a long drink from his glass. "It was all claws and fangs and glowing eyes. But there was nothing clear. When I see someone's thoughts, it's not like a video camera replaying a movie. It's all filtered through that person's emotions and prejudices."

He looked back at me then. "So, it's what Seth perceived, not necessarily what it actually was."

"So what does that mean?" I asked.

He sighed. "It means that it could've been anything that attacked Seth."

The screen door creaked behind me, making me jump, and Mom brushed past me, her deck of tarot cards in her hand. She didn't look at me, but she didn't tell me to leave either, so I decided to stay.

"Are you okay?" Mom asked, gently touching Gideon's forehead, as if he had the flu instead of the ability to read people's minds and see their most horrific memories.

"I'm all right." He stood up rather abruptly. "I should get changed before we do the reading."

Mom nodded and watched Gideon until he disappeared into his bedroom at the far end of the trailer. Then she took a fortifying breath and sat down at the table. With the cards in her hands, she began to shuffle them slowly, but her gaze rested on me.

"How are you doing, *qamari*?"

I shrugged, unsure of how to answer. "I'm okay."

"I'm sorry about last night," Mom said, referring to her outburst before everything had happened with Seth. Her cheeks reddened slightly with shame, and she lowered her eyes so her dark lashes rested on her cheeks.

"It's okay." I tried to ease her worries. "I understand."

"It's not okay, Mara," she said harshly, and shook her head, then she looked back up at me. "But I'll do better. I promise you. Things will get better."

I forced a smile. "I know."

"And I'm sorry that you found Seth like you did this morning." She set the cards aside. "I know the two of you were friends."

Seth had been traveling with us for five years now, so we'd practically grown up together. Two summers ago, we'd briefly tried our hand at dating and exchanged a few kisses, but it felt wrong to me, like dating my brother. But Seth had always been kind to me, and quick to help anyone who needed it.

I'd often thought of him as a gentle giant, and I could still remember the strength of his arms when he had pulled me to him for a kiss. He could've crushed me if he'd wanted to, but I'd never felt anything but safe with him.

And something had attacked him, something strong enough to take him down and leave him so weak he could barely squeeze my hand.

"All right," Gideon said as he came back, pulling me from my thoughts. "Shall we do the reading, then?"

He sat down across from my mom, and I felt weird just standing and gawking at them, so I sat down in the chair beside my mom. I was careful to be as quiet as possible, because if I proved to be a distraction, I knew they would send me away.

"It's been so long since I've done a reading for you," Mom mused as she handed Gideon the deck. Whenever she did readings, she always made sure her clients handled them first. She said they needed to get a feel for the cards, and the cards needed to get a feel for them.

"It has been," Gideon admitted.

Years ago, before the readings had begun taking their toll on my mother, she would do readings for him often, getting a sense of where we should go and helping make decisions for the carnival. But once Gideon saw how badly they affected her, he'd stopped.

"What kind of spread did you have in mind?" Mom asked as he shuffled the cards.

"Just a simple three-card one."

"Do you know what you want to ask?" Mom asked.

He nodded. "I have a question in mind."

"You don't wish to share with me?" she asked, trying to keep the pain from her voice.

He set the deck in front of her. "Not this time, love, if that's all right."

"If it's what you wish."

She broke the deck three times, so it sat in three piles before her. With a three-card spread, the first card would represent the past, the middle card the present, and the final card the future.

Mom took a card from the first deck, and laid it in front of Gideon. It depicted a full moon in a dark purple sky, shining above a few trees. Hidden in the very bottom corner of the card was a white wolf, right above the name of the card—The Moon.

The second card my mom flipped over was upside down, so it faced her, which meant it was in the reverse position. It showed a man draped in robes of gold and purple, holding a ball of lightning above his head—The Magician.

The final card she turned over, she saw it before Gideon did, and I heard her breath catch in her throat. It showed a skeleton in a black robe riding a white horse over a graveyard—Death.

Mom folded her hands before her, staring down at the cards. "Do you know what the cards mean, or shall I do the reading?"

"Do your reading." Gideon leaned back in his chair. "I want to know what you're sensing."

"I'm not sensing as much as I'd like, but I'll do my best." Mom tapped the first card with her long fingers. "The Moon in your past represents a confusing, dark time. You may not have always understood your actions, and the world may have put a heavy burden on your shoulders.

"On its own, it means nothing negative," she continued, moving her fingers to the next card. "But when paired with the Magician, it means that someone or something destructive is manipulating your choices, and you may pay a price."

Her shawl had slipped off her shoulder, revealing the large sun she had tattooed on her dark skin.

"The Magician is a man of great power and talent, with the ability to cross between the spirit world and the world of humanity, but in reverse, it represents a blockage of that path," Mom went on. "And if the Magician is not careful, he can lose everything that matters to him.

"Death, as you know, does not usually mean death," she said, but she didn't touch this card. She'd tapped the first two, but this time, instead, she pulled her shawl up around her again. "It simply means that something is coming to an end. It can be a positive, that the darkness and financial loss that have plagued us these last few months might be lifted."

Gideon stared thoughtfully at the cards for a moment, then asked, "Do you get any other senses about what it all means?"

"It's not clear, Gideon. There's something . . . *here*." She gestured widely around us, referring to Caudry as a whole. "I think that's why my headache was so bad before I'd hardly even done any readings. There's another energy fogging everything up."

"So you can't get a good sense of things?" he asked.

She shook her head grimly. "No. I'm sorry."

"No, it's all right, love," he brushed it off, and continued staring down at the cards.

"Do you feel it too?" I asked.

"What?" He looked up at me, as if he'd forgotten I was there.

"Mom said she's feeling foggy. What about you?" I asked.

He leaned back in his seat again. "I'm definitely getting a weird energy here, but I'm not sure if 'foggy' is how I'd describe it."

"Then how would you?" I pressed.

"Do you know what a divining rod is?"

I shook my head. "No."

"My grandfather used to use one," Gideon explained. "He swore by it, though he swore by a lot of things I'm not so sure of. He would use a stick branched out in the shape of a Y, and that would be the divining rod.

"Then he'd grab on to each end of the Y and walk into fields," he continued. "The idea is that the rod would be able to sense water or metal or oil or whatever other worthy substance it was searching for."

"Did it?" I asked.

Gideon nodded. "Sometimes, yeah, he did discover something of value. And sometimes it works like that for me."

"What does?"

"It's how I was able to find Lyanka." He pointed to my mom, a small smile playing on his lips. "And all the other *special* people in the sideshow. I'd get a sense about them. Just something inside, and I knew that they were like me. Like *us*. So I'd ask them to join."

I crinkled my forehead. "So you're, like, a supernatural divining rod?"

"Something like that," he said, then wagged his fingers in the air. "Except now, I seem to be getting false positives everywhere."

"How can you be sure?" I asked. "Maybe everyone here is secretly supernatural."

"That I might consider, but I'm getting senses from things that certainly aren't—like a rock or a bush or the tigers or Hutch," Gideon elaborated. "The rock and the bush, maybe something had rubbed off on them, but certainly, the tigers and Hutch didn't suddenly gain some kind of power in the last twenty-four hours."

"Do you think the tigers had something to do with this?" I asked.

"I don't know." Gideon shook his head. "There's something strange about this town. Maybe that's making the tigers act crazy."

"There is something dark here," Mom said.

Gideon stood up, startling both my mom and me. "And it's about time I got to the bottom of it."

"Where are you going?" Mom asked.

"To see Leonid Murphy."

15. blue moon

For the second day in a row, I found myself in Gideon's beat-up truck on the short ride from our campsite at the carnival on the outskirts of town to Caudry town proper. This time, Luka had been enlisted to join us, and I sat between him and Gideon.

Whenever Gideon went to deal with someone who might be trouble—like a vendor who refused to pay us our dues or an unsavory biker gang that kept messing with Roxie and Carrie at the peep show—he brought along Seth and Luka with him. Seth because he was so strong, and Luka because he healed so quickly, he could handle just about anything.

While I knew I wouldn't be much of a replacement for Seth, I wanted to help. Truthfully, I think Gideon let me tag along on the off chance that I sensed something he missed, that I could pick up things like my mom did.

We drove through Caudry until we reached the other side, driving on a wide road lined with cypresses and willows until we reached a building nestled right up against the swamp. The porch out front looked like it had seen better days, but the fresh coat of navy blue paint and new windows suggested that it was in the process of being fixed up.

Along the top was a sign that looked brand-new, and the words *Blue Moon Bar & Grill* were written in big bold letters next to a painting of a crescent moon.

"This is it?" I asked as Gideon parked in front of it.

"This is a restaurant," Luka said, pointing out the obvious. "Leonid can't live here."

"Well, this is the address he gave me." Gideon picked up the tattered postcard from the dashboard.

The front showed an alligator, its mouth wide open and ready to snap down and take a bite. The back had Leonid's chicken scratch, promising us riches if we came to Caudry. He tapped the address Leonid had scrawled on it—*867 Brawley Boulevard*, and the numbers on the side of the building were printed clearly as 867.

"He told me to look him up when I came into town," Gideon added.

"I guess we should check it out, then," I said, since there didn't seem to be any other way to find Leonid, and he was our only real connection to this town.

A sign on the window had the word CLOSED in bold red letters, but that didn't stop Gideon. He gave the door a good tug and it opened, so we went inside.

The place was dark, dimly lit by a few bulbs over the bar, and it appeared about the same as it had on the outside—newer tables and vintage artwork in shiny frames, but the floors were gray and warped. The bar in the back had a marble counter-top, but the stools in front were worn and faded. The whole place felt as if it was in mid-renovation.

The swinging doors to the kitchen pushed open and a man came through, holding a dishrag in his hands. He was tall, with a full head of thick wavy hair sprinkled with hints of silver. His skin was the color of dark caramel, and the lines around his eyes and mouth suggested he was in his early forties.

"We're closed," he said, and his voiced rumbled with a strong Latino accent. "We open at four on Sundays, so if you come back in two hours, I'll be happy to seat you."

"Thank you, but we're not here to eat," Gideon explained. "We're looking for a friend."

The man had been walking toward us, but he stopped and tilted his head. "Someone who works here?"

"I don't know, actually. This is the address he gave me." Gideon gestured to the restaurant. "He's called Leonid Mur-phy."

"Leonid?" An odd smile spread out across the man's face. "There's a small apartment just above the bar, and Leonid rents it from us. If you go around to the south side, you'll find a stair-case alongside the building that leads up to it."

"Thank you." Gideon offered him a small wave, and we started making our exit.

"Are you with the carnival, then?" the man called after us, stopping us just before we reached the door.

Gideon paused for a moment, then turned back to face him.

"Yeah, I'm Gideon Davorin. I run it, actually." He motioned to me, then Luka. "This is Mara Beznik, and Luka Zajíček. They work there too."

"I'm Julian Alvarado." He put his hand to his chest, and my mind instantly flashed to Gabe. His name was Alvarado, and in a town this size, I had to wonder if they were related. "This is my place.

"I've heard a lot of great things about the carnival, but I haven't been out to see it yet," Julian went on, and I wondered if the good things he'd heard had come from Gabe. Had he spoken of me? "The restaurant keeps me busy."

"I would imagine," Gideon replied with an uneasy smile.

"But listen, if you guys or any of the carnival workers want to stop out here, you can have a drink on the house." Julian pointed to the bar in the back. "It's always great to have entertainers like you in Caudry. It breathes a bit of life into the old town."

Gideon thanked him again, and I hurried outside before Julian said anything more. He'd seemed nice enough, but I was terrified that Julian may be Gabe's father and that he could make a connection I didn't want him to make. If Gabe had mentioned me by name, "Mara" was uncommon enough that Julian would figure out that I was part of the carnival.

There was so much going on, I knew that I shouldn't even be worrying about what Gabe thought of me, or if I really would see him again. But I couldn't help it. I hadn't meant to make a connection with someone just when everything at home seemed to be falling apart.

"You okay?" Luka asked, noticing me dash out of the restaurant.

"Yeah, I'm fine." I smiled to reassure him. "Let's just go see Leonid."

Gideon led the way up the rickety stairs, and it was obvious that any repairs being done hadn't extended beyond the front of the house for the bar and grill. Before we'd even reached his door, I could smell something off—like acetone mixed with sulfur.

"Gross." Luka wrinkled his nose. "It's like someone spilled nail polish remover on a pile of rotten eggs."

"That means this is Leonid's place," Gideon said under his breath, and knocked on the door. He glanced back at Luka and me. "You guys hang until I see how Leonid is doing, all right?"

Leonid Murphy had traveled with the sideshow for many years, and I didn't know the full extent of the reason he'd left three years ago, but there had been very strong rumblings of drugs. I knew that Gideon didn't seem to care when Blossom or Doug smoked pot, so I figured it had to be something harsher and more complicated than that.

At any rate, Leonid had left on amicable terms—Gideon had given him a handshake, a few hundred dollars, and wished him all the best. That's why, despite Leonid's sketchy history, Gideon had trusted his old friend's postcard. Well, that and desperation.

"Just a second!" Leonid's nasally, slightly high-pitched voice wafted through his door.

Moments later, the front door flew open, and Leonid was exactly as I remembered him. He towered half a foot over Gideon, who was quite tall in his own right, and Leonid had answered the door shirtless, so I could see every rib and bone protruding through his pale skin.

His skeletal frame had nothing to do with any alleged drug use—it was the reason he'd joined the carnival. No matter how much he ate, he'd never gained a pound. He'd worked as a contortionist, and I'd seen him dislocate all his joints and bend himself up into a shockingly small pretzel.

"Gideon!" Leonid exclaimed, and without warning, he threw his arms around Gideon in one of the most awkward embraces I'd ever seen.

Then his eyes drifted over to Luka and me, and I noticed his normally green eyes had gone muddy. The left one, in particular, looked glossed over, like glaucoma had set in, even though Leonid couldn't have been more than twenty-seven or twenty-eight.

"Mara, Luka!" Leonid shouted, letting go of Gideon. "Oh gosh, the gang's all here. It's so great to see you all. I'm so glad you came."

"Well, you did invite us," Gideon told him, and he'd stepped back, leaning against the stair rail so he'd be a bit farther out from Leonid's reach.

"I did. Of course, I did." He moved back into the doorway, and motioned for us to come in. "Come on in. Welcome to my home."

Since he was so tall, he had to hunch over to invite us in and he kept his long arms folded up so we could pass. He looked very much like a praying mantis, and suddenly, I heard Blossom's voice in my head—as crisp and clear as if she were standing beside me—reading aloud from a book of poetry, " 'Will you walk into my parlor?' said the Spider to the Fly."

16. the hermit

Inside the stench was stronger, and I wanted to plug my nose, but I didn't want to appear rude. Luka had to wipe his eyes, since they'd begun to water. The kitchen below must have had its own more appetizing scents strong enough to block out whatever Leonid had cooking up here.

Leonid's apartment was small and cluttered, but not particularly dirty. Stacks of magazines, newspapers, VHS tapes, and records filled most of the space. A ratty old couch sat across from a massive floor television. The coffee table beside it was mostly cleared off, with only a few books and a small stack of papers on it.

The windows at the back of the apartment were open, but the air felt stale and musty. In the distance, a lone bird sang a mournful song.

"Sorry about the mess," Leonid said, then pointed to the couch. "Y'all can have a seat. Take a rest."

I took a seat in the middle, and the worn-out cushions felt

like I was sitting on a blanket thrown across a two-by-four. Gideon and Luke sat on either side of me, and Leonid disappeared into the front room before returning with a plastic kitchen chair.

"Do you need anything? Want a drink? I think I have some sardines I could spread on crackers if you're hungry," Leonid offered.

"No," Luka said too quickly.

"That's quite all right," Gideon replied more gently. "Thank you for offering, though."

"Yeah, just let me know if you change your mind." Leonid set the chair across from us, and he made like he was about to sit, but something occurred to him. "Oh, yeah, I should show you this. This is why I told you to come here."

"Show me what?" Gideon asked.

"I'll get it, I'll get it." Leonid went over to a pile of papers in the corner and began riffling through them. "I know it's here. I was just looking at it, because I heard there was a carnival in town, and I thought it might be you. I *hoped* it was, anyway."

"Yeah?" Gideon asked. "I thought you might stop by, if you were around."

"I would've. I want to. I've just been so busy." He shrugged his bony shoulders. "You know how life gets."

I tried to imagine what Leonid could be busy with. I wanted to ask him if he had a job, but that sounded too forward.

"Ah-ha!" Leonid held up two pieces of paper, both of them yellowed with age. "Here it is." He hurried back over and handed them to Gideon.

The first one was a black-and-white flier with a picture of Leonid on it. The headline read, *Come See One of the Marvels of the World!* Below, in smaller print, it read *Leonid the Human Skeleton.*

Below the picture was the day and time where people could see Leonid in the Caudry town square. It was dated only a few months ago, during a celebration the town was having for New Year's. That made it all the more curious that the paper had gotten so yellow in such a short amount of time.

"That's where I made all the money." Leonid tapped the flier. "I know it doesn't look like I'm living high on the hog, but you know how things go. I take the work where it comes, and I actually haven't worked since then, and I'm still getting by just fine. It had quite the turnout, and people paid to take their picture with me."

"Good on you," Gideon said. "You always were a talented performer."

Leonid smiled broadly at the minor compliment, his mouth spreading so wide it looked like his face might split apart, and he sat back in the chair.

"That other thing, that's why I invited you here," Leonid said, gesturing to the paper below the flier. "I got that letter a couple weeks after I did my show."

I leaned closer to Gideon, reading over his arm.

Dear Leonid Murphy:

Thank you for the wonderful performance last week. It was so amazing to see you, and I know that everyone got a real thrill out of meeting you. You're a very special man,

Leonid, and I hope that you can appreciate all the talent that you have.

While you were performing, I heard you mention that you'd traveled with a carnival where there were all kinds of people like you, each with unique talents of their own. I was wondering if you could put me in contact with them, or perhaps extend an invitation yourself? I know that if we could get something like that here, we could get the entire parish to turn out!

I would love to have the carnival here to signal the coming spring, perhaps around the week of March the thirteenth?

If your friends in the carnival can make it then, I can promise them a hefty payday, along with a bonus for yourself. As a gesture of good faith, I've enclosed a check for $500 as a finder's fee.

Thank you again for your wonderful show, and I'm so happy that you've decided to make Caudry your home.
Sincerely,

Della Jane

I didn't even have to read the name. I already recognized the loopy scrawl from the woman who'd given me her number yesterday.

"I hope you don't mind that I didn't tell you about the finder's fee." Leonid shifted in his seat. "Since she promised you a payday, I didn't think it would matter either way."

"No, it's fine," Gideon assured him.

From what I understood, Gideon had spoken to someone at

the mayor's office after he'd received Leonid's postcard. They'd agreed upon the dates and promised Gideon a flat rate of several thousand dollars if we performed nine days, plus everything we earned from the concessions.

So far, it promised to be a larger wage than we'd earned in years.

"We really appreciate you sending the work our way, Leonid," Gideon said. "You know how work can dry up, especially in the winter, so it was very kind of you to think of us."

"Of course, of course. You know you guys are always family to me." His eyes flitted away then, staring at some distant point on the wall.

"This isn't purely a social visit, though." Gideon set aside the letter and flier on a pile of records stacked beside the couch, and Leonid looked sharply at him. "There is something I wanted to ask you about."

"Oh?" Leonid's eyebrow arched so high, it looked like it might spring off his forehead.

Gideon took a deep breath. "I don't know how to explain it exactly, but we've all felt it." He looked to Luka and me, and we both nodded our confirmation. "There's just something . . . strange in the air. Something playing with our senses."

"No, I know exactly what you're talking about." Leonid nodded feverishly and scratched at his protruding collarbone. "Something around here plays with the *senses*."

Gideon leaned forward, resting his arms on his knees. "Do you know what it is?"

"I don't know *what* it is, but I know that it *is*. It exists." He swung his long arm back, pointing at the swamp through the cracked windows at the back of his apartment. "Do you know what the swamp is called?"

"Um, Mystic Swamp?" Luka guessed lamely, causing us all to give him an odd look.

"No." Leonid shook his head. "It's called the Nukoabok Swamp. Nukoabok means 'mad river,' according to the Choctaw Nation."

"Wait. Wait." Luka held up his hands. "Are you saying that's like an old Indian burial ground?"

Leonid snorted—a rather mucus-y sound that traveled through his long nose. "No, of course not. Don't be ridiculous. You've been watching too many scary movies."

"Well, what exactly are you saying?" Gideon asked.

"The Choctaw Nation were the first people to live here, centuries ago." He stood up and began pacing as he spoke. "But when they lived here, all that time ago, it was a river flowing fast and strong. Even then, though, they felt *it*. They sensed it the way any person senses it. I bet the animals feel it too."

"What's 'it'?" I asked.

"I don't know." Leonid gestured wildly. "Whatever it is that you're feeling, that I feel." He pointed at that swamp again. "It comes from there. I guarantee it."

"Then why do you live so close to it?" Gideon asked. "Wouldn't you at least want to live on the other side of town?"

"The rent's cheap here, for one thing," Leonid explained. "And for another, the water's harmless. I mean, yeah, I believe it has a power of its own, but so do we." He motioned to us. "We all have some kind of power that everyone else would claim is supernatural. But that doesn't make us bad or dangerous, right?"

When none of us replied, he asked again, more insistently this time, "Right?"

"Right, of course not," Gideon said, his tone soothing to help quiet Leonid's agitation. He looked to Luka and me, and we both smiled. "We're not dangerous."

"Right." He nodded, as if to convince himself. "It's growing, I think." He scratched his head, his long fingers tangling with his stringy hair, and looked back at the swamp. "It's getting bigger. I mean, I know it's gotten bigger since the Choctaw Nation moved on."

"*Bigger?*" I echoed.

"It used to be a river, but the silt slowed it down, and now it's a nearly stagnant tributary." Leonid stared out the window at it. "The water used to move through, but now it just sits." Then he turned back to us with a too-wide smile plastered on his face. "But it's just like you said. Just because it's powerful and supernatural don't mean it's dangerous."

But he gulped when he said it, like he wasn't quite sure he believed it himself.

17. mad river

The midway opened at ten, but our part of the carnival—the sideshow with the acts and the oddities museum—didn't start until four, when more of the crowds began arriving. We'd gotten back from visiting Leonid a little before three, so Gideon called a meeting at the top of the hour.

With the cheerful music wafting over from the rides, we gathered in the middle of the campsite. A few lawn chairs had been set in a circle, and my mom sat front and center next to Betty Bates. I felt wired, like an electrical current was running through my legs, and I didn't think I could sit if I wanted to. So I stood off to the back, next to where Roxie, Hutch, and Luka sat on top of a picnic table.

Just before the meeting was set to begin, Tim Phoenix hobbled out of his trailer. A beige Ace bandage was wrapped tightly around his knee, and Luka leaped off the table and rushed over to help him.

"What happened?" Luka asked him in a frantic whisper as he hooked an arm around Tim's waist.

"I just fell during practice." Tim tried to shrug it off as Luka helped him to a seat. "It's nothing."

It would be nothing, if Tim was an average acrobat. But he wasn't. Tim, his older brother, Brendon, and Brendon's daughter, Alyssa, all had the power of levitation—meaning they could float, suspended high above the ground, from sheer power of will.

In all the years they'd been traveling with us, I'd never once known any of them to fall.

"Are you all right, Tim?" Gideon asked. He'd taken his position, standing in front of us, and his dark eyebrows pinched as he studied Tim.

"Yeah, it's just a sprain." Tim shrugged again. "I'll be fine for the show tonight."

"But you fell?" Gideon pressed. "While you were performing?"

"Yeah." Tim shifted in his chair, and his face began to redden. "I lost my grip, and then I just . . . I couldn't catch the air, I guess."

Gideon seemed to consider this for a moment, then he shook his head, clearing it of whatever had been filling it. As he surveyed the crowd, his eyes were light blue, and I found some relief in that.

"As you all probably know by now, I visited with Leonid Murphy today," Gideon said, speaking loudly as he addressed the carnival. "There have been strange things going on here. Those of you with extra senses have most likely felt it."

People began murmuring then, adding their own stories to the ones I already knew—my mom's excessive mania, Gideon's faulty divining rod, Roxie's weak fire. Luka said that his badly scraped knee had healed up just fine yesterday, only to reopen for a while this morning before healing again.

Even those without extra senses, like Betty the Bearded Lady and Zeke the Tiger Tamer, complained of problems. Betty had been having headaches, and Zeke had been having nightmares.

"Maybe that's what happened with Seth," Tim said, his voice just above a whisper. "Maybe his strength went out the same way my flying did, and he couldn't fight off whatever attacked him."

"So we've all felt it?" Gideon asked, drawing everyone's attention back to him. "Leonid thinks this strange energy comes from the water here, specifically the swamp and tributaries that surround Caudry."

"What is it?" Betty asked, her usually confident voice trembling.

"Is it dangerous?" Brendon added.

"Leonid claims it isn't, and he's been living here for some time, as have the people in Caudry," Gideon explained as best he could. "With our extrasensory abilities, I believe we're more sensitive to it than the average townsperson."

"What about Seth Holden?" Brendon's wife, Jackie, asked. She sat clutching their young daughter in her lap. "What happened to him? You can't say that that wasn't dangerous. And Blossom Mandelbaum is still missing."

"Blossom isn't 'missing.'" Roxie used air quotes. "She's just . . . not here. And if this *energy* or whatever is affecting all of us, it had to have been messing with her, and her telekinesis is extrasensitive. She probably got agitated and took off to hang out at the music festival. She'll be back before we leave."

"You don't know that," Jackie said, her voice growing sharper as she spoke. "And that still doesn't explain Seth."

"It stands to reason that if the energy is affecting us, it's most likely affecting the tigers," Gideon replied carefully.

Zeke was instantly on his feet. "My tigers would never do this!"

"Zeke, calm down," Gideon said. "No one is saying your tigers are at fault. Whoever spray painted my trailer probably thought it would be funny to leave their gate open, and with everything going on, the tigers were probably spooked and reacted. Seth just got caught in the middle."

"Gideon—" Zeke started, but Gideon held up his hand.

"There isn't a better explanation right now," Gideon said firmly. "I'm not proposing we get rid of the tigers—not yet— but we do need to take greater precautions. While we're here, there will be no tiger shows, and that gate is to be kept locked at all times." Zeke lowered his head. "Is that understood?"

"Fine," Zeke relented, and sat back down.

"Now, I know some of you probably think we should pack up and cut our losses," Gideon said.

Only a few murmured their agreement, with Jackie Phoenix being the loudest.

"Our contract stipulates that we don't get paid until Sunday the twenty-second, the last day of our show." Gideon spoke loudly so his words would drown out the protests. "The midway has made some money, but we've only had one night of shows. We haven't even made enough to cover the cost of getting out of here.

"I won't force anyone to stay," Gideon said. "Everyone is always free to go, whenever they choose. But I am staying." He paused. "Would any of you like to leave now, before you've gotten paid?"

Someone coughed, and a few chairs creaked as people shifted their weight. But no one raised their hand or stood up. Everyone was staying.

"We do need to take extra precautions, beyond the ones I mentioned with the tigers," Gideon went on. "You cannot count on your extra senses, since they've been going out. For those of you that perform, you need to do things the old-school way—no tricks to save you or help you.

"I'm also instituting a buddy system," Gideon said, and this was met with groans and eye rolling. "At least when it's dark out. Don't go anywhere alone. There's no reason to risk it.

"All right. Any questions?" Gideon asked, and when there didn't appear to be any, he said, "Let's go to work, then. Everybody try to have a good time, and stay safe."

We all had jobs to do, but everyone seemed slow to clear out. Gideon had given us a lot to take in, even if I already knew some of it.

Roxie muttered as she stood up, "This sucks." Then she raised her arms over her head, stretching, and the short pink top she wore rose high, revealing her taut belly.

"It sure does," Hutch agreed, letting his gaze linger on her exposed skin. Roxie noticed, so she swatted him on the arm. "Sorry."

"At least it explains what happened with me the other night. Sorta." Her brow furrowed, and she pursed her lips for a moment, then turned to me. "What about you? Have you felt anything?"

Gideon had asked me the same question after we left Leonid's, and I told him I hadn't. At least not at Leonid's. Since we'd gotten to Caudry, I'd had these weird flashes of cold, especially in my chest, but that was all. There I was, mere feet away from this super-powerful water, and everyone else's senses were going wacko.

That was all the proof I needed that I didn't have the same "gift" as my mother. The chill I felt wasn't anything more than nerves or a cold draft.

"No," I answered Roxie. "But I never do."

18. lust

You're gonna be late if you don't head out soon," Roxie told the mirror, but the reflection of her blue eyes was locked on me. The red sequins on her slinky two-piece outfit glinted under the light from the globed bulbs of her vanity, and her bleached-blond hair was teased out as large as it could go.

Tacked up on top of the mirror were a few photo-booth snaps of her and Carrie, along with another one of me, Roxie, and Blossom. Next to the pictures was a flier for Roxie's solo show, which featured a drawing of scantily clad Roxie standing in a ring of fire with the words *Foxy Roxie Plays with Fire* written in flames across the top.

"What if you need my help?" I asked, but I glanced at the clock and saw that it was already 7:56.

I sat on the tattered fold-out sofa in the back of Roxie's Airstream, watching her get ready under the guise of helping. I'd already done my gathering for the night, and for the moment, nobody needed my help.

"The show doesn't start for a half hour, and I'm already practically ready." Roxie gestured to her attire and heavy makeup. "I'll be fine."

"I know . . . but Carrie isn't here," I said.

Usually, Roxie and Carrie performed together in a sort of burlesque show. They danced provocatively in skimpy outfits, but never took their clothes off, and they usually incorporated some element of magic. Roxie played with fire, and Carrie did tricks with hoops and made flowers appear and disappear.

But with Seth still in the hospital—recuperating very slowly, according to the doctors—Carrie remained posted at his bedside, meaning Roxie was doing the act by herself.

"I'll be fine," Roxie repeated, and turned to face me. "Why don't you want to go meet Gabe?"

"It's not that I *don't* want to see him."

In fact, my heart skipped a beat every time I thought of him, and I wanted nothing more than to see him and talk to him and feel his lips against mine.

"Then what is it?" Roxie pressed.

"With everything going on, I feel bad," I explained lamely. "Like I shouldn't be out having fun."

Roxie folded her arms over her chest. "So, you think if you weren't out having fun with a cute guy for a couple hours, Seth would magically be all better? And all the weird vibes going on here would disappear? And the carnival suddenly wouldn't be going broke?"

I lowered my eyes. "Well, no."

"If you didn't go meet Gabe, what would you be doing?" Roxie asked. "Hanging out in your trailer, reading a book and waiting around to see if someone needed a hand—even though you know that nobody will, not until it's time to close up for the night."

"But—" I started to protest.

"No." Roxie held up a finger to silence me. "This town sucks. *Somebody* should be having fun, and if it's not me, it might as well be you."

"You're right." I stood up and took a deep breath. "How do I look?"

Even though I'd been debating whether or not to meet him, I'd still gotten ready like I'd planned on it—I wore a thin white sleeveless top that just barely showed my white bra underneath, a handkerchief skirt with a bold tribal pattern, and a few layered necklaces and bracelets.

Roxie tilted her head as she studied me. "You look amazing, but you're missing one thing." She reached back and grabbed a tube of lipstick from the piles of makeup she had strewn about the vanity counter.

"Thanks," I told her after I'd applied a coat of bloodred lipstick. "Now I should probably run, if I want to meet him."

I smiled at her, then dashed out the door. I ran all the way through the campsite with the full moon lighting my way, but I slowed down once I made it through the hole in the fence. Running to Gabe out of breath wasn't exactly the kind of impression I wanted to make.

It was as I made my way down onto the midway that I realized Gabe and I had never decided on an exact meeting place. And, to make matters worse, it was packed. Well, worse for my love life at least.

Then, just as I was feeling frantic—stalking down the gravel pathways, my eyes darting everywhere—I finally spotted him. He was standing a few feet away from my mom's fortune-telling tent, exactly where I saw him last.

His back was to me, with a fitted leather jacket pleasantly hugging his broad frame. I'd seen him only a couple times, so it should've been harder to recognize him just from his silhouette. But I knew it was him all the same.

When he turned around, he was already smiling, like he knew I was there. Like the first time I'd seen him, sitting on his balcony, and somehow, he'd been able to see me hiding in the shadows.

"Hey," he said as I reached him. "I thought you might've changed your mind."

"No, I got held up for a minute." I smiled up at him. "Sorry."

He shook his head. "Don't worry about it. I'm just happy you're here now."

My mom's tent was mere feet from where we were standing, and even though the curtain was closed—meaning she was with a client—it was still dangerous to be this close to her. If she spotted us, I couldn't handle the lecture, or the ensuing embarrassment of my fortune-teller mom chewing me out in front of a townie.

So I knew that we should move, that I should direct Gabe to go anywhere else, really. But, for a moment, I felt too . . . mesmerized? In lust? Enchanted? Frozen?

His eyes were the same rich golden brown they always were, but tonight they seemed brighter and bigger, like a gemstone catching the sun. Even his smile seemed somehow sexier than before, and the wicked edge to it felt sharper. Everything about him had my heart racing even faster than normal.

I narrowed my eyes at him, trying to understand what could be different. "Did you change something? Maybe your hair?"

Gabe laughed, smoothing back his thick hair, then glanced up at the night sky. "No. Nothing's changed."

"Sorry." I pulled my gaze away from him and shook my head. "I'm just having a weird day."

"Maybe we can turn that around with a fun night?" Gabe suggested.

"That sounds like the perfect plan." I took the opportunity to start walking away from my mom's tent, and Gabe followed, his steps matching mine.

"What do you have in mind?"

"Well . . . I thought maybe we could hang out here again," I suggested.

Truth be told, I would've loved to have gotten out of there, away from the prying eyes of everyone I knew. But I couldn't. Gideon had assigned Roxie as my buddy, so technically, I wasn't supposed to be leaving her alone. The only way I could really justify seeing Gabe was if I didn't get too far away that I wouldn't be able to help Roxie if she needed me.

"Cool." Gabe grinned. "I'm up for anything as long as it's with you."

"Anything, eh?" I arched an eyebrow.

"I have an adventurer's spirit," he proclaimed. "I can take on any challenge, and I'm not afraid of anything."

"Wow." I widened my eyes with feigned amazement. "I bet you rule at Truth or Dare."

"I really do," he admitted, then stopped short. "I can tell that you don't believe me, so I'm going to prove my bravery."

"Oh really?" I smirked. "How, pray tell, are you going to do that?"

"I'm going in there." He pointed to the long black trailer at the end of the midway, where a name had been written in bold red paint—*Terrifying Curiosities & Oddities of Past & Present*.

I kept my smile plastered on my face and gulped down my unease. Of course, there was nothing terrifying at all about what the museum contained—unless you counted Hutch, who I did not trust to not accidentally let on to Gabe exactly who and what I was.

But I couldn't tell Gabe that, and I didn't want him to think that I was the kind of person who was too afraid to go into a place like that, because I absolutely wasn't.

So, with my smile still in place, I said, "Let's do it."

"Excellent." Gabe held out his hand to me, so I let him take mine in his. His skin felt hot—almost uncomfortably so—but I didn't see any appearance of being overheated. No sweat, no flushed skin. Just an easy smile and a glint in his eyes.

As we walked toward the museum, he said, "To paraphrase the great Ray Parker Jr., I ain't afraid of no curiosities or oddities."

19. curiosities

Hutch ran the museum, but he didn't even notice Gabe and me right away.

He was supposed to be selling passersby on the museum, calling out to them and telling them to step right up and see the horrors inside. Instead, he leaned against the black podium near the door, absently chewing on his dirty fingernails, his shaggy brown hair flopped over the neon sweatband he wore around his forehead.

When he caught sight of me, walking with my hand in Gabe's, he straightened up and offered the best showman smile he could manage.

"Are you brave enough to face the horrors within?" Hutch asked Gabe, but his eyes flicked to me for a second. I smiled at him and hoped I didn't look as nervous as I felt.

"Yeah, I think we can handle it." Gabe held up two fingers, making a peace sign. "Two tickets, please."

"Five dollars," Hutch said, and he kept casting nervous glances my way as he and Gabe made the exchange.

"Is it really that scary in there?" Gabe asked.

"Some people have lost their minds after going through," Hutch told him loudly, hoping to attract more customers. "You better hang on tight to your lady."

"Will do." Gabe laughed, but he squeezed my hand tighter.

He went first, going up the metal staircase into the trailer, and I looked back over my shoulder at Hutch. I mouthed the words "thank you" to him, for not outing me, but he just grinned and waved me off.

The museum was nothing more than a semitrailer that had been painted black and dimly lit, so everything inside would seem spookier than it was. Black curtains strung across rods provided the labyrinthian pathway and blocked off the less-exciting parts of the trailer.

A spooky record played over the speakers, covering up the low hum of the AC. It was nice during the dog days of summer, because we had to keep it air-conditioned, so I spent many a sweltering afternoon in this trailer.

The first few "exhibits" sat under glass cases on black tables. They were basic fodder you'd find at any place like this. A two-headed snake floating in formaldehyde in a jar. A skeleton pieced together from a fish and a monkey that appeared to be a mermaid. A glittering horn that allegedly belonged to a unicorn.

"I expected unicorns to be larger," Gabe commented on the horn, which I suspected came from a goat.

"Maybe it was a baby unicorn," I suggested.

Gabe scrunched up his face. "That's depressing, then."

As we rounded the curtain to the next half of the museum—the part with the live performers—Gabe put his arm loosely around my waist, so his hand rested on my hip. Even through the fabric of my skirt, the heat from his skin was palpable. In the cool air-conditioning of the trailer, I would've thought he'd cool down some, but it apparently hadn't had any effect on him.

I was about to suggest he take off his jacket, but a girl farther down in the trailer screamed, and instinctively, his arm tightened around me, pulling me closer to him.

This half of the museum devolved into more of a haunted house. Performers sat in little curtained cubicles with a spotlight above them and a pane of plexiglass separating them from the audience. In front of them was a plaque that explained who they were and why they were here, but the performer remained perfectly motionless—that is, until a spectator leaned in to get a better look at the plaque.

Performers varied from day to day. Sometimes Luka would be in here, shoving stakes through his hands, and before the incident, Seth would lift heavy weights.

People like Betty the Bearded Lady and her husband, Damon the Three-Legged Man, were usually here, although Betty preferred to wave and apply makeup, while Damon tended to lurch around his space like a caged monster, terrifying the spectators.

I kept my head down in an attempt to avoid recognition, but I jumped at all the right times, relishing the way it felt when Gabe held me closer to him. I wasn't scared and didn't need him to protect me, but I'd take any excuse to end up in his arms.

When we neared the ending, where the bright lights from the

carnival shined in through the open door, Gabe stopped suddenly. He looked around, so I did the same, but I didn't see anyone. We were alone in the narrow walkway, and he leaned down to kiss me.

I wanted to kiss him, but someone could round the corner any minute, catching us in an embrace, and I didn't want to risk it.

"Come on," I said. I stepped back, holding one of his hands in mine, and I pulled back the curtain behind me, revealing crates of random junk we used to set up the museum, like tools, different props, and extra black fabric.

His lips curved into a smile, with a devilish curl in the corner—the one that warned me that I should be afraid, that he was someone I should not be inviting to take me into the dark shadows. But I didn't care.

The fire in his skin had somehow spread to me, with a heat radiating deep inside me. Soon, I'd be gone, and I would never see him again. But now I was with him, so I needed to savor every moment and really be *with* him, tasting his lips and feeling his hands on my body.

Gabe followed me behind the curtain, pushing me back until I was pressed against the cold metal wall of the trailer. His mouth was on mine, kissing more ferociously than he had before. One of his hands slid up my shirt, his fiery fingers pressing into my side as he held me, and I wrapped my arms around his neck.

The feel of his body—firm and hot—pressing against me, mixed with the feel of the metal—cold and unyielding—pressed against my back. He felt so hungry, and I wanted him to devour me. I wanted to consume him, to feel him on every inch of my flesh—

—then I felt an icy dagger piercing my heart. A brief agony tore through me, and my chest felt frozen, with the cold blasting through me.

"Mara?" Gabe sounded breathless and panicked.

I blinked as the cold subsided, and his hand was on my cheek, gently forcing me to look up at him. Even in the shadows of the trailer, his dark golden eyes seemed to glow as they searched my face.

"Are you okay?" Gabe asked, and I managed to nod. "What happened? You just . . . froze up."

"I don't know." I lowered my eyes, because I couldn't explain it.

"I'm sorry if I was being too aggressive." His voice was low and pained.

"No, no. It wasn't that." I smiled weakly at him and took his hand. "I liked *that*. I like kissing you."

He smiled crookedly. "I like kissing you too."

"Good. I'm glad that's settled, then."

"Maybe we should get out there and get some air." Gabe motioned toward the exit behind him.

He stepped back then and bumped right into a crate, sending it clattering to the floor. He bent down, scrambling to pick everything up.

"Hey! Nobody's allowed back here!" Luka barked, and he pushed back through a curtain. He must've been in the back, getting ready to take over and give Damon a break. But then he saw me and confusion spread out on his face. "Mara? What are you . . ."

Then his eyes darted to Gabe, and Luka's eyes widened with realization.

Gabe had straightened up, giving up on cleaning the mess, then motioned between Luka and me. "You two know each other?"

"Shit. I'm sorry," Luka apologized, but it was too late. My secret was out.

20. the fool

L et's talk outside," I told Gabe with my head bowed. He tried to take my hand, but I pulled away and walked ahead of him.

Outside the darkness of the trailer, the lights felt blinding, and I blinked as I waited for my eyes to adjust.

"What's going on?" Gabe asked, but I kept walking ahead of him, wanting to get as far away from the bright sounds and flashing lights and curious eyes as I could. "Mara!"

I stopped then, just on the other side of the booths and tents. My back was to the carnival, and I could see the campsite through the chain-link fence. I could just about make out the shape of my old Winnebago, the dusty trailer I'd called home for the past several years, and my mind flashed onto the beautiful mansion that Gabe lived in.

"Mara, if I did something wrong, you can tell me," Gabe said. "If you want me to slow things down, I can. I just—"

"You didn't do anything wrong," I said, and I turned to face him. It wasn't cold, but I wrapped my arms around myself.

"Was that guy your boyfriend?" he asked tentatively.

I shook my head. "No. It's nothing like that."

He relaxed then—the lines of his body slacking—and let out a breath. "Then what's going on?"

"That guy was my coworker." I motioned to the midway. "I work here." Then I pointed to the Winnebago. "And I live there."

"You . . ." His brow furrowed, deep creases stretching out in his smooth skin above dark eyebrows. "You travel with the carnival?"

"That's right." I smiled bitterly. "I'm a carnie, and I work with a freak show."

He looked at me, and I felt the shift in his gaze as he tried to search out what I did in the freak show. What thing made me a freak.

And I couldn't talk to him anymore. I couldn't bear the thought of hateful words coming from his lips, the same lips I could still taste on mine. I'd heard all the insults before, and they shouldn't hurt, but they still did, and so far Gabe had been nothing but sweet to me. I didn't want to tarnish that memory by hearing him call me something that could never be taken back.

"And I shouldn't even be out with you." I started to back away, toward the fence. "I have work I should be doing, so I really don't even have time to see you."

"Mara," Gabe began.

"Don't worry. I'll be gone next Sunday, and you won't ever have to see me again."

"Mara," he repeated, and took a step toward me, so I turned and started running.

I didn't really have anywhere to go, so I ran until I found the gap in the fence, and I slid through it. The pointed edges scraped my skin, but I didn't care. I kept running until I got to my Winnebago, and I never looked back.

Once I was inside, I leaned against the counter and struggled to catch my breath and slow the racing of my heart. Gabe and I hadn't known each other that long, but I liked him, and it hurt knowing I wouldn't be able to see him again.

What hurt the worst was knowing that he wouldn't think of me the same way. For a while, he'd seen me as a real person. He'd really seen *me*, and he'd liked me. But now I was reduced to a disposable, forgettable, dirty freak. An accidental foray onto the other side of the tracks, one that wouldn't be repeated.

"Mara?" Gideon's voice came through the screen door, his British accent softening his words. "Is everything all right, love?"

"Yeah, everything's fine," I lied as I bit back tears.

"Are you sure?" Gideon asked, and his voice was closer now, right on the other side of the door.

"Yeah." I sniffled. "It's just been a long day, and I need to go lie down."

"All right." He sounded reluctant to let it go. "Let me know if you need anything."

"I will," I told him, and to ensure the conversation was over, I walked back to my bedroom and rattled the beaded curtain as loudly as I could.

I threw myself onto my bed, causing the thin mattress to

bounce. The shelving above my bed was filled to the brim with books, and when I flopped into bed, it knocked a book loose and it fell onto my head.

"What a perfect way to end a perfect night," I muttered to myself.

I rolled onto my back and picked up the book. Enough light was streaming in through the beads from the kitchen that I could read the title, embossed in gold on a pale red cover. It was a book of poetry by Mary Howitt.

My stomach soured as I turned the brittle pages, and the book opened almost immediately to "The Spider and the Fly." I'd gotten the book last summer for a nickel at a yard sale, and one day, a couple months back, Blossom had pulled it out.

We'd been stuck in some dry town, with nothing to do and nowhere to go. I'd been sitting at the kitchen table, playing a game of solitaire, and Blossom lay stretched out on the floor, with a rolled-up sweater under her head like a pillow.

And as I played, she'd read the poems aloud. I could almost hear her voice now, reading in an exaggerated falsetto, " 'O no, no,' said the little fly, 'for I've often heard it said,/They never, never wake *again, who sleep upon* your *bed.*' "

I slammed the book shut and set it on my nightstand before rolling over onto my side, putting my back to it. I closed my eyes tightly, trying to push away all my thoughts about anything.

Blossom being gone, Seth's attack, Leonid's claims, Gabe's kisses, the coldness in my chest, and the fact that I'd never kiss Gabe again. All these things swirled inside me, and I pushed them all down until finally sleep enveloped me, quieting all the things that hurt and frightened me.

21. shadows

I opened my eyes to the blackness. Darkness engulfed me, wrapping me up in the nothingness. There was no ground below me, no sky above. Only the black, and the cold.

The icy cold was coming from within me, spreading out from my chest and freezing me from the inside out. I wanted to scream, but the words were frozen in my throat.

Then a face began to take shape before me, and I realized it was *her*—the old woman from my nightmare. Her gray hair swirled around her head like a halo as she floated across the nothingness toward me.

Her mouth hung open with her long talonlike fingers extended toward me, and she began to scream. Again her words came too quickly in a language that I didn't understand, but they were insistent and angry, echoing inside my brain.

I couldn't move or speak, so I closed my eyes, trying to will her away. And then I felt her hands on me, gripping my shoulders painfully and digging her nails into my flesh as she began shaking me.

Her breath felt cold on my face, and she smelled musty and tangy, like rotten fruit. I turned my head to the side, squeezing my eyes shut as tightly as I could, and her hands were like a vise on my shoulders.

She began screaming the same phrase over and over, right in my ear. My arms felt like they were going to snap as she tightened her grip, and I couldn't take it anymore.

I opened my eyes, expecting to see her rotting face floating in front of me, but instead it was only the ceiling of the Winnebago, tinged slightly brown from an old leak in the roof.

Gasping for breath, I sat up with her words still ringing in my head. I had no idea what it meant, but it sounded like she was saying "id-hab-bee-in-who-nah" again and again. I rubbed my arms, trying to convince myself it was only a dream, but my arms still ached from where she'd grabbed me.

My mom snored softly in the twin bed across from mine, and I had no idea what time it was, but I had to talk to her. If these nightmares I was having were anything more than simple dreams, Mom would know.

I got out of bed and went over to where she slept. "Mom?" I shook her gently. "Mom? I need to talk to you."

"Not tonight, Mara," Mom mumbled, her voice thick with sleep, and she buried her face deeper into her pillow. "My head is still throbbing, and I need to sleep."

"It's okay," I told her softly. "It can wait until the morning."

"I love you, *qamari*," Mom said, and within seconds, she began snoring again.

After the nightmare I had, I knew sleep wouldn't be an option. I was still wearing the skirt and top I'd gone to bed in, so I changed into a more comfortable tank top and baggy pajama pants before heading out into the kitchen/living room.

I flicked on the small light above the kitchen sink, bathing the trailer in dim yellow light. Using my grandma's ancient kettle, I put a pot of tea on the tiny stovetop. I grabbed my still-unfinished V. C. Andrews novel and settled back on the couch, preparing to spend the rest of my night reading and drinking a cup of tea.

I'd only just finished reading a page when I heard a strange sound outside. The nights were cool, so all the windows in the motorhome were open. Setting the book aside, I tilted my head, listening more closely, and it came again—a hushed hissing sound, not entirely unlike the one I'd heard right before Seth was attacked.

Last night, I'd assumed it had been the punks spray painting the trailer. They could be back to cause more havoc. Or maybe it was something else entirely.

Then I heard a loud clattering sound—metal on metal—and I jumped to my feet. I'm not sure what exactly I planned to do, but I had to see what was going on, so I threw open the screen door.

"You woke up Mara," Luka grumbled, speaking barely above a whisper, probably so as not to wake anyone else in the campsite.

With the aid of the full moon and the streetlamp on the

other side of Gideon's trailer, I could easily see in the dark. Luka stood with his arms crossed over his chest, while Hutch sat on the ground beside him, struggling to untangle himself from a lawn chair.

"It's not my fault that Betty didn't put away her chairs before she went to bed," Hutch protested.

I climbed down the steps of the trailer and walked over to them. "What are you two doing?"

"Luka thought he heard a noise, and he made me go out with him to investigate." Hutch shot a glare up at Luka. "Stupid buddy system."

Luka held up his hands. "These are Gideon's rules, not mine."

"*You* didn't have to go out and check out the noise. It's seriously like you've never seen a horror movie."

Hutch grimaced because he still hadn't freed himself from the chair, so I crouched down and helped him. I pulled apart the plastic slats, and his foot was finally able to slide free.

"Thank you," he whispered before standing up.

"Sorry about accidentally outing you with that guy," Luka said to me. "Since you spent the rest of the night holed up in your Winnebago, I'm assuming that it didn't go well?"

"Don't worry about it." I shook my head and tried to ignore the painful lump in my throat. "It's not like it could last forever, anyway, right?"

"I know, but it still sucks when things have to end abruptly like that," Luka said.

"So what was the noise that drew you out of your trailer?" I asked, changing the subject.

"It was like a hissing, kind of, like the air being let out of a very large tire," Luka explained.

"That wasn't you guys?" I glanced around the campsite, realizing that it meant that we weren't alone.

"Why would we hiss?" Hutch asked incredulously. "People don't hiss."

"Exactly," I said under my breath.

"*There!*" Luka said, managing a whispered shout. He pointed frantically to the far side of the camp, where Gideon's trailer butted up to the overgrown swamp behind us.

"What?" Hutch asked, but as soon as the words were out of his mouth, I saw it.

A dark, low shadow moving quickly behind the trailers. I couldn't tell if it was a dog, a bear, or even a man. It was just a blur of darkness running around the campsite.

Without thinking, I sprinted after it, and Luka ran beside me. We raced around Gideon's trailer, following the shadow, but we were always too many steps behind to really see it. We chased it around the periphery of the campsite, and when it turned beside Betty and Damon's trailer, I knew we had it. Beyond their trailer was just the open field that backed up against the chain-link fence. There was nowhere for it to hide.

I sped up, my legs pumping as quickly as they could beneath me. I rounded the trailer with my heart pounding in my chest, knowing I'd finally have caught sight of whoever—or whatever—it was that had probably attacked Seth.

But then there was nothing. The field was completely empty, and there wasn't any sign of the shadow running anywhere. It was just gone.

MONDAY, MARCH 16, 1987

22. apologies

The motorhome smelled like coffee, and that's what pulled me from my sleep. After the shadowy thing had disappeared, Luka, Hutch, and I had sat on the picnic table in the center of the campsite, waiting for it to return. But it never had.

Eventually, when the sun began to rise, I decided to call it a night and head back to my camper. Hutch had actually fallen asleep on the picnic table, lying on his stomach on the bench, and Luka woke him up and dragged him back to their place.

I curled up on the dinette bench, propping my head on the cushions, and attempted to read my book, but I must've dozed off, because I woke up to my mom brewing coffee and humming an old Fleetwood Mac song. A quilt had been draped over me, the same one that Blossom used whenever she crashed on our couch.

"Morning," Mom said without looking back at me, as if she could somehow sense me waking up behind her.

"Morning," I mumbled, and pushed myself up so I was sitting. "What time is it?"

"Eight thirty." She kept her back to me as she put a pan on the stovetop. "Are you hungry?"

"Not really. I could use a cup of coffee, though."

"I already poured you one." She pointed behind her to a mug sitting on the table beside me, and grabbed two eggs from the fridge. "Why are you sleeping out here? Did something happen last night?"

I gulped down my coffee—bitter, warm, and black, just the way I liked it—before answering. "Nothing happened, exactly, but I did have this really strange dream."

There was no point in telling her about the thing that Luka and I had chased, because it wasn't even really a *thing*. We hadn't actually seen anything, and in the bright light of morning, it made me realize that it had probably been nothing more than our own paranoia.

Or maybe it was the peculiar power of the Nukoabok Swamp that seemed to be affecting everyone around here. It would make sense that it played tricks with our imagination, and that even explained the bizarre nightmares I'd had since I got here. Zeke claimed he'd been having nightmares too.

"What was it about?" Mom asked.

The old woman flashed in my mind, screaming her string of angry syllables at me—*id-hab-bee-in-who-nah*. I shook my head, trying to clear my thoughts of her. "It's . . . nothing. Just a bad dream."

"Dreams can be an important way of our spirit telling us things that we need to know . . ." Mom trailed off and leaned forward so the skull key fell out of her blouse. She liked to wear it under her clothing, close to her heart, but she didn't even notice it had escaped as she looked out the small window above the stove. "There's a boy."

"What are you talking about?" I asked.

"There's a strange boy in the campsite, and he's coming over to our motorhome." Mom looked back at me, like I should understand what was going on.

I set down my coffee and tossed off the quilt. I'd only just gotten up, and by then he was close enough to our screen door that I could see him.

Gabe.

I didn't move. I didn't even breathe. I could only stand, petrified, hoping that he would move on before he saw me or my home.

When he knocked, his fist rapping loudly on the metal door, I nearly screamed. Mom moved to get it, but I rushed past her and answered it before she could. I held the door open, but I didn't go outside or move so he could come in. The height difference of the trailer meant that I was actually taller than him, looking down at him.

"Hi." Gabe smiled sheepishly up at me. "I hope I didn't wake you."

"No, I was awake," I said through lips that felt numb and clumsy.

I was acutely aware of the haggard appearance of everything. The once avocado-green carpet of the motorhome had become a sickly shade of brown, and it was balding in patches. The cupboards behind me were duct-taped to keep them from falling open, and cushions on the dinette were patched with old pieces of my mom's dresses.

Not to mention how unkempt I looked personally—no makeup and dark circles under my eyes, my black hair pulled back in a messy ponytail, and my rumpled pajamas with no bra.

And Gabe stood before me without a hair out of place, designer jeans, and black-and-safari-patterned Nike sneakers that easily cost more than my family made in a month.

"What are you doing here?" I demanded, because I couldn't possibly imagine what he wanted with me, or how he had even known which motorhome was mine.

"I was wondering if we could talk." His eyes were imploring me, absent of any glint I'd seen in them last night.

I looked past him, to the campsite, where everyone was beginning to wake up and start their day. Damon was standing shirtless outside his trailer, grilling up some type of sausage for breakfast, and Brendon kept giving Gabe the eye as he hauled acrobatic equipment out of his trailer.

Talking to him outside wouldn't be good, but going into the motorhome, where my mom lurked a few feet away, wouldn't really be any better.

"Mara, invite your friend in," Mom commanded with a weary sigh. "I have business to attend to in Gideon's trailer anyway."

"Come in," I said, since I didn't have a choice. I stepped back to let him in and folded my arms over my chest.

Even though it was first thing in the morning, Mom had already put on a long, flowing dress and adorned herself in jewelry, from earrings to necklaces to half a dozen rings. Her long black hair cascaded around her in waves, and she held her hand out to Gabe.

"I'm Lyanka Beznik, Mara's mom," she said as she shook his hand.

"Gabe Alvarado, Mara's friend." His eyes flitted to me briefly. "I think."

"Gabriel?" Mom asked, raising one eyebrow, and I sighed inwardly at my mom's strange insistence on calling everyone by their full given name.

"Gabriel is my full name." He glanced at me, looking caught off guard. "Most people call me Gabe, though."

"Gabriel, then," she repeated. She smiled thinly, then her gray eyes rested on me. "Be good."

With that, she left us alone, standing awkwardly in the small, dingy Winnebago. I felt his eyes on me, but I wouldn't look at him directly.

"I don't understand." Gabe rubbed the back of his neck. "I feel like you're mad at me, but you're the one that lied to me."

I bristled. "I didn't *lie*."

"Fine. I'd categorize it as a lie by omission, but whatever. You left something out. I don't care how you want to think of it," he said in exasperation. "The point is that *I* didn't do anything. So I don't understand why you're mad at me."

"You didn't have to do anything." I shook my head. "I saw it in your face."

His brow furrowed in confusion. "Saw what?"

I swallowed hard. "Contempt."

"Contempt?" He scoffed. "Why the hell would I look at you with contempt?"

"Because." I stepped back from him, hating the twisted pain that grew in my chest when I thought about the names I'd been called by guys who I had thought liked me, by people I'd thought were friends, and by strangers who didn't even give me a chance.

"Because why?" Gabe pressed.

"Because that's what they all do!" My voice was quavering, and I was practically shouting. "Once people know who I am, and they see that I'm just some poor loser traveling with a freak show, it all changes. I become like subhuman garbage to them."

"I am sorry if anyone has ever made you feel that way, Mara, I truly am," he said, and the softness of his expression and the hurt in his eyes made me believe he really was. "But those are just really shitty people, and I am not them."

I shook my head, fighting back tears. "You can't lie to me. I saw the look on your face when I told you what I really was."

"That wasn't contempt. It was the realization that you were leaving." He shrugged his shoulders helplessly. "I was sad, and I was a little angry that you knew you weren't going to be here very long, and you didn't tell me."

I lowered my eyes. "I didn't think you'd care."

"Why wouldn't I care? I like you." He moved closer to me. "And until last night, I thought you liked me too."

"I like you," I said softly. He put his hands on my waist, gently, warmly, and I lowered my arms to my sides and let him pull me closer. "But it doesn't change anything. I'm still leaving soon."

"So?"

I looked up at him. "So?"

"You knew you were leaving since the day you met me, and you still kissed me. And you kept seeing me. Why?"

"I don't know." I raised one shoulder in a lame shrug. "I just wanted to be with you."

"Let's just be together then, for as long as you're here."

I smiled despite myself. "Okay."

"Good." He bent down, kissing me on the mouth, and just when I put my arms around him, he abruptly stopped and stepped back. "Sorry. I just feel like your mom is gonna walk in at any moment, so I thought I should stop that before things get too heated."

"Good call." I laughed.

"Why don't I take you out on a real date tonight?" Gabe suggested. "We can see something outside of the carnival. I'll show you everything that Caudry has to offer."

"I have work to do, but I could probably be done by six," I said. "And I'd have to be back by eleven to help take things down."

"So, between six and eleven tonight, you're mine."

23. bedouin

Gabe had been gone for all of thirty seconds before my mom came back into the Winnebago, meaning she had been waiting and watching. I'd already turned, pushing aside the beaded curtain to go into the bedroom.

"So you're not gonna tell me what that was about?" Mom asked.

"You mean you didn't hear it all from wherever you were spying?" I asked, but I was mostly teasing.

I knelt on the floor and opened the drawers underneath my bed to rummage through my clothes. Mom waited on the other side of the curtain, so I couldn't really see her, but I knew exactly how she was standing—arms folded over her chest, toe tapping anxiously on the floor, her lips in a thin line and her eyes cast down in a mixture of anxiety and feigned indifference.

It wasn't that my mom didn't care. In fact, it was the opposite—she cared far too much. But we were now at that awkward stage in our relationship where I was legally an adult, but still a teenager who lived under her roof, albeit a small and no-madic roof.

Not to mention that her job was taking a toll on her, so she wasn't able to do as much as she once had. That meant many of the adult responsibilities—like cooking and cleaning—had fallen to me.

"I only watched through the window of Gideon's trailer," Mom said, as if she hadn't had her nose pressed to the glass. "I wanted to make sure you were safe."

"Gabe's perfectly safe," I told her, but the second the words were out of my mouth, I wondered how I could be so sure. So far, everything in Caudry wasn't exactly as it seemed, and every-thing had a sinister edge to it.

Finally, Mom had enough of talking to me through the cur-tain, so she pushed through the beads and sat down on her bed behind me.

"Then why haven't you told me about him?" she asked. Underneath her concern, I heard a pained current.

I temporarily abandoned my search for an outfit, and I sat with my back still to her. "I don't know."

"You know, everybody knows everybody's business around here," she said quietly, as if everyone was crowded outside our doors, listening. "That means I've known for *days* that you've been running around with some boy, a rich townie, and I've been waiting for you to tell me. And you never did."

I turned to face her. "I wasn't trying to keep it from you. I just . . ." I sighed. "I knew it wasn't anything serious, and I didn't want you to lecture me about not being safe or getting too attached."

"Oh, *qamari*." Her mouth curved into a sad smile. "You're a young woman. You want your own life, your own dreams, your own loves. I wouldn't expect any less from you.

"When I was your age, your grandma Basima was still dragging me around the country, chasing the promise of riches or love from yet another snake-oil salesman." My mom affected the same weary tone she always did when she talked about her mother.

I hadn't known my grandma all that well, since she'd died when I was three. By the time I was born, Grandma Basima had already started spiraling. Mom claimed that Grandma had overused her powers as a necromancer, and it drove her crazy.

Around the time I was born, she developed dementia-like symptoms, and my mom had to put her in a special home. It was impossible to care for my grandma and me while traveling on the road.

The only thing else I really knew about my grandma had to do with the skull key with the ruby eyes my mom wore around her neck. I couldn't see it now—it was tucked safely beneath her top, so she could wear it next to her skin—but I knew the key was there. It was always there.

The key belonged to Grandma Basima's steamer trunk that I'd only seen a handful of times, despite the fact that we carried it with us always. My mom kept it in the cargo area of the Winnebago, below the floor.

When I was young, if I tried to touch it, Mom would slap my hands and tell me to never touch it. *It's not for play*, she had warned me, and as I got older, she explained to me that the trunk contained tools of the dark arts.

"She'd had hundreds of boyfriends and thousands of jobs,

and none of them were ever the right one," Mom explained. "So I promised myself that one day I would settle down, fall in love, and have a family."

She forced a smile so pained, I was afraid she might crack. My mom always tried to hold herself with such dignity, despite our circumstances, but underneath, I knew how much she hurt.

"But I didn't know how to escape, so I gave in to temptation and used the *gift* your grandma passed down to me," Mom went on. "The spirits never left me alone, making it impossible to hold down a steady job, and your father . . ."

She trailed off, letting that hang in the air for a moment. "Well, your father couldn't handle the life of a *bedouin*, but not many can."

"It's not a bad life," I said, and that was true.

My life with a traveling sideshow had been chaotic, and we'd always been on the edge of poverty. But we all took care of each other and looked out for one another. I was never alone, and no one here ever treated me like I was a freak or different, because I wasn't. I was just one of them.

"Mara." Mom held up her hand to me. "I want you to have the things I could never have, that I could never give you. That means that someday you'll find love and make a home. And that's why you must never, ever open your mind to the spirits."

I did my best not to roll my eyes or look annoyed. "I know, Mom. You've only told me that about a thousand times."

"Mara, I am serious," she snapped. "This place"—she gestured vaguely around, wagging her fingers in the air—"the energy will tempt you, but you mustn't let it. That's why I'm happy you're seeing this boy."

"Why?" I asked. "He's from here. Kinda."

"Yes, but he'll keep you distracted while we're here, so you can avoid whatever it is that's pulling everyone else in all directions." She cast a derisive glance out the window, at the swamp that lurked behind the campsite. "And when the week is up, you'll say your sad good-byes, and we'll move on. Then you'll find a nice boy you can *really* fall in love with."

I tugged at a lock of hair that had come loose from my ponytail and stared down at my lap. "But Gabe is a nice boy."

"He seemed nice enough, and very respectful," Mom allowed. "But there will be other boys, nicer ones. Ones that aren't too wealthy and don't live in a place filled with a dangerous energy."

Still staring down, I chewed my lip. "Is that supposed to make me feel better?"

"No, but it's the truth, and the truth rarely makes anyone feel better." Mom got off her bed and sat down beside me, putting her arm around me as she did. "I'm sorry, *qamari*. I didn't mean to make you sad.

"I only meant to tell you that I understood and that you didn't need to hide things from me," she went on. "And now I've only succeeded in convincing you the opposite, I suppose."

"No, you didn't." I leaned into her, allowing her to hug me close.

"It's only a few more days, and then we'll be out of here and off to somewhere brighter and better," Mom promised, but that thought hurt so much more than it would've before we got to Caudry. Before Gabe.

24. tigris

Hutch leaned against a black trunk marked *Gideon's Magic Act* in white paint, and caught his breath. The cargo trailer filled with supplies for Gideon's act appeared to be half empty, but Hutch already looked exhausted.

It didn't help that the temperatures were already over eighty with humidity that made it feel like the air was sticking to my skin. Hutch was shirtless, and his wiry frame was covered in a thick layer of sweat.

But I understood it. I spent the morning practicing with my crossbow at the edge of the camp. It was an old crossbow, with the stock literally held on with duct tape. It was all that we'd been able to afford, but it still shot straight, so that's what mattered.

It'd been hard taking aim with sweat dripping down my forehead and stinging my eyes, but I managed to hit every target I aimed for.

"I come bearing gifts from Betty," I said as I reached him and held out a big glass of lemonade.

"Thanks," he said, and gulped it down within seconds of me handing it to him.

"Where's Gideon?" I asked, peering into the trailer with another glass of lemonade in my hand.

"He's down at the tent, setting stuff up." Hutch wiped his forehead with the back of his arm. "You can leave his glass here, if you want. He'll probably be back up in a few minutes."

I set it down on the trunk beside him. "Do you need help with anything?"

"Not unless you can get Seth back here." His joke felt empty, and his mouth twisted into a grimace. "Sorry. This just really sucks without him. I didn't realize exactly how much we relied on his strength."

"Gideon called the hospital today, and it sounds like Seth's on the mend, so that's good," I said, relaying what I'd heard from my mom. "I don't know when he'll be back, though."

Hutch squinted, staring off at nothing for a moment. "Do you think that thing we saw last night was the same thing that attacked Seth?"

"I don't even know what we saw last night." I shrugged. "I'm not even sure we saw *anything* at all."

Hutch looked at the ground and muttered, "I saw something."

"If it was anything, it was probably a dog," I said.

"Luka thinks it was a coyote." He scratched absently at his knee through a hole in his jeans. "At least that's what he told Tim when they were arguing this morning."

"They were arguing?" I asked.

He nodded. "Tim's angry that Luka was chasing after this

thing, and it could be a rabid animal or a psycho from town. Tim pointed out that we still don't know who spray painted 'freeks' on Gideon's trailer."

"Well, we'll probably never know. It's not the first bit of unsolved vandalism we've come across, and it probably won't be the last."

"Maybe." He stretched as he stood up. "But I hope that we'll at least figure out what the hell is hunting us."

For some reason, the hair on the back of my neck stood up, and a chill ran down my spine. "'Hunting us'? Don't you think you're being a little extreme?"

Hutch shrugged. "That's just how it feels to me."

I couldn't think of anything else to say to that, so I wished Hutch good luck on the rest of his unloading, and I walked across the campsite to work on my own chores.

The tigers were restless, with Mahilā making mewling sounds. I hooked the hose up and hauled it over to their pen, hoping that a cold pool would help them relax and fight the heat.

When I walked over, Zeke was already there, leaning against the fencing and watching his tigers. His fingers hooked onto the thick metal bars, and he watched as Mahilā paced. The thick scars that marred her soft golden fur looked more pink than normal. As she turned and rubbed up hard against the fence, sending tufts of fur flying, I realized that must be why her skin looked so irritated.

Since Safēda was older and hadn't had such an abusive past, she was usually calm, preferring to lie in the shade or splash in the pool. But today she couldn't seem to sit still.

She'd walk across the pen, then she'd turn quickly and walk back toward Zeke and me. Safēda stopped right in front of Zeke and stared up at him with her wide blue eyes.

"What is it, Saf?" Zeke asked. He reached his hand through the bars, and she leaned in toward him, allowing him to stroke her white fur. But only for a moment. Then she turned and darted across the pen again.

"The tigers are acting strange," Zeke told me, keeping his eyes on the big cats.

"Do you think the heat's getting to them?" I asked. "Heat can make anyone act crazy."

"I don't know." He pointed to the kiddie pool in the center of the pen. "I just filled that up a half hour ago. They drank some, but then went back to the pacing."

"I could spray them down with the hose. It might help."

"I don't think so." He finally pulled his eyes off Safēda and looked at me. "I already told Roxie this, but now I'm telling you too—I don't want you feeding the tigers or cleaning up after them or going in the pen at all. Not until we're out of town. Is that clear?"

"But—" I began.

"I'll take care of everything," Zeke interrupted me. "I'll make sure they have enough water and food."

I paused, trying to wrap my head around what he was saying. "Does that mean that you think the tigers had something to do with what happened to Seth?"

"It means that my tigers aren't happy, and when they aren't happy, people can get hurt," Zeke growled. "I don't want to see anything happen to Safēda, Mahilā, or anybody else here. So just stay away from them. Okay?"

"Okay." I nodded. "I got it."

I looked over at Mahilā, still continuing with her plaintive song, and I couldn't help but wonder what the tigers knew that we didn't.

25. secrets

The sun had begun its descent toward the horizon, and the sounds of the carnival played like a familiar song behind me. I waited just outside the main gates, on the edges of the gravel parking lot.

To keep my hair off my neck, I wore it in a side braid. The air had begun to cool, but only slightly, so I wore a light dress. The humidity still left a halo around the lights, making everything appear to glow more than normal.

Just when I began to worry that Gabe had changed his mind and wasn't going to show, a cherry red Mustang pulled up in front of me.

"Ready to go for a ride?" Gabe asked, grinning at me.

"Definitely." I hopped in the car, and he turned down the INXS that was blasting out of the tape deck.

We sped out of the parking lot. The T-top were off, so the wind blew through my hair and cooled my skin. When we hit the streets of Caudry proper, Gabe slowed a little so he could tell me about various landmarks in town—like the small local grocer, a diner that served the best crawfish in all of Louisiana, and the car dealership that Logan's parents owned.

Then he turned, taking us away from the center toward the outskirts. We continued on a narrow road, with overgrown grass and wildflowers growing up around us, until the Mustang pulled to a stop on an old stone bridge that curved up over a river.

With the sun dipping completely below the horizon, the sky had become a dark shade of blue that shifted to purple to almost white just before it kissed the ground. Stars twinkled brightly in the dark parts of the sky, and the moon looked bright and fat hovering just above us.

Gabe got out of the car first, but he left the engine on, so the music played softly for us. He came around to open my door. I smiled and murmured *"thank you"* before following him over to the stone wall of the bridge. Then, like a good tour guide, he took on a loud explanatory voice and motioned to the river beneath the bridge.

"This is the Brawley River," he explained.

I leaned over the wall, the stones pressing into my stomach, and stared down at the black water flowing beneath us. About a quarter mile ahead, I could see where the river met a large and equally dark lake.

"The Brawley River flows from Lake Tristeaux"—he pointed to the lake—"back to the Nukoabok Swamp, which surrounds the entire north side of Caudry. Lake Tristeaux is salt water, since the Gulf of Mexico bleeds into it. Since the Brawley River is a small river, it ends up being mostly salt water."

I straightened up and looked over at him. "That's cool."

"I don't know if it's cool or not, but that's not why I added it to your Caudry Tour."

I arched an eyebrow. "Why did you?"

"Two reasons. The first is because Brawley is my mom's maiden name." He looked back down at the river, and something dark flickered across his gaze for a moment. Then he shook his head, and his smile returned. "This river was named after my family."

"Wow." My eyes widened. "Your family must be pretty special."

He laughed darkly. "I don't know if special is the right word. My family's just been in Caudry for a very long time, and they've had money for a very long time. The combination of the two means that things get named after us."

"I still think it's cool," I said, but he only shrugged. "And your uncle sounded pretty cool too." He looked up at me in surprise. "Didn't you tell me that he used to have huge parties where people from all over would come?"

"Yeah." Gabe nodded, and an easy smile spread out across his face. "Uncle Beau was kind of legendary. He was larger than life, and everyone loved him. He was a local celebrity, actually, but he traveled all the time. He worked as a consultant for some oil company or something, so he went all over the country. And everywhere he went, he'd always make himself new friends."

"He sounded like a great guy," I said.

His expression turned somber. "Yeah, he was."

"So what was the second reason you showed me the river?" I asked after he lapsed into silence.

He glanced up at the sky, then down at the watch on his

wrist. "I thought I timed this better, but I guess we need to wait a few more minutes."

"Okay?" I gave him a quizzical look.

"Trust me. It'll be worth it."

"I trust you."

His smile fell, and he quickly looked away, staring down at the river again. "My uncle Beau used to tell me that since the water had salt in it, sharks would swim up the river. I never saw any when I was a kid, so I don't know if it's true."

"It's nice that you know so much about your family," I said.

"It's only my mom's side," Gabe explained. "My dad is from Venezuela, so I never even met most of his family."

"My dad is from India, but I don't really know that much about him or his family. He left when I was three."

"I'm sorry." Gabe reached out, putting his hand over mine, and the heat spread through me.

"No, don't be. It was a long time ago." I shook my head. "The only thing I really know about him is that he chose my name. My middle name, Varali, means 'moon' in Hindi." Then I lowered my eyes. "That's what he used to call us—my mom was his sun, and I was his little moon."

"At least your middle name is cool," Gabe said, his tone playful to lighten the mood. "I got my uncle Beau's middle name—Bardau."

I raised an eyebrow. "Bardau?"

He rolled his eyes. "It's French or something. My mom claims it's been in the family for generations."

"Having heritage is cool," I told him. "You get to carry all the history of your family, and you have a legacy."

In the fading light, his whole face darkened, and he swallowed hard. "Maybe. But sometimes that legacy just feels like a prison sentence."

"You're old enough that you can make your own choices."

"As my mom is quick to point out, just because I'm nineteen doesn't mean I can do anything I want." He stared wistfully down at the river. "It's so much more complicated than that."

My mind suddenly went to the conversation we'd had on the Ferris wheel, the one where Gabe promised to tell me his secrets on our fifth date. The look on his face now—his jaw tense under his smooth skin, his eyebrows pinching together, and his lips pressed together—made me realize his secret was much darker than mine.

"What do you mean?" I asked.

Suddenly his head shot up. "It's starting."

"What?" I asked, but he was already pointing toward where the river fed into the lake.

"Just watch." Gabe moved closer to me, so he was nearly standing behind me, and I felt his hand on my waist, hot through the sheer fabric.

I scanned the darkening sky with no idea what I should be on the lookout for, and I was about to ask him again when I saw something. A small flash of purple—like a neon lavender—floating a few feet above the water.

It only lasted a second, so I couldn't even be sure that I saw anything. Then it happened again, several feet away from the first one. Slowly, it began to build up—both in number and frequency—until the sky was dotted with several dozen flashing purple lights.

"What is it?" I asked breathlessly.

"Purple fireflies." Gabe's voice was low in my ear, and I could hear his smile. "Caudry is the only place in the whole world that has them."

I pulled my head back so I could look up at him. "Really?"

"Really," he said, so I turned my attention back to the glowing fireflies. "Back in the fifties, some scientists came to figure out why they were purple. They never did find out exactly why, but they eventually decided it had something to do with what the fireflies ate here.

"My uncle Beau always said it was the water," Gabe finished.

He wrapped his arms around me, hugging me to him, and I leaned into him. He felt so strong and warm and wonderful, and his lips brushed against my neck, softly but deliciously, and the heat surged through me like an electric current.

Behind me, the Cure sang about a night like this, and in front of me, the sky was filled with dancing fireflies. The moment felt so perfect and magical, I wished it would never end.

26. freak

The bulbs above the marquee flickered every few seconds, but the names of the movies playing in the tiny theater were still visible: *Some Kind of Wonderful*, *Lethal Weapon*, and *Evil Dead II*.

"Lady's choice," Gabe said, motioning up to the marquee.

We'd hung out at the bridge for a little while, talking and watching the fireflies, before heading back to eat supper. Gabe suggested the diner that had the best crawfish in the state, and they really were the best crawfish I'd ever had.

Since there wasn't much else to do in Caudry, we headed over to the movie theater. It had been ages since I'd seen a movie in theaters. Usually I just watched whatever Luka or Hutch had on the VCR in their motorhome.

"What are you in the mood for?" I asked. "Romance? Action? Campy horror?"

He moved closer to me, looping his long fingers through mine, and although I should've been used to it by now, the heat of his skin surprised me. He'd ditched the leather jacket tonight, but he still had to be at least ten degrees warmer than me.

"Since I am on a date with you, I would say that I'm definitely in the mood for romance," Gabe said with his usual sly grin.

I stared up into his eyes—they were the color of burnt caramel, and so big and bright despite the darkness of the street. They still had a glimmer, a glint of something wicked, but tonight I could see something else lurking behind them, something that looked like hunger.

I'd felt it inside the museum trailer last night, when his kisses had felt ravenous.

"What's your secret?" I asked suddenly.

His smile instantly fell. "What?"

"Before, we promised to tell each other our secrets, but you already know mine."

He looked away from me, and though he kept his hand around mine, he stepped back, putting distance between us. "We agreed on the fifth date, but this is only, like, our third date."

"Fourth," I corrected him.

"Right." He smiled but it was weak and didn't quite reach his eyes. "Next time, then."

I opened my mouth to argue that there wasn't a point in waiting another day, and it didn't exactly seem fair that he'd already found out that I was with the carnival. But before I could get anything out, a horn blasted loudly on the street beside us.

A Mercedes pulled in sharply, parking at a ridiculous angle beside Gabe's car on the street right in front of us. The windows were rolled up, but I could hear Guns N' Roses thumping through the car stereo.

"Shit." Gabe cursed softly under his breath.

The passenger-side door opened, and Troy Gendry hopped out. His blond hair was slicked back, and when he flashed us a toothy smile it made his beady eyes appear even smaller.

"Gabey-baby!" Troy shouted as he walked over, causing Gabe to grimace.

Logan Montgomery got out of the driver's side more slowly, carrying a can of beer in his hand. His Ray-Ban sunglasses were pushed to the top of his head, and the collar of his polo was popped.

Logan leaned up against the hood of his Mercedes. "What are y'all up to?" he asked, managing to sound entirely bored and indifferent to his own question.

"It looks like these two are on a date." Troy grinned like a jackal. "But that can't be right, can it?"

Gabe moved an arm protectively around my waist. "We are on a date, actually, and we were just heading into a movie."

"Why are you on a date?" Logan asked, then he pointed to me with his beer can. "Isn't she running off with the circus in a couple days?"

My cheeks flushed with warmth, but I held my head high. The disgust in Logan's voice and Troy giggling like a drunken fool wouldn't make me cower.

"I told Selena that Mara worked for the carnival," Gabe said through gritted teeth. "But Mara's here now, so we're hanging out, and I don't really know why that's any of your business or why you'd care."

"If you wanna slum it, that's your thing." Logan shrugged. "But I might marry your sister someday, and I don't want to have any little carnie bastards for a niece or nephew, so just be sure you wrap it up."

Gabe inhaled through his nose, and he stepped away from me. I tried to grab his hand, to keep him beside me, but he slipped easily through my grasp as he walked up to Logan.

Logan, for his part, stood up and tried to look intimidating, but that was nearly impossible to do against Gabe. Despite being older, Logan was much shorter and not as broad shouldered or muscular.

Not to mention the look on Gabe's face—the intensity of his eyes and the way his lip curled back as he glared down at Logan.

"Gabe," I said, but his penetrating gaze was focused solely on Logan.

"You're never marrying my sister," Gabe growled. It was low and throaty, and Logan visibly gulped. "And if I ever hear you say anything like that again about Mara, I'll bust your face in."

Logan's mouth hung open dumbly as he struggled to think of a comeback, but he just ended up looking like a fish gasping for air as his lips moved and nothing came out.

"Come on, Logan," Troy said, rescuing his friend. "We're almost out of beer. Let's get to the liquor store before it closes."

"Let's get out of here," Logan said. He tried to sound tough and aloof, but it fell flat, and he hurried around to the driver's-side door a bit too quickly.

"We don't need to waste any more time with these *freaks*," Troy sneered just before he got in the car.

There was something about the way Troy said that and the way he looked at me when he said it. I knew then that he and Logan had been the ones who had spray painted "freeks" on Gideon's trailer.

Luka'd said that they'd been drunk and hassling him shortly before the carnival closed. They must've still been pissed off—and even more drunk—so they came back in a lame attempt to settle the score.

As Logan sped off in his Mercedes, Troy flipped us off, and I wondered exactly what they'd been up to on Saturday night. Had they attacked Seth?

That didn't seem likely, given the way Logan cowered in front of Gabe, who didn't possess the kind of supernatural strength that Seth did. But I couldn't help but wonder if they knew something more about what was going on here in Caudry.

"I'm so sorry about that," Gabe said, returning to my side now that Logan and Troy were gone. "My sister always dates assholes."

"It's okay." I brushed it off. "Believe it or not, I meet a lot of assholes in my line of work."

He frowned. "You shouldn't have to deal with that."

"I meet a lot of nice people like you too," I assured him with a smile. "So it's all worth it in the end."

27. slumber

S o how was the date?" Roxie asked. In the darkness of the campsite, her face was nearly hidden, other than the ember from her cigarette.

I'd gotten back to camp just in time to help the carnival close down, and then I'd helped make supper for everyone. Now, everyone else had gone to their motorhomes for the night, except for Roxie, who sat on the steps outside her door, smoking, while I put away lawn chairs.

"It was good," I said, since I didn't know how else to answer. "We're seeing each other again on Wednesday."

I liked Gabe a lot, and I was liking him more the more time I spent with him. But the run-in with Troy and Logan had left a blemish on the whole evening. Not to mention the fact that I felt Gabe was hiding something from me.

But did I even have a right to be upset that he was keeping some kind of secret from me? I'd be leaving in less than a week.

I would never be able to know everything about him anyway, so what did it hurt if he wanted to keep a few things to himself?

"That's good," Roxie said. "I'm glad you're having fun."

I walked over and sat down beside her. After her shows tonight, she'd showered away all the makeup and hair products, so her blond hair hung wet down her back against her oversize T-shirt.

"I thought you quit smoking," I commented.

"I did." She let out a heavy sigh. "I'll quit again once we leave this place."

"Yeah, I think this town is wearing on everyone," I said, looking out at all the darkened motorhomes. Normally, people would stay up a bit to talk and unwind, but since we'd been in Caudry, as soon as the meal was over, everyone went inside and locked up.

"It's just so weird being in the trailer by myself." She flicked her ashes and chewed her lip. "Ever since I joined this carnival, I've never been alone."

That was the good and the bad about growing up the way I had. People were always around—looking out for you, caring for you, telling on you, invading your privacy. It was a mixed bag.

"When Carrie started dating Seth, he was always hanging around our trailer," Roxie went on. "And Blossom started staying half the time at your place, but she was still here a lot. I was always tripping over one of them. And now . . . they're all gone."

"Carrie and Seth are just in town at the hospital, and

they'll be back soon," I reminded her. "And you keep saying that you're sure Blossom will turn up at the end of the week."

"I know, but . . ." She trailed off and the silence hung in the air. "I'm a little envious of you, actually."

I looked at her sharply. "What? Why?"

She shrugged and stared down at the ground. "Everything's so easy with you and Gabe."

I scoffed. "It has not been easy."

She shook her head. "No, I know. I just mean you like him, and he likes you, so you're together, and you kiss and talk and do all the things couples do."

"Well, not *all* the things," I corrected her softly.

"Sometimes, I have crushes on people." When she said it, her eyes lingered for a long time on the trailer that Luka and Hutch shared.

I'd suspected for a while that Hutch had a crush on Roxie, but I could never quite get a read on how exactly Roxie felt about him. She teased him a lot and always kept him at arm's length, but Roxie kept pretty much everyone at arm's length.

"If you like someone, you could just tell them," I suggested.

"I know." She shook her head again. "But I'm just not ready." She took a long drag of her cigarette and exhaled a big plume of smoke. "Ever since what happened with my stepdad . . . I don't think I'll ever be ready."

Roxie had lost control of her pyrokinesis. Her house burned to the ground, and, thankfully, other than her stepdad—whose hands had been burned to crisps—no one had been hurt.

That was the night that Roxie took off, and she kept running until she finally found the carnival.

"You'll be ready when you're ready," I told her gently. "And if someone really cares about you, they'll understand, and they'll wait until you are absolutely certain that you're ready."

"I hope so," she said.

Abruptly, she threw her cigarette on the ground and stomped it out with the heel of her bare foot. "I should head inside, I guess."

"I can stay with you tonight," I offered. "If you want."

Roxie seemed to consider this for a moment, then nodded. "All right. You can stay in Blossom's bed."

I ran over to my Winnebago to let my mom know that I was just staying at Roxie's, so she wouldn't worry, and I changed into pajamas. When I went back into Roxie's Airstream, all the lights were off except for her bedside lamp.

Her room was in the back, with her narrow twin bed across from Blossom's. She sat cross-legged on the covers and brushed her long platinum-blond hair.

There were three young women sharing a small trailer, so their stuff was crammed everywhere. All of the drawers were overflowing, and the door to the closet could never completely close. Posters and pictures covered every inch of the wall. One of Seth's shirts lay on the sofa that folded out into Carrie's bed.

It had to be really strange staying alone with the ghosts of Carrie and Blossom.

"I don't think we've ever had a slumber party," I said, hopping into Blossom's bed.

"This is the first time I've ever really had the room for it." Roxie set aside her brush and crawled under the covers. Then she flicked off the light. "Night, Mara."

I expected to lay awake for a while, since I was sleeping in a new place, and I still had so many details of my date with Gabe running through my mind. But it had been a very long day, and exhaustion set in quickly, so I was out within minutes.

I didn't stay asleep long, though. My stomach turned sour, twisting up inside me, and I woke up feeling like I'd throw up any second. I sat up in the strange bed, trying to decide if I needed to run to the bathroom or not, and I heard something that scared me to the core.

Mahilā the tiger let out a long and pained roar.

TUESDAY, MARCH 17, 1987

28. assault

Roxie's bed was on the side of the trailer that faced the tiger pen, and I jumped from my bed and leapt into hers.

"What the hell, Mara?" Roxie shouted, sitting up with a start.

"Something's wrong with the tigers," I told her as I pushed back her blinds.

The streetlamp was on the other side of Gideon's trailer, which cast the tiger pen in a dark shadow, but the full moon was bright enough that I could see fairly well. Unfortunately, there wasn't much of a view of the tiger pen from this angle.

Mahilā let out another sound, more of the guttural mewling she'd been doing since we got to Caudry.

"I've gotta go check on them," I said, climbing off the bed.

Roxie grabbed my arm, stopping me. "Mara, no. If there's something that's hurting those tigers, what do you think it will do to you?"

"I can't just let the tigers get hurt. Listen to them!"

"I know, I love the tigers too, but Zeke has a tranq gun and Gideon has a shotgun. They need to be the ones to deal with this."

I climbed back on Roxie's bed and pushed aside the shades. "Where the hell are they? Other people in the camp have to be hearing Mahilā too."

Roxie crouched down beside me so she could peer over my shoulder. "I don't know."

The lights on Luka and Hutch's trailer flicked on, and a few seconds later, the front door opened. Luka stepped out first, holding a devil stick, which was a large baton he used in tricks. Following a few paces behind him was Hutch, holding two other devil sticks.

"Idiots," Roxie said under her breath. "Go back inside, go back inside."

Instead of going inside, they decided to split up. Luka went right, going toward the tiger pen, and Hutch went left, going away from it.

"At least Hutch is smart enough not to walk *toward* the danger," Roxie muttered.

As Luka walked toward the tiger pen, he had to pass the Phoenixes' trailer. And then I saw something—that same thing I'd seen last night. A dark blur of a shadow, but this time it seemed . . . more real somehow. The darkness was less abstract and more of a shape—something low to the ground and very fast.

Roxie gasped. "Luka's walking right toward it!"

I jumped off the bed and ran toward the door. Roxie cursed, and I heard her footsteps as she ran after me. As soon as we got outside, we separated, with Roxie going after Hutch, and me bolting toward Luka.

The air felt thick, like a humid blanket wrapped around me and slowing me down. Beneath my feet, the grass was slick and cool with dew, and I struggled not to slip as I rushed to Luka. Clouds were gathering overhead, and soon the light of the moon would be blocked out.

Surprised, Luka struck out at me with the devil stick, but I ducked, barely missing it. Then I grabbed Luka's arm and started running toward his trailer.

But there it was, in front of us. It was hidden around the corner of the Phoenixes' motorhome, as if it had been circling the trailer, but the creature cast a shadow out in front of it in the moonlight.

With nowhere else to run, I decided that we should hide. I pushed Luka to the ground and we crawled underneath the motorhome. It sat only a foot or two off the ground, and I could only hope that whatever was stalking the campsite was too big to get under the motorhome.

Lying on my belly in the dirt beside Luka, I held my breath as my heart pounded in my chest, and my stomach lurched.

Only a few feet in front of me, I could see the feet of the creature. Four huge feet with long toes, almost like fingers, and razor-sharp claws at the end.

"What the hell is that?" Luka whispered.

"Is anyone out here?" Gideon shouted. He sounded nearby, but I couldn't see him, not from where I was hiding. "If you're out here looking for trouble, you need to know that I have a gun."

The feet in front of the trailer moved quickly, once again

moving in a shadowy blur impossible to see clearly in the darkness of the night.

"Hello?" Gideon called again.

Then there was nothing but silence for a few moments. It was long enough for me to consider climbing out from under the trailer and letting Gideon know we were close.

"Holy shit!" Gideon yelled, and the air cracked like thunder as he fired his shotgun.

29. inhuman

The silence that followed felt more deafening than the gun-shot. I didn't dare move or breathe, and I couldn't see any-thing. I felt trapped in a void, where I could only imagine all the worst things that could have happened.

"Zeke!" Gideon shouted, and the world fell back into motion again. "Get out here!"

If Gideon was calling people to come out, then he must've thought it was safe. I crawled out in a hurry, not waiting to see if Luka followed.

I ran toward the sound of his voice and discovered that the fencing around the tiger's pen had broken. The metal tines were bent and twisted, creating a gap large enough for a bear to fit through.

Gideon knelt on the ground with his shotgun in one hand, while his other was pressed against a wound in the tiger's abdo-men. Safēda's blue eyes were wild with fear, and her white fur had been stained red with blood.

Mahilā stood at the other side of the pen, howling.

"What happened?" I asked.

Gideon looked back over his shoulder at me. "Get in your trailer. Tell everyone to stay inside."

"But what happened?" I persisted. "Did you shoot Safēda?"

"No." He shook his head. "I found her like this. I fired the gun to scare away whatever had attacked her."

"So you didn't see it?" I asked.

"Mara!" Gideon snapped. "Get back in your trailer! Lock the door!"

I knew I wouldn't be able to get any more from him, so I did as I was told. Though I skipped my trailer, instead deciding to hole up in Luka's trailer with him, Hutch, and Roxie.

We sat at the windows, watching as Zeke rushed around to gather blankets and basic first aid. A few people came out to ask Gideon what was going on, but he sent them all back to their trailers with no more information than he'd given me.

Then Zeke and Gideon loaded Safēda into the back of the truck, and Zeke sped off, presumably to get her the medical care she needed.

Finally, the sky began to lighten, and people began filtering out into the campsite. Normally, most of us weren't up this early, but I don't think anyone had gone back to sleep. Not that I blamed them. Gunfire wasn't a common occurrence in the camp.

"Did you guys get a good look at it?" Hutch asked, not for the first time. "You saw the thing, right?"

He sat in the dinette across from Luka, while Roxie poured herself another cup of coffee. I sat in the swivel chair by the window, with my chin resting on the back of the chair, so I could watch everything that happened outside.

"We didn't really see much of anything." Luka repeated the answer he'd been giving Hutch since we'd gone into the trailer a couple hours ago. "It was dark, and we were under the camper."

"But you think it was an animal?" Hutch pressed.

"It wasn't human, so it must be an animal," Luka replied wearily.

"You know those aren't the only two options," Hutch said.

"Hutch!" Roxie snapped. "Just let it go for a while, okay?"

The camp looked gray and dull, since the sun hadn't risen fully yet, and everyone moved slowly as they started their morning routines, looking like zombies in a horror movie. Then the campsite was suddenly flooded with red and blue, and Hutch jumped to his feet to look out the windshield.

"Holy crap," Hutch said. "There's a cop here."

A black-and-white car pulled into the center of the campsite. *Caudry Sheriff's Department* had been painted on the side in bold blue letters, and my heart sank when I saw Deputy Bob Gendry getting out of the driver's seat.

Gideon was already walking toward him, his lips pressed together in a grim line. Blood stained the white ribbed tank he was wearing, and I realized that he'd already lost a lot of clothes to bloodstains this week.

I moved slowly, opening the door to the motorhome and waiting at the bottom of the steps so I didn't intrude. Mahilā growled, and I looked over to see her locked up in the traveling cage.

"What can I do for you?" Gideon asked.

"We've had some complaints about gunfire and possible animal attacks." Deputy Bob stood with his hands on his belt, emphasizing the fact that he had a gun holstered on his hip.

"We've had some problems with an animal harassing our campsite," Gideon explained carefully. "I fired a gun to scare it off."

Deputy Bob looked over at the mangled tiger pen, and his full lips pinched into an annoyed pucker. "It seems like you've had some problems with your tigers."

"It's not our tigers," Gideon corrected him. "It's something from around here—something from Caudry—that attacked the tigers."

"What kind of tiger is that?" Deputy Bob narrowed his small eyes as he watched Mahilā pace her cage.

"She's a Siberian tiger," Gideon replied.

"I don't know much about exotic animals, like what you've got here." The way Deputy Bob gestured when he said that, it seemed as if he was including all the people who lived in the carnival.

"I doubt very much that your knowledge extends beyond the limited things you've seen inside of your little backwoods town," Gideon said, not bothering to even mask the irritation in his voice.

Deputy Bob laughed then, a loud braying sound that echoed through the campsite. "You don't know anything about Caudry, do you?"

"I know that I'll be glad when we get out of here," Gideon countered.

"The sooner the better, don't you think?" Deputy Bob asked with a raised eyebrow.

Gideon stood up taller. "Our contract is up on Sunday. We'll be leaving then."

"The thing is that I don't think Caudry is zoned for that type of animal." Deputy Bob pointed to Mahilā. "And I was willing to let it slide, but now that it seems you can't control—"

"We have control of the tigers," Gideon cut him off and pointed his finger at the deputy. "There is an animal here, some type of oversized coyote, and it's messing with us. *You* need to get control of *it*."

"I'm a deputy." He smirked and tapped the badge on his chest. "Not animal control. And once you get these tigers out of here, I'll see about sending the animal control boys out here to have a look at your claims about alleged coyotes."

"You think my tiger attacked herself?" Gideon countered.

"No, I think you have two tigers, and the one that's left doesn't look too happy about being here," Deputy Bob said. "They're wild animals, maybe even rabid. And if you don't get them out of here by the time the carnival opens this afternoon, I'll have to shut you down."

Gideon gritted his teeth, but he nodded. "Fine. The tigers will be gone."

Deputy Bob grinned. "Glad to hear it. Now I hope y'all can enjoy the rest of your stay in Caudry."

The deputy turned and went back to his car, so I walked over to Gideon.

"Why'd you let him make you get rid of the tigers?" I asked as Deputy Bob got in his car.

"Whatever's been bothering us seems attracted to the tigers," Gideon explained. "It'll be safer for them if they're gone. Maybe with the big cats gone, we'll get some peace and quiet around here."

Deputy Bob finally turned off his flashing lights and backed out of the campsite. When he turned out, Carrie Lu walked in. She watched the police car leave, then looked over at the crushed tiger pen.

"What the hell is going on here?" Carrie asked no one in particular.

30. the hierophant

People immediately began peppering Carrie with questions about Seth and what she was doing and how she was doing, but her appearance really said it all.

Her black hair had been pulled into a ponytail, and her deep-set eyes had dark bags underneath, contrasting with her pallor. With her shoulders hunched and her arms hugged against her chest, it was like she was trying to fold her slender frame into herself.

Roxie pushed her way through the small crowd of people that had gathered around Carrie, then she looped her arm around her roommate's shoulders.

"Seth is awake, and he's doing better," Carrie said. "The doctors say he should be well enough to be released tomorrow."

"That's great news," Gideon said. He stood a few feet back, away from the well-wishers, but his low rumbling British accent pushed through the murmurs of everyone else. The exhaustion of this place was wearing on him, but he looked relieved and even managed a small smile.

"It's been hell sleeping in the hospital, though, so I just came back to catch a nap and grab some of my things," Carrie explained.

"Give her space, people," Roxie commanded, and began leading Carrie to their trailer. "She can talk to you when she wakes up."

"Actually, I was just going to call a meeting," Jackie said, and everyone turned to look at her in surprise, including Gideon and her husband, Brendon.

She stood in front of her motorhome, already dressed in a jumper with her blond hair curled even though it was barely seven in the morning. Behind her, her daughter, Alyssa, was inside the trailer with her face pressed against the glass door, making her nose smoosh up like a pig's snout.

"I would like it if you would join us for the meeting, Carrie," Jackie said, resting her blue eyes on Carrie. "I understand if you need your rest, though."

Carrie nodded numbly. "I can stay for the meeting."

"Are we having it now, then?" Gideon asked with a cocked eyebrow. He glanced around the campsite, looking skeptical and annoyed. As the head of the carnival, he was usually the one who called the meetings.

"Since Carrie is here now, I think it would be best." Jackie tried to keep her voice even, but I heard a slight nervous tremor running through it.

Gideon turned and shouted, calling for everyone to join us

in the campsite for a meeting. Most people were already outside and awake, but a few stragglers made their way out. Hutch scurried around to set up lawn chairs, and I rushed to help him.

Roxie led Carrie to a picnic table in the back, while Gideon took a seat front and center. Mom finally emerged from our Winnebago with a shawl wrapped around her shoulders and sat down next to him.

"What's all this about?" Brendon asked his wife while everyone took their seats.

"I think it'd be better if you just sat down with everyone," Jackie whispered.

He eyed her warily, but he complied, sitting down next to his brother near the front. With the whole campsite here, we were actually a couple chairs short, so Hutch and I chose to stand in the back.

"Thank you all for coming out here so early, but in light of everything that's happened, I think it's best that we talk about it all now," Jackie began.

"As you all know, there was a police officer that came into the campsite this morning. He said he came here because they'd had a complaint." She paused, clearing her throat. "I called in that complaint."

A few people gasped, and Brendon cursed under his breath.

Gideon stood up slowly, and Jackie took a step back. He wasn't as tall or as strong as Seth, but the scars on his back and arms proved that he never backed down from a fight. His hands were big and rough from years of manual labor, and he'd balled them into fists as he seethed at Jackie.

"You had *no* right to do that," Gideon said, and Jackie flinched. He didn't raise his voice at all, but the anger in his words was palpable.

"I did what I had to do to protect my family," Jackie insisted.

"If you're worried about your family, you come to me," Gideon snarled. "You do *not* go to the outside! You do not bring them here!"

"Gideon," my mom said quietly, in a vain attempt to calm him.

"I did go to you and you didn't listen!" Jackie shot back. Her nostrils flared as she glared up at him. "There is something attacking us—*targeting* us—and you're doing nothing!"

Gideon took a deep breath and unclenched his fists. When he spoke, his voice was restrained and tight. "What else would you have me do? We have precautions in place, and the tigers will be gone this afternoon."

"I don't feel safe here, Gideon," Jackie admitted, and her shoulders sagged as she deflated. "I think we should leave."

"I already told you, Jackie. You're not a prisoner here. You and everyone else who wants to go is free to go." He turned away from her and looked at the rest of us, sitting and watching. "But I cannot leave a paycheck behind here. I am staying until Sunday. The carnival is staying."

With that, Gideon turned and walked back toward his trailer. There was nothing more to be said, so the crowd slowly broke up and went about their business.

My mom paused outside Gideon's door, pulling her shawl more tightly around her shoulders, then she shook her head and walked to our Winnebago instead.

I promised Carrie I would help her gather anything she might need for herself or Seth later, then I left her with Roxie and hurried into my motorhome. Mom was sitting at the dinette, her worn tarot cards spread out before her.

Her brow was furrowed, and the creases around her dark eyes seemed to stand out more. She barely glanced up at me, but I saw that her eyes were the color of a stormy sky. Her long red nails tapped anxiously on the table, and I slid into the booth across from her.

"What do you see?" I asked, looking down at the spread of cards before her.

She gathered up the cards before I could get a good look at them, but I'd already spotted a few—The Devil, the Three of Swords, and the Moon. In their simplest terms, they could be read as bondage, pain, and fear.

"Nothing." She shuffled the cards back into a deck. "They're all nonsense. I haven't been able to get a good read since we've arrived in Caudry."

"Do you think we should leave?" I asked.

Mom sighed and stared down at the table. "Not yet. We only have a few more days, and if we do the things Gideon suggests, I believe we'll be safe."

"Jackie said that she thinks the creature is targeting us."

"*Creature?*" Mom snorted. "You're proposing a monster is hunting us?"

I shrugged. "I don't know. I don't know what it is, but it didn't look like any coyote I've ever seen."

"This place is playing tricks on all our minds." Mom gestured vaguely to the air, then she reached across the table and took my hand. "I've been alive for thirty-seven years, and I have seen all kinds of things that defy the laws of nature. But I've never seen a monster. Only those that are misunderstood and mistreated."

My mom had grown up during a time when men and women with deformities and extra senses had been kept in cages like animals. She'd told me horror stories about the abuses and exploitation she'd seen in other circuses and sideshows, things that Gideon strived to protect us from.

"Do you think it's an illusion, then?" I asked.

"I don't know, *qamari*," Mom admitted wearily. "But what I do know is that while we're here, you must stay safe. Don't go out alone at night. I want you in this trailer, sleeping in your bed, every night by midnight. And if you must see that boy in town, do so in the afternoon. So far, daylight seems to have kept our troubles at bay."

I nodded but didn't say anything. Gabe and I'd made plans to see each other Wednesday at seven, but as long as I'd be back in bed by midnight, I didn't see the harm.

31. strength

Seth Holden looked too large for the hospital room. The bandages around his chest and arms bulked up his already thick frame, and he was nearly six and a half feet tall, so his feet were pressed against the wooden footboard.

Roxie and I stood in the doorway to his room, unsure of how to proceed since Seth was snoring softly. Carrie was still at the campsite, packing up Seth's things, and Luka and Hutch would be bringing her later. Roxie and I decided to visit Seth on our own, so we wouldn't crowd him too much, but now we were beginning to regret our decision.

"We have to wake him up," Roxie said finally. "This is ridiculous."

Carrying a vase of daises we'd picked up at the only floral shop in town, Roxie walked into Seth's room. I followed a step behind her, so she'd be the one to wake him and not me.

"Seth?" Roxie asked quietly, setting the flowers on the bedside table. "Seth? Are you awake?"

Sunlight streamed in through his open blinds, onto the carnation-pink floor tiles and white sheets. In some places on his bandages, the white had turned a shade of pink, where he must be bleeding underneath.

But, other than that, Seth didn't really look that terrible. The bandages were hiding the worst of his injuries, so the only real visible wound was a narrow scratch running along the bottom of his chin, and it didn't even require stitches.

Slowly, Seth's eyes opened and he blinked a few times. When he saw Roxie and me, his mouth spread out in a sleepy smile.

"Hey, guys. It's so great to see you."

"How are you feeling?" I asked, and Roxie sat down in a pale blue recliner next to the bed.

"Great." He gestured to an IV dripping into his arm. "They have me hooked up to the good stuff. Tomorrow, if I'm released, I think they'll be sending me home with some very nice pills."

"Well, I'm glad you're not in any pain." I sat on the edge of Seth's bed, since the room didn't have any other chairs.

"How is the carnival going?" Seth asked. "How is everyone?"

I glanced over at Roxie before replying with, "Good, I think everyone's doing really well."

That was mostly true. Seth and Safēda had been the only two injuries, and I didn't want to burden him with the suspicions and paranoia back at camp. He'd already been through enough.

"It's been really busy at the carnival," Roxie said cheerily. "I think we're actually gonna make bank here."

"That'll be great, since I have these hospital bills to pay for now," Seth said, but he didn't sound that upset about it.

In part, because of morphine, and in part, because he'd probably never actually pay them. When we went to hospitals while traveling, we used fake names, and then we were gone. It wasn't the best way to live, but it was the only way we could afford getting help when we needed it.

"Carrie called from the payphone outside the camp." Seth's blue eyes grew serious as he looked between Roxie and me. "She told me there's been some strange things going on there."

I shrugged, trying to downplay it. "There's something weird about the town. There's a bad energy."

"My pyro hasn't been working right at all," Roxie added, and rubbed the palm of her hands where her fireballs usually sprouted from.

"That explains how I was overpowered by a big coyote," Seth muttered to himself.

"A big coyote?" I asked. "You remember it attacking you?"

He shook his head. "No. I don't remember the attack at all. Carrie just told me that's the theory going around, though. Some kind of big coyote."

"That's one theory," Roxie said under her breath.

"You'll be getting out of here tomorrow," I said, quickly changing the subject. "That must be exciting."

"Yeah." Seth paused before adding, "Carrie and I are actually going over to Texas. We were thinking we could wait in Houston and meet up with you guys when you're done here."

"You're leaving?" I asked in surprise.

"I can't work." Seth gestured to his bandages. "And I'm weak as hell. This place seems totally bugshit. So we thought, why not go someplace safe and quiet to recuperate?"

I forced a smile to hide my growing unease. "That makes total sense."

"A campsite is no place to heal," Roxie chimed in. "And I doubt there's a good hotel anywhere in this town."

Seth began talking about Carrie's plan to pawn some of her jewelry and Seth's videos and cassettes so they would be able to afford to stay in a decent place in Houston for a few days, and he wondered aloud if Gideon would be able to advance him some cash.

While he spoke, Roxie cocked her head and eyed the daisies we'd brought with growing suspicion.

"You know what's weird?" she asked when Seth finished talking. "There's only one floral shop in this whole town."

I shrugged. "So?"

"When we came in, the town sign said there were, like, thirteen thousand people or something," Roxie elaborated. "And there's only one flower shop and a small grocery. It's not large enough to support that much business. Yet every day, the carnival is totally packed. Where are these people coming from? And why?"

"I think you answered your own question, Roxie," I said. "It's a small town. There's nothing else to do."

"Maybe," Roxie said, but by the way she narrowed her eyes at the daisies, I knew she wasn't convinced.

WEDNESDAY, MARCH 18, 1987

32. wicked

I awoke in my own bed with a dog-eared copy of *Something Wicked This Way Comes* lying beside me and my crossbow on the floor, in case I needed it. I sat up and peeled back the curtains, expecting to find the carnival in ruins, but instead, the campsite looked normal.

After Roxie and I visited Seth, we came back to the carnival and got to work. It was a full crowd again, but relatively uneventful. When nightfall came, I sat posted at the window, watching and waiting for the creature to come back again.

But it never had. There had been no strange noises. No monsters. No bad dreams.

So, I got up and got ready and went about my day helping where I was needed. The camp felt strange and silent without the tigers. Zeke had picked up Mahilā, and he was taking her and Safēda to Houston to see an exotic animal specialist.

The Phoenixes had done their afternoon show in the tent.

Despite Jackie's growing concerns about Caudry, it seemed that for now they were staying.

The rain started in the afternoon, and though it showed no signs of letting up, the lines of people kept getting longer. So far, the showers were light enough that the rides could stay open, but people flocked to the shows to stay dry.

To help expedite the lines because of the weather, I stood outside of the main tent with Hutch and took tickets. It was a large red-and-white-striped tent that looked exactly like it came out of an ad for Barnum & Bailey's Circus.

Usually, Zeke would do a show with his tigers in the big tent on Wednesdays, but with them gone, Gideon had stepped up to do another magic act. Posters on the side of the tent and around the carnival depicted him in a sharp tuxedo replete with a red bow tie and top hat, under the banner of *Gideon Davorin— Master of Illusions and Dark Arts.*

Once in costume, Gideon smiled and dazzled as he performed. Under his working-class exterior, a real showman lurked. Sometimes I'd sit in the back of the tent, watching his act, and the audience always sat in rapt attention.

The length of the lines to his shows was evidence of his talent. Even when the weather wasn't bad, repeat viewings weren't uncommon.

Fortunately, the tent had a large overhang, so Hutch and I were able to stay dry as we collected tickets. The line was getting near the end when I heard someone squeal, *"Mara!"*

I looked over to see Selena standing a few feet away under an umbrella held by Logan, and she waved wildly at me. Her hot pink rainboots matched her lipstick perfectly, and her black hair was perfectly styled.

"I think I can handle these last few folks if you wanna go say hi to your friend," Hutch said, gesturing to where Selena continued to grin broadly at me.

"Thanks," I said, but I didn't really know how grateful I felt. So far, Selena had been nothing but nice to me, but Logan had proved himself to be quite the jerk.

But since she was standing there, waiting for me, I couldn't exactly ignore her, so I jogged over to them. Though her umbrella was large, it wasn't quite big enough for me to stand under without squishing against them, so I stayed just outside, letting the rain dampen my clothes and hair.

"I was hoping I would see you here tonight," Selena said, then she seemed to notice the drops of water splashing on me. "Oh gosh, I don't want you getting soaked. Let's move over here where it's a bit drier."

Selena stepped a few paces over toward the midway, with Logan dutifully following to keep the umbrella over her. A blue tent reached out past a ring toss with goldfish as the prize, so we stopped just under it, leaving room for customers to play the game.

"That's better," Selena said, turning her doe eyes to me. "So, how are you doing?"

"Fine, I guess." I ran my hand through my damp hair, trying to smooth it, since I felt decidedly unglamorous in my hand-me-down dress compared to her. "It's been busy out here, so I've been working a lot."

"At least it looks like the dog didn't get you," Logan muttered. He wasn't looking at me when he spoke, instead preferring to sneer at a little girl who was crying because she failed to win a fish.

Selena's cheery demeanor instantly fell, replaced by a worried frown and frantic eyes. "What dog? What are you talking about?"

"Didn't you hear?" Logan chuckled and turned his attention back to his girlfriend. "They're *claiming* that there was some kind of coyote attacking their tigers. Troy's dad had to come and check it out."

Her tawny skin paled, making the rouge on her cheeks stand out more. "There's a coyote?"

"No," Logan scoffed. "Troy's dad thinks they're just trying for insurance fraud."

"It is not insurance fraud," I snapped, and glared at Logan, not that it fazed him. Nothing seemed to faze him, except Gabe's threats of violence. "Something really attacked the tigers."

Logan held up his hands in a gesture of peace, but the arrogant smirk remained plastered on his face. "Whatever you say. You guys must be the only carnies out there not scheming or looking for a quick buck."

"*Logan!*" Selena swatted him in the arm hard enough to make him actually flinch. "Be nice to her! She's my brother's girlfriend."

My irritation with Logan momentarily disappeared when I heard the word *girlfriend*, and I felt my whole body flush. I'd kissed boys and gone out with them before, but I'd never hung around anywhere long enough for me to really be someone's girl-friend.

Even now, seeing Gabe nearly every day since we'd gotten to town, I wouldn't really consider myself his girlfriend. That was a title reserved for something more serious, something that lasted longer than a week.

Still, a warmth grew in my chest and butterflies filled my stomach at the thought of actually calling Gabe my boyfriend.

"Why don't you go make yourself useful and get me a drink?" Selena suggested to Logan, who'd just stared sullenly at her since her outburst.

"Fine," Logan agreed.

He tried to take the umbrella with him, but Selena snatched it from him, so he pulled his jacket over his well-manicured blond hair as he walked into the rain. He muttered something under his breath that I couldn't hear, but it caused Selena to nar-row her eyes at him.

"I'm sorry about Logan," Selena said, still glaring after him. "He's a grump sometimes."

"Yeah, I figured that," I said, since I didn't know Selena well enough to ask her what she saw in Logan or why she was dating someone who was so obviously a massive jerk, when she seemed so nice.

She turned her attention back to me, giving me a sympathetic smile. "So everything is okay? I hadn't heard anything about the animal attack."

"I think everything's okay now."

"Good." She nodded, then repeated it to herself again. "Good." A bright smile returned to her face. "I just thought I'd say hi and see how you were doing. I wanted to get to know the girl that has so totally captured my brother's attention and his affection."

I smiled because I couldn't help myself, and my cheeks warmed with embarrassment. Unsure of how else to respond, I lamely replied with, "I like your brother too."

"He told me that you're leaving on Sunday," Selena said. "Have you thought about staying?"

"I . . . um, I . . ." I stammered, unable to tell her what I was really thinking.

I'd love to have a home base somewhere, with a house that isn't on wheels, and I'd love to see Gabe every day, not just for this week but the week after that and the week after that.

But there was no way that I could stay in a town like Caudry. It felt small and claustrophobic, with people like Logan, who knew everybody's business and looked down on them for it.

And that was without even getting into the supernatural issues with the Nukoabok Swamp and purple fireflies and the creature that stalked our camp.

On Sunday, regardless of how I felt about Gabe, I would be leaving Caudry forever.

"Sorry, I'm being nosy," Selena said quickly, apparently noticing the distress in my expression. "That's something you should talk about with Gabe, not me."

"It's okay," I told her, and forced a smile.

"Anyway, I should go find Logan before he gets himself into trouble." Selena glanced around, looking for her boyfriend.

"It was nice seeing you again," I said.

"You too." She started walking away, but then she paused

and turned back to me. "And, Mara, if you have any more prob-lems with that animal, you should let Gabe know. I'm sure he'd love to help you, if he can."

"Thanks," I said, but something about her expression felt very strange.

In fact, the whole day had felt off and strange, like the un-comfortable stillness before a storm hits, and I realized that I didn't want to be at the carnival a moment longer.

33. lusus naturae

I was soaked through by the time I reached Gabe's. As I'd walked up the cobblestone driveway toward his house, the branches from the willow trees seemed to be reaching out for me.

Despite the warmth of the air, I felt a chill run through me as I walked up his steps. I took the heavy iron knocker in my hands and stared up at the white mansion that loomed over me.

The appearance of the antebellum architecture meant it was most likely hundreds of years old. There had to have been so much that happened inside the walls of the house. So much life, and so much death.

And then I heard it, the voice from my nightmares, coming from inside my head. The old woman screaming shrilly, *"id-hab-bee-in-who-nah!"*

The front door opened, and I stumbled as I took a step back. A hand reached out, steadying me, and as Gabe helped me up, I realized with some dismay that I didn't remember knocking. I took the knocker in my hands, but the house had distracted me before I could do anything more.

"Mara?" Gabe asked, holding my arm warmly in his strong hands. "Is everything okay? I thought I wasn't picking you up for another two hours?"

"No, you're right. I just . . . I wanted to see you." I tried to smile, but everything felt off, like I was just waking up from a dream I couldn't remember.

I stared at his crimson-red front door and the cast-iron door knocker.

"How did you know I was here?" I asked, and looked up at Gabe.

"I thought I heard someone outside," he replied vaguely. "You're soaking wet. Why don't you come inside and dry off?"

I followed him into his house, trying to shake off the increasing chill growing in my chest. The last time I'd been here had been in the middle of Selena's party, and I'd been doing my best to take in the full beauty and opulence of the mansion by stealing glances around party guests.

"I'll grab you a towel," Gabe offered, leaving me to stand dripping water onto the hardwood floor.

Gabe returned a moment later and draped a thick fluffy towel around my shoulders before handing me another for my hair.

"Who decorated your house?" I asked Gabe as I dried my hair.

"My mom, mostly, but Selena helped a bit."

"It's so stylish and hip," I commented as I spied a Jackson Pollock painting hanging in the grand entry. "Whoever decorated like this seems like they'd have a very cosmopolitan sensibility." I paused. "One that clashes with the way of life down here."

There was clearly a culture clash growing inside this house. The crown molding and antique chandeliers contrasted sharply with the furniture in bold primary colors and modern art. It was like a mashup of *Pee-wee's Playhouse* and *Gone with the Wind*.

"I think my mom would've been happier in New York," Gabe admitted.

"Then why did you move back here?"

Gabe let out a deep sigh. "The Brawley legacy." He looked around the entry at the grand staircase and refurnished fixtures. "This house has been in our family for nearly two centuries. My mom couldn't let it go."

"Well, I'm glad," I said. "If she had, you wouldn't be here with me now."

He looked at me then, his deep golden eyes meeting mine, and I saw a heat in them that I felt reflecting in my own. It wasn't lust or the hunger I felt when he kissed me or even the way my pulse quickened every time he was near.

It was something deeper. The comfort that I found in his presence and the way my smiles felt easier when he was around. The way I wanted to know everything about him, and how I wanted to tell him everything about me, even the things that I'd never told anybody.

I realized that's why I'd come over here today. Everything about today had felt off and wrong, and I knew that Gabe would make me feel better, safer, happier.

He reached out, taking my hand in his, and his skin felt even warmer than normal, nearly scalding.

"You're freezing!" His eyes widened with alarm. "At the risk of this sounding like a line, I think you should get out of those clothes." I arched an eyebrow, so he added, "I'll throw your dress in the dryer, and in the meantime, you can put on some of my warm, dry clothes."

I smiled. "That sounds fair."

Gabe took a step back toward the staircase, still holding my hand as he did. "My clothes are upstairs in my room."

"Why do I feel like you're always looking for excuses to get me into your bedroom?" I teased.

"Maybe because I always am," Gabe admitted, making me laugh again.

He led me to his spacious bedroom, where the wallpaper was carefully concealed with a multitude of band posters. His bed was unmade, hidden beneath a pile of blankets and pillows. The blue teddy bear I'd won him sat on his dresser next to his Nintendo, causing me to smile.

With his back to me, he rummaged through his closet looking for something suitable for me to wear. I pulled my dress up over my head, and since it was sopping wet, I didn't want to just drop it on his floor.

"So I think this will—" He started turning around, holding a T-shirt in his hand, but then he saw me standing in my white bra and panties, and he just stopped, gaping at me.

Then he shook his head and lowered his eyes. "Sorry. I didn't know you'd already taken off your dress."

"Don't apologize." I laughed. "I knew you were right there when I took my dress off."

He lifted his eyes slowly, as if expecting there to be some kind of trick, but when I didn't freak out, he brightened up and said, "Hey, there's your other tattoo."

I glanced down at the tattoo that was scrawled across my abdomen in large bold letters.

Lusus Naturae

It'd been my first tattoo, one I'd had to use a fake ID to procure at a rundown tattoo parlor in Denver when I was only fifteen. Roxie had gone with me, and she'd held my hand when it hurt.

Gabe moved closer to me, filling in the few steps that had been between us, and he tilted his head. "What does that say?"

"*Lusus naturae*. It means 'freak of nature' in Latin," I explained.

He shook his head, and his forehead creased. "Why would you get that?"

"Growing up in a circus sideshow, I always felt that way." I shrugged, but his reaction made me feel self-conscious, so I hugged my wet dress to me, hiding the tattoo.

"I'm sorry," Gabe said hurriedly, realizing that his words had stung. "I didn't mean it like that. You're just so beautiful and wonderful and kind, and I can't imagine anyone ever making you feel like less than that."

I didn't say anything, because I didn't know how to respond. I'd been called beautiful before, mostly by my mother, and by a few clumsy boys who'd said it as they fumbled with my bra hooks. But I'd never had anyone call me beautiful and wonderful, and *really* mean it, not the way Gabe did.

There was a weight in his words, and a look in his eyes, and a softness in his touch. The way when we walked together, he always slowed his pace to match mine, and he tilted his body toward me whenever he was close.

"I should get your dress in the dryer," Gabe offered, since I wasn't doing anything but staring at him. He reached out to take it, but I put my hand over his, stopping him.

"Wait," I said, breathy and desperate.

His eyes met mine, confused and worried. "Why?"

Then, so I wouldn't have to explain it to him, I dropped the dress and moved toward him. Gabe caught on then, wrapping his arms around my bare flesh and pulling me toward him as his lips found mine.

He picked me up, making me squeal in delight, and carried me back to his bed. As he laid me back down on the softness of his blankets, I realized just how badly I wanted to be with him. The few moments he parted from me—standing up to take off his shirt and reveal the wonderful sculpting of his body—felt like an eternity.

Then he was with me, his bare skin pressing against mine, and his mouth felt hungry as it trailed down from my lips to my neck. As his hands and lips warmed my skin, my body flushed with heat. For the first time since I'd gotten to Caudry, I didn't feel a chill hiding anywhere inside me.

Somewhere in the distance—back in the real world, away from where Gabe had me enveloped in his arms, my hands clinging to his back—I was only vaguely aware of the sound of a door slamming.

"Gabe!" a woman's voice called in a Southern drawl, and that snapped us both back.

"Shit," he said under his breath, and sat up, kneeling between my legs on the bed. "That's my mom. My parents are home."

34. family

My dress was still soaking wet, so I quickly pulled on the Joan Jett T-shirt he'd grabbed for me. It was too big, but it was still very obvious that I wasn't wearing any pants.

"You like Joan Jett?" I asked.

He looked at me over his shoulder as he hastily searched his dresser drawers. "I love Joan Jett. Doesn't everyone?"

"Gabe?" his mom yelled up the stairs.

"I'll be right down!" Gabe shouted back, then as he handed me a pair of sweatpants, he whispered an explanation. "I know that we're adults and we can do what we want, but I am living at home for the moment, and I really didn't want my parents' first impression of you to be them thinking they caught us having sex."

"Me neither," I agreed, but my thoughts had gotten tripped on the words *first impression*. The addition of the word *first* implied there would be a second or more, that his parents would actually get to know me.

I understood for the first time that Gabe was treating this like a real relationship and me like a real girlfriend. That was part of what I liked so much about him, that he treated me like a real person, and not just a stopover as he went on with the rest of his life.

But the problem was that this couldn't be a relationship. His sister asked me if I might consider staying, and I realized with great dismay that she'd probably asked because Gabe had brought up the prospect.

"Are you ready?" Gabe asked after I'd finished tying the drawstring of the sweatpants.

He stared down at me, his eyes wide and nervous. Then it hit me, making my breath catch in my throat and my stomach twist.

I was going to break his heart when I left.

Swallowing back the painful lump in my throat, I nodded. "I'm ready."

Gabe went first, and my steps were filled with lead as I followed him. As we descended the stairs, I heard the click-clack of high heels on the hardwood floor, so I heard his mom before I saw her.

Then she walked into the entryway, her head down as she looked at the mail in her perfectly manicured hands. Her hair was a blond mass of curls, adding much-needed height to her petite frame, and she wore a pencil skirt made of red satin with a matching blazer.

Without her even looking up, I already recognized her. Gabe's mom was Della Jane, the woman who had helped Gideon and me at the police station four days ago.

"Gabe, honey, have you been reapplying to NYU, because you've gotten another—" Della Jane had been looking down at the mail, but her words died on her lips the second she looked up and saw me coming down the stairs behind her son.

"Oh, I'm sorry. I didn't realize you had a guest," Della Jane said, smiling thinly.

Making matters worse, Gabe's father walked in from another room, presumably the kitchen based on the freshly opened bottle of beer in his hand. It was just as I'd expected when I met him at the Blue Moon Bar & Grill—Gabe's dad was Julian Alvarado. His salt-and-pepper hair was still damp after coming in from the rain, and the top two buttons of his dark shirt had been left undone.

Julian narrowed his eyes when he saw me, probably wondering how the girl he'd met a few days ago had turned up in his house, and Della Jane held the letters in her hand so tightly, they'd begun to crumple.

Since we'd reached the main floor and the situation felt increasingly awkward, Gabe decided to make introductions.

"This is Mara, the girl I've been seeing." Gabe gestured toward me, and for a moment—for one second so quick I'm not even completely certain that I saw it—Della Jane looked horrified. But then it was gone, and she was smiling at me, looking like an ordinary, friendly but caught-off-guard mom.

"Yes, we've already met, actually," Della Jane replied in her warm Southern accent. "A few days back at the sheriff's department."

"I've met her too," Julian added, looking at me quizzically.

"You have?" Della Jane asked, her smile faltering a bit.

"She came into the bar with other folks from the carnival, looking for her friend that rents the apartment upstairs," Julian explained, and now Gabe was giving me a bewildered look that matched his father's.

Seeing them all so close together, the resemblance between them was uncanny. Gabe had his dad's height and broad shoulders, but he had his mom's cheekbones and wide smile.

"Caudry's a small town, so I guess I get around a lot," I said sheepishly, since everyone was looking at me like I was a puzzle they were trying to solve. The air was bubbling over with unasked questions.

"I guess you do," Gabe agreed, but there was a tightness to his tone that made me realize that this was something we'd talk about later.

Della Jane cleared her throat and tugged at her ruby earring. "What, um, were the two of you planning to do tonight?"

"Mara walked over in the rain, and I was just getting her something dry to wear," Gabe explained, as if it wasn't obvious that the outfit I was swimming in didn't belong to me.

"Gabe, where are your manners?" Della Jane scolded him. "Why didn't you pick the young lady up?"

"I just wanted to go for a walk and get some air," I said quickly. "I didn't realize how hard it was raining until it was too late."

"Well, if the two of you wanted to stay in tonight and avoid the weather, we could all watch a movie." Della Jane pointed to a gaudy big-screen TV that took up a huge chunk of floor space in the sitting room adjacent to the entryway. "Selena just rented *Top Gun* and *Weird Science* from the video store."

"Actually, I think I should probably get going home," I said, and Gabe looked at me sharply.

Della Jane clicked her tongue. "Oh, that's a shame," she said in such a way that I couldn't tell for sure if she meant it or not.

"You sure?" Julian asked. "You're more than welcome to stay for supper, and I make a mean steak."

"Sorry, but I'm sure," I said. "I have to work tonight."

"I'll pull the car around," Gabe offered, and he wouldn't look at me as he went over and slipped on his tennis shoes.

While he went out to get his Mustang, he left me waiting inside with his parents, and it was feeling increasingly claustrophobic. Julian put his arm around his wife's waist and told me about the restaurants he'd owned in New York, and Della Jane just kept a strained smile plastered on her face.

Gabe had this life that was solid and real, with a house that had been in the family for generations and married parents that loved each other and applications to NYU. He had a past, and more important, he had a future.

I was a girl with nothing more to my name than my name itself. If I were Della Jane, I wouldn't want me dating her son either.

After awkward good-byes, I hurried into Gabe's car, and I wasn't surprised to see the tension had carried over. He sped out of the driveway without saying anything until we were almost to the edge of town.

"If you didn't want to stay in with my parents, I totally get that," he said finally. "But you didn't have to leave. It's not even seven yet."

"I know, but I do need to get back. There's a lot going on at the carnival," I said, and that wasn't completely a lie, and my mom would be happy that I was back so early.

"Like what?" Gabe asked, sounding exasperated. "You tell me hardly anything about your life and what's going on. Like how you met both my parents."

"I didn't know they were your parents," I corrected him icily. "They didn't exactly introduce themselves and say, 'Oh, by the way, in case you decide to date Gabe, I'm just letting you know that he's my son.'"

Della Jane hadn't even given me her last name—and while I had suspected that Julian might be related to him, there hadn't really been an organic way to bring it up in the two minutes we'd spoken.

"Fair enough," he allowed, and his hands relaxed slightly from how tight they'd been gripping the steering wheel. "But you've apparently been going on all these adventures around Caudry." He sighed. "I know you don't have to tell me every little thing about your life, but I just feel like you're keeping so much from me, and I don't know why."

There wasn't some big awful reason. I just hadn't wanted to tell him about going to the police station to try to report that my friend may or may not be missing, or about visiting a former co-worker and probable drug addict who believed that this town had a supernatural pall over it.

Neither of these stories was glamorous or normal or the kind of thing you tell someone on a first date.

We'd reached the carnival parking lot, and he pulled over as rain pattered down on the Mustang. He turned to look at me, waiting for me to explain myself or just say anything.

I stared down at my hands, blinking back tears, and finally said, "I was embarrassed, okay?"

"Embarrassed?" Gabe reached out and took my hands in his. "You don't have to be embarrassed with me. If I've done anything to make you feel ashamed about any part of your life—"

"You don't get it." I shook my head. "We only have a week together, so I just wanted to keep us nice and shiny and *separate* from all the crap in my life that never quite works."

He didn't say anything for a minute. He just held my hand, rubbing the back of it with his thumb, and stared down at his lap.

"I know exactly what you're talking about," he said at length. "I've done the same thing before." He lifted his eyes to meet mine. "But I don't want to do that with you. I don't want to keep you separate from anything."

I closed my eyes, trying to steel myself from the depth of his words and the pain they brought with them. Here was someone asking me to share my life with him, and I couldn't.

"Gabe, you're not listening." I opened my eyes. "I'm not your girlfriend." My voice cracked, but I kept going. "I will *never* be your girlfriend. A week just isn't enough time."

"It's actually ten days," he corrected me softly.

"I have to go." I pulled my hand away from his and opened the car door.

"Mara, wait," he said, but I was already out the door. He got out too, and I didn't want him following me into the carnival, so I stopped. "When will I see you again?"

"I don't know." I started backing away. "I'll let you know."

"How? You don't have a phone."

"I know where you live. I'll find you when I'm ready," I replied simply, and I hoped that that would satisfy him because I couldn't keep having this conversation. I turned and jogged away, and at least the rain helped mask my tears.

35. gambit

an you grab me one too?" I asked Hutch as he pulled a
beer out of the fridge in the trailer he shared with Luka.

Luka was sitting across from me in the dinette, and he gave
me a look over his cards. "That's your second beer tonight, and
you're not usually a drinker."

We'd finished taking down the carnival for the night, and
Roxie, Tim, Luka, Hutch, and I were all relaxing over a game
of poker and a few beers. We used tokens from the digger crane
games on the midway as poker chips, each with a theoretical
value of a penny, though we rarely actually enforced payment.

"Your date with Gabe must've gone *really* bad," Roxie commented as Hutch handed me a beer. She sat beside me in the
booth, playing with her tokens. "Especially considering you
won't even talk about it."

"There's just nothing to talk about." I rubbed my temple.
"And it's been a really long week, and that has nothing to do with
Gabe."

I wasn't actually lying about that. While things with Gabe had taken a depressing turn tonight, one where I wasn't sure that it would be fair to him if I saw him again, it was mostly the carnival and Caudry and everything around it weighing down on me.

"I will drink to that!" Tim lifted his beer up, like he was toasting, and then took a long drink.

Luka put one hand on his boyfriend's leg. "How are you feeling?"

"My leg's still sore, and I'm only levitating about a third of the time," Tim said.

"Yeah, it's about the same for me." Roxie grimaced. "My pyro is a frickin' joke right now. Like, I hated it when I first got it, but now my whole act is based around it, so I need it. This whole place sucks."

Hutch sat at the end of the table, rocking on a crate that he used for a chair since the table didn't comfortably seat five. "Is Jackie still planning on leaving?"

"I don't know." Tim set his cards facedown on the table and slumped back in his seat. "She wants to, but my brother is refusing to go right now, and I don't think she'll leave without him. At this point, though, I'd honestly be happy if we just packed up and left."

Roxie folded her arms and leaned forward. "You know what my theory is?"

"What?" Hutch asked, looking up at her.

"That thing—whatever it is—is targeting us because we have supernatural powers," Roxie said, like this was a theory she had worked out in her head even though I hadn't heard it before.

Luka scoffed. "That doesn't make any sense. The only things that have been 'targeted' so far were Seth and the tigers, and the tigers aren't any more supernatural than any other cat."

"Whoa." Hutch sat back, and his eyes widened. "What if Safēda did have extra senses like you guys did? I mean, she was particularly well-behaved and nice for a tiger."

"That's not what I meant, but maybe." Roxie shrugged. "Or maybe the thing just attacked them because they were outside and available."

"Let's say I buy your theory that we're being targeted," Luka allowed, but he did little to mask the skepticism in his voice. "What is this thing allegedly doing the targeting, and what's its motive?"

"Gideon seems to think it's some type of coyote, so maybe it is," Roxie said, which only caused Luka to roll his eyes. "We all agree that Caudry has bad vibes going on, and it's messing with all of us. Even those without extra senses have been having strange dreams."

"Last night I dreamt that I had the head of a bear, and when I tried to talk to people nobody could understand me and they all ran away screaming," Hutch interjected.

"So, it's reasonable to assume that whatever 'power' is at play here is screwing with the local flora and fauna," Roxie went on, ignoring Hutch. "This place could drive a wild dog or a coyote mad and cause them to lash out, especially at anything that they sense has supernatural powers."

"You're making big leaps on what it's 'reasonable to assume,'" Luka said dryly.

"They have purple fireflies here," I said, remembering how magical that date had felt and pushing down all the feelings that went along with it. "Gabe showed them to me."

"*See?*" Roxie glared at Luka, vindicated.

"Purple fireflies are a big stretch to supernatural-hunting-coyote," Luka said.

I started peeling off the label of my beer bottle as something occurred to me. If Roxie was right about the flora and fauna being affected, and the purple fireflies suggested that she was, then Gabe would probably fall under the category of local fauna.

"Do you think Gabe likes me so much because this place is screwing with his head?" I asked quietly, interrupting Roxie's argument with Luka about what constituted reasonable.

"No, he likes you because you're likable," Roxie said, looking at me like I was an idiot. "Is that what your deal is with him? You're freaking out because a boy actually likes you?"

"I'm not freaking out, but that's not the problem." I lowered my eyes. "It's because he likes me, and I'm leaving, and I don't want to hurt him."

"Not to ruin your touching moment here," Tim interrupted, and his blue eyes landed softly on me. "I am genuinely sorry for the mess you're in, Mara." I waved it off, so he continued. "But if Roxie is right, doesn't that mean that we should all leave immediately, before someone else gets hurt?"

"No." Roxie shook her head so hard, her ponytail bobbed wildly behind her. "We'll just take precautions, like Gideon said."

"So you're saying it's dangerous, but it's not?" Luka asked.

"No, I'm saying it *is* dangerous, but it's not too dangerous that I can afford to leave," Roxie elaborated. "I don't know if or when Blossom is coming back, and with Seth out of commission, there's a chance that Carrie might not want to travel for a while. Which means all the expenses fall back on me. I need the money."

We sat in silence for a moment, letting the weight of Roxie's words sink in. We were all basically in the same boat, Luka and Hutch more so because Seth was their roommate. But we'd each made choices in our life that led us to a place where we couldn't leave a dangerous situation because we couldn't afford to.

"So . . ." Hutch said. "Do you guys think that it might be a bear doing the attacks and not a coyote? Because that would explain my bear dream, right?"

"Sometimes a dream is just a dream, Hutch," Luka told him, and picked his cards back up.

THURSDAY, MARCH 19, 1987

36. hunted

In the blackness, I knew she would be coming for me.

The air felt cold and electric already, and lurking in the darkness, I sensed her before she appeared. As she floated toward me, I didn't cower or cringe. I wouldn't back down from her anymore.

This time, she said nothing as she approached, and she drew closer to me than she ever had before. Her skin hung against her skull like gray plaster, flaking and falling off. I realized that her eyes weren't black—they were missing. Where her eyes should've been were two empty sockets somehow staring back at me.

Her lips had pulled back, revealing yellowed and missing teeth. She was nothing more than a smiling skeleton before me, draped in old fabric with tufts of thinning, white hair floating above her.

She reeked of decay—of spoiled fruit and must and something sulfurous that reminded me of Leonid's apartment.

"What do you want?" I asked, since I didn't want to stare

into the abyss of her eyes any longer than I needed to. I wanted to get this dream over with.

Then she opened her mouth and began to shriek, her song of sounds and syllables sounding like nothing but nonsense to me.

"Id-hab-bee-in-who-nah!" she screamed frantically in my face, repeating the same words over and over again.

I wanted to tell her I didn't understand, but she began to howl. Her voice took on a manic, agonized quality, growing louder and more high pitched. I covered my ears with my hands, trying to block it out, but it was coming from inside my head and reverberating all the way through me.

I was so focused on trying to block out her voice that I didn't notice that she'd moved even closer to me. Not until she reached out for me, and then it was too late. Her long fingers tore through my chest and wrapped around my heart, freezing it completely.

Unable to move or breathe, I could only gape at her. With her face mere inches from mine, she softly said, "Mara, id-hab-bee-in-who-nah."

And then I sat up in my bed, gasping for the breath that my lungs had been deprived of. My whole body felt cold, like I'd been dumped into a bath of ice water, and I shivered.

In the twin bed across from me, Mom was sleeping soundly. Since Caudry was taxing to her, I didn't want to disturb her, not now, but the second she woke up, I would tell her about this dream. I'd been putting it off, and it was only getting worse.

I pulled the covers up around me, wearing them like a shawl, and I walked out into the kitchen. After that nightmare, sleep would no longer be an option for me.

I grabbed the old quilt off the couch and wrapped it around me over my other blankets. I needed as much warmth as I could get, but I didn't think anything could drive this cold away. It felt embedded deep inside me, in my bones and coursing through my veins.

Based on the bluish glow of the sky outside, I guessed it was just before dawn. I went about making myself a cup of tea, hoping to help thaw my insides. As I filled up my gramma's antique teapot, I looked out the window above the sink and noticed the door to Luka and Hutch's trailer opening.

Roxie came out first, pulling a hooded sweatshirt around her to keep the night's chill at bay, and Hutch followed a few steps behind her. His dark hair stuck up at odd angles from sleep, and he shivered in his muscle shirt.

Concerned that something might be wrong, I abandoned my teapot in the sink and opened my front door. Roxie paused when she saw me and offered a small wave.

"Is everything okay?" I asked, leaning on the rusted doorframe of the Winnebago.

"I was getting a crick in my neck from sleeping on the couch." Roxie stuck her thumb back toward Hutch and Luka's trailer. "I wanted to get back to my own bed to get some shuteye before the day started, and Hutch insisted on walking me back."

"The rules are that you're not supposed to be out after dark," Hutch replied, suppressing a yawn. "I'm just making sure that you're safe."

"But then who will protect you when you're back on your own?" Roxie asked. "This just becomes a never-ending cycle."

Hutch pointed at me. "Mara will keep an eye on me."

"I'm like a neighborhood watch here," I replied dryly.

"See?" Hutch asked, but Roxie just shook her head and started walking.

Since I'd agreed to watch Hutch for safety, I kept my post at the open door and watched as they walked across the campsite. Besides, my stomach had started to sour, twisting and turning inside me, and I didn't feel like I could just go back inside and sit down.

Hutch stumbled once, tripping on a divot in the grass, but Roxie caught his arm and steadied him. When they reached Roxie's Airstream, she stopped just outside the front door and turned back to talk to him. I could hear their voices, but they were too far away for me to understand what they were saying.

Behind Roxie, her motorhome rocked so subtly I wasn't sure that anything had happened at first. Then it happened again, jerking more forcefully, and the trailer creaked audibly.

Hutch grabbed Roxie's arm and they both stepped back from the motorhome. Roxie glanced around, probably checking to see if any of the other trailers were moving, but they weren't. Something was happening *inside* her trailer.

Then I saw a rustle in the window above her bedroom. A curtain moved, blowing out through broken glass.

"Roxie, Hutch!" I shouted. "Get away from there!"

They both turned to run away, but it was too late.

A dark blur of teeth dove out the broken window. It landed right on Hutch, knocking him to the ground and choking the scream that had started escaping from his lips. There was the awful sickening sound of ripping flesh and gnashing teeth.

Roxie faced the creature, holding her palms out toward it,

and two fireballs burst out from her hands. One was small and orange—a pitiful shell of what Roxie was usually capable of with her pyro—but the other was a large, blue ball that flew right at the animal.

That was enough to frighten the thing, and it disappeared into the protection of the swamp behind the campsite.

37. justice

The air around Roxie's trailer still smelled of sulfur and blood.

Inside, it was a mess. Broken glass, shredded cushions, even some of the pictures on the wall had been torn up. Roxie was still at the hospital with Hutch, so my plan had been to clean up the trailer before she came back.

"This is . . . *bad*," Luka said, echoing my thoughts.

He stood behind me with a garbage bag, but this was far more than just picking up trash. Cupboard doors had been ripped off their hinges. Costumes had been shredded, so glitter and sequins covered everything.

"She's not gonna be able to sleep in here for a while," I said.

"She can stay with me and . . ." Luka trailed off, choking back Hutch's name. "He'll be okay, right?"

My thoughts flashed to this morning, to Hutch lying facedown in the grass. His back had been covered in blood, and his left shoulder appeared to be missing a chunk of flesh and muscle. I'd wrapped him in the old quilt, trying to hold his body together.

Roxie and I tried to help Hutch to his feet, and he'd only groaned at first. He made a few attempts at words, but they sounded like nonsense. We'd half-walked him, half-carried him to Roxie's truck and loaded him in.

"Do you think that was the bear from my dreams?" Hutch asked before Roxie sped off, taking him to the hospital.

"Yeah," I told Luka now. "I think he'll be okay."

"What the hell kind of animal does this?" Luka asked, gesturing to the mess around us. "What was it even after? There's hardly any food in here."

Our conversation was interrupted by the loud wailing of sirens. I peered out the broken window above Roxie's bed. It was just after eight in the morning, and the sun was already blazing down on us, and the air was thick with humidity and mosquitoes.

Everyone in the camp was already awake, thanks to the attack on Hutch just before dawn. Gideon had come out, shotgun in hand, and while Roxie and I had gotten Hutch up and out of here, Gideon had been patrolling the area for whatever had attacked Hutch.

He'd come back an hour later with nothing to show for his search and told everyone to go about their business. There had been some grumblings that something else should be done, but with Hutch at the hospital and the animal/creature/thing gone, there wasn't much that *could* be done.

So I wasn't entirely surprised when the police car pulled into the middle of the campsite with its lights flashing and sirens blasting. Gideon came out of his trailer to greet the car, but it was still a couple more minutes before Deputy Bob finally turned off the sirens and stepped outside.

Luka and I went out to get a better vantage point on what was happening, as had everyone else. My mom sat next to Betty Bates at a picnic table, helping shuck corn we'd be eating for lunch, and Jackie Phoenix cradled her young daughter against her.

"I'm here to shut y'all down," Deputy Bob announced loudly and proudly. His small, shifty eyes were hidden by dark aviator sunglasses, and he smirked as he surveyed the campsite.

A few people gasped and murmured, and my mom actually shouted, "You can't do that!" Gideon held his hand up, silencing everyone, and kept his cool gaze on Deputy Bob.

"On what grounds?" Gideon asked.

"The hospital reported another animal attack," Deputy Bob explained. "It seems this area is unsafe for humans, so we can't have you camping out here or having innocent townsfolk coming out and getting mauled by some kind of wildebeest."

My mom snorted and returned her attention to shucking the corn. "A wildebeest is a kind of antelope," she said dryly, loud enough that Deputy Bob could hear her clearly. "I sincerely doubt that whatever is going on here has anything to do with an *antelope.*"

The deputy pushed his sunglasses down so he could glare at my mom over them, but she didn't pay him any mind.

Gideon stood before the deputy, not saying much and picking absently at his hands, big and leathery from years of hard labor. His white tank top was stained with oil and dirt and red paint, and the thin suspenders he wore accentuated his broad shoulders. Black tattoos trailed down his thick biceps, and he towered over Deputy Bob.

"What are *you* doing to protect my people?" Gideon asked quietly, still staring at the ground.

Deputy Bob pulled his eyes from my mom to look at Gideon. "What?"

"*You* have a problem." Gideon lifted his head to meet Deputy Bob's gaze, and his voice was low and rough, like gravel crunching beneath tires. "Whatever has been hurting my people is your problem, not mine. All the blood that's been spilled is on your hands."

Gideon stepped closer to Deputy Bob. "So you need to take care of your problem, or you need to pay us what we're owed."

The deputy swallowed, and his eyes darted around at the semicircle of carnival workers glaring at him. He pushed his sunglasses up and opened his pouty lips, but no words came out. For the first time, he seemed to realize the gravity of the situation.

"Wait, now!" a Southern accent floated from behind the campsite, and I looked over to see Della Jane struggling to hurry toward us with a manila folder in her hand. "Dang it, Bob, I told you to wait for me."

"You and the mayor do not give me my orders," Deputy Bob snapped at her.

"Oh, don't get yourself in a tizzy," she told him.

Della Jane stopped, leaning a hand up against the Phoenixes' trailer, and pulled off her baby-blue pumps that were giving her so much trouble. Without the added heel, I realized that she was actually about an inch shorter than me.

As she walked through the campsite toward him, she stopped and smiled and said hello to everyone she passed. When she saw me, she gave me a small wave and beamed at me like we were old friends.

"What are you even doing out here, Della Jane?" Deputy Bob folded his arms over his chest. "This doesn't concern you."

"You know damn well it does, Bob," Della Jane barked, then she offered an apologetic smile to Jackie and Alyssa. "Pardon my French."

She stood beside Gideon, who appeared to be some kind of giant next to her, and glared up at the deputy. "I have a contract with these people. I agreed to pay them a sum of money for ten days' worth of work, and you wanna go kicking them out after less than a week."

"Della Jane—" the deputy began, but she cut him off.

"We've got New Orleans right to the southwest of us, and we've that big equinox festival going on one parish over," Della Jane went on. "The mayor wants us to have a place on the map, with attractions and tourists to make us a real destination spot. Shutting down the events we do have isn't going to make the mayor too happy."

"It's unsafe," Deputy Bob said, but his words lacked the conviction they had when he began.

"If it's unsafe, then make it safe," Della Jane retorted. "That's *your* job."

The deputy exhaled through his nose. "I didn't make the call, and I'm not talking about this with you here anymore. If you got a problem with this, take it up with the sheriff." Then, speaking louder as he looked at the rest of us, he added, "I suggest the rest of you get out of here before sunset if you don't want to end up under arrest."

Deputy Bob went around and got back in his car, and Della Jane cursed at him. She exhaled deeply, blowing her blond curls out of her eyes.

"I am so sorry about this mess," Della Jane said, and turned back around to face us. "It wasn't supposed to be like this, I swear."

"Well, it is," Gideon replied simply.

"I know, I know, and I'll take care of it all," Della Jane persisted. "I'll get animal control to do their jobs and take care of whatever's been harassing you out here, and I'll get the cops to lay off you."

Gideon scratched the side of his head and seemed to consider it for a moment. "Perhaps we should just cut our losses. We can accept half the agreed-upon payment, and we'll head out."

"The contract's very specific, and I don't think the mayor would just let you out of it." She frowned. "Unfortunately, it's all or nothing.

"But we can fix this," Della Jane went on excitedly. "If you come down to the sheriff's office around"—she paused, checking her gold Rolex—"eleven, we can talk to them and get this all cleared up. How does that sound?"

"Doesn't seem that I have much of a choice," Gideon muttered. "I'll be there."

Della Jane shook his hand, promising that this would all be taken care of soon, and it'd all be worth it. She waved as she left, like a beauty contestant in a parade float.

"You heard all of that, so there's no reason to recap," Gideon said, speaking to anyone who might be listening. "Open up today, like normal, and I'll try to have this all taken care of by tonight."

"I'm not opening up," Jackie said, shaking her head. "It's not safe for a child here. I'm not staying."

Gideon nodded once. "If you still want to be a part of this carnival, we'll see you in Houston." He paused. "Anyone else that wants to join her, go ahead. I won't have your blood on my hands. But I'm staying, so I can keep a roof over our heads."

38. rotten

I t's like a ghost town," Roxie said, staring out at the half-empty campsite. Luka stood a few feet in front of us, waving wildly at his boyfriend, who was inside the retreating trailer along with the rest of the Phoenixes.

Almost half the carnival had pulled up stakes and gotten out of town, including Betty Bates and her husband, Damon. That didn't count Carrie, Seth, Zeke, and the tigers, who had already gone to Houston.

Most of the midway workers stayed, since Doug Bennett refused to pay anyone anything if they left, but Gideon offered partial compensation to all who felt too threatened to stay.

Gideon had left for the meeting at the sheriff's office a half hour before, around the same time Roxie returned with Hutch. The doctors had stitched him up and assured him that he'd be no worse for wear, and Hutch was now doped up on pain meds and sleeping soundly in his motorhome.

"I must be crazy for staying," Roxie said with an exasperated sigh.

"What else are we gonna do?" Luka asked, walking back over to us since the Phoenixes' trailer was out of sight. "Your trailer is trashed, and I'm the only one working now to support three people."

"We need to find this thing and stop it." I'd been sitting on the steps in front of Roxie's Airstream, but I stood up now. "We need to get it before it gets us."

"That is a great idea, but how exactly are we gonna do that?" Roxie asked. "We don't even know *what* it is."

"When we visited Leonid Murphy, he seemed to have a few ideas about what was happening in Caudry," I said.

"Yeah, but he also seemed kinda crazy and a little strung out," Luka reminded me with a grimace. "Not to mention that his apartment reeked really bad."

"The creature is getting bolder. It broke through the window right above Roxie's bed." I pointed to the shattered glass, and Roxie shivered involuntarily. "We have to stop it before somebody gets killed."

Roxie chewed her lip for a moment, then nodded. "We can take my truck."

"I'll stay back with Hutch," Luka said. "There's no way I want to deal with that stench again."

I hurried to tell my mom where I was going so she wouldn't panic, but she didn't really have much to say. She was otherwise preoccupied with trying to get the carnival going when half the acts had skipped out.

As we drove through town in Roxie's beat-up Chevy, she

sang along to Madonna. I leaned my elbow out the window, relishing the way the wind helped cool the sweat that clung to my skin. Despite the heat, I felt a permanent chill inside me, like my heart had frozen solid.

"What are we gonna do if Leonid doesn't know anything?" Roxie asked once the song ended.

"I don't know." I shook my head.

We'd reached the Blue Moon Bar & Grill, and, at my request, Roxie parked her truck on the far side of the parking lot, where Gabe's dad would be less likely to notice me. She turned off the ignition, but we both sat inside for a minute.

"What if we're blowing this all out of proportion?" Roxie asked, staring straight ahead at the dashboard. "When I was in the ER with Hutch, he kept asking about bears, and the doctors fixing him said there were some bad animal attacks about a dozen years ago or so. He said that Caudry attracts some crazy wildlife."

"If this is all just a bear or a coyote or a big, furry alligator," I said, causing Roxie to wrinkle her nose at the mention of the gator, "then we just let animal control and the police take care of it. Della Jane sounds like she's gonna light a fire under them, and they should have captured or shot it real soon."

"But why does this Della Jane person even care so much?" Roxie turned to face me. "We're just a dinky rundown little carnival. It's not like we're the Beatles or something."

"The carnival has been packed every night." I shrugged. "It's sorely lacking in entertainment around here. She's trying to build this town back up, and she's gotta start somewhere, and apparently that's with us."

"I guess," Roxie said, but she didn't sound convinced.

Not that I blamed her. I didn't completely understand Della Jane's passion to protect us either. I'd neglected to tell anyone that she was Gabe's mom, mostly because I didn't want to talk about Gabe.

I had finally decided that it wouldn't make any sense for me to see Gabe again. That was painful enough to think about, and I knew it would only hurt worse to say it aloud. Between the animal stalking us and the seriousness of Gabe's feelings for me, it all felt like a disaster waiting to happen.

But disaster or no, it didn't change the fact that I actually felt something for Gabe, and my chest ached at the realization that I'd never see him again.

"Come on," I said, opening the truck door.

As we ascended the rickety stairs along the restaurant, I breathed in deeply, preparing to get my last good breath before the stench of Leonid's apartment overwhelmed me. But as we kept climbing, I realized that I didn't really smell anything. No sulfur or acetone.

Roxie was ahead of me and reached the landing before I did. She wrinkled her nose. "Luka was right. It *does* stink here."

I inhaled through my nose, and I smelled what she was talking about—tangy, pungent, sickly sweet, and utterly wretched—and while it did make me want to gag, it didn't smell anything like it had before, and it was much fainter.

I shook my head. "No, this isn't it."

"Well, whatever. Let's get this over with." She knocked on Leonid's door while I tried to place the scent. I was certain I'd smelled it before.

When Leonid didn't answer, Roxie knocked loudly again, pounding on the thin wooden door so hard the frame began to splinter.

"Roxie, take it easy." I put my hand on her arm before she broke the door down. "He's probably not home."

"Or maybe he is home, and he's hiding because he knows he's the reason we came to this godforsaken hellhole!" Roxie shouted at the closed door.

"Maybe," I said as calmly as I could. "Or maybe we should just come back later."

"*No!*" Her blue eyes were wild, and her jaw was set. "I can't take this damn town anymore! I'm not leaving until I get some answers."

I was about to ask what she planned to do, but she slammed into the door with her shoulder. It didn't give yet, but the frame splintered and cracked. It wouldn't take much more for her to break it down.

It was then that the smell finally hit me. Last summer, when we were packing up to leave, I'd discovered a cooler sitting behind the campsite. I opened it up to discover ten pounds of rotting meat that had been for the tigers. Zeke had forgotten about it, and it had been sitting in the sun for a week.

That was the smell coming from Leonid's apartment— rotting flesh.

"Roxie, I don't think you should—" I started, but it was too late. The door gave way, and the noxious air billowed out.

"What the heck, Leonid?" Roxie asked, and began gagging.

Since she was struggling to suppress her gag reflex, I went into the apartment first. I'd pulled my T-shirt up over my nose and tried to breathe in only through my mouth, but I didn't have to go in very far to see the problem.

As I walked in, I noticed that all the stacks of newspapers and magazines that clogged the pathways had been written on. A single word in bright red marker, over and over again in Leonid's chicken scratch.

SORRY

Beyond the stacks of papers in his living room, I discovered him.

Hanging from his ceiling like a forgotten fly strip, was Leonid. The noose had been made from braided electrical cord, and his head hung only a few inches from the ceiling to keep his long legs from touching the floor. His head lolled to the side with his swollen tongue hanging out of his mouth, and his skin had turned an angry purplish-red.

Then, as if she were standing beside me whispering in my ear, I heard Blossom's voice saying, *"They never, never wake again, who sleep upon your bed."*

39. the hanged man

My skin was damp from my shower, but I still felt unclean.

Roxie and I had fled Leonid's house, with her speeding like a maniac all the way back. We hadn't even considered calling the police, because neither of us wanted to get mixed up with the Caudry authorities any more than we absolutely needed to.

The second Roxie got out of the truck, she threw up, and I went to my motorhome to shower. I didn't want the scent of Leonid's decaying flesh stuck to me for a moment longer.

"Mara, *qamari*." My mom brushed my wet hair back from my face. "What's happened?"

I was sitting at the dinette, nursing the cup of hot tea Mom had put in front of me, and she hovered beside me. Her eyebrows were pinched with worry, and darkness clouded her smoky gray eyes. Her long black hair was pulled up in a loose bun, and since she'd been doing manual labor today, she'd exchanged her jewelry for old denim overalls.

The air conditioner rumbled in the window behind me, barely held in place by duct tape and a bungee cord. Mom turned it on to keep out the oppressive heat that enveloped Caudry, but it only made the persistent chill inside me take hold even deeper.

"Leonid Murphy is dead," I told her finally.

She gasped. "What? How?"

"He hung himself in his apartment," I said, and unbidden, the image of his body dangling in his living room filled my mind. His pale skin covered in flies that crawled over his protruding bones.

"You and Roxanne found him?" Mom asked, slowly lowering herself onto the bench across from me.

"He'd written 'sorry' everywhere." I shook my head, trying to chase away the memories. "Something really bad is going on here. I think we need to get out of here."

"I know, I know." She lowered her eyes. "I've been thinking that no matter what Gideon accomplishes today, you should leave. You could convince Luka and Hutch to go, and ride with them."

I scoffed. "Mom, I'm not leaving without you."

"Gideon can't leave, Mara," she told me wearily. "With Roxanne's motorhome messed up, and Seth out of work, and the tigers injured, we're in even worse shape than when we got here, and we were in very bad shape then."

"But it's not just Leonid or even the attacks." I moved my cup of tea to the side and leaned forward on the table. "I've been having these dreams."

Mom instantly went on high alert—her shoulders rigid,

her lips pursed together, and her eyes narrowed. "What kind of dreams?"

"It's all dark, and this old woman comes at me. I don't recognize her, but she looks like she's decaying," I explained. "She screams at me, and I can't understand what she's saying. Then I get this icy cold feeling in my chest."

"That's the dream?" Mom asked, still sitting severely, and I nodded. "What does it sound like she's saying?"

"Um . . ." I concentrated, trying to remember the exact string of syllables she screamed at me. "It's like . . . *id-hab-bee-in-who-nah*, I think."

"*Id-hab-bee-in-who-nah?*" Mom repeated, then her entire face fell. She let out a pained gasp and closed her eyes. "Oh hell."

"What? What is it?" I asked.

"I tried so hard to keep this from you." She shook her head, her eyes still closed tightly. "I didn't want this life for you. I never wanted you to have this *gift*." She laughed darkly, the way she did anytime people referred to her extra senses as a gift.

"What are you talking about?" I asked, and my voice was gaining a nervous tremor. "What's going on?"

The large skull key she wore around her neck had come free from her shirt, and it lay on her chest, rising and falling with each of her breaths. The rubies of its eyes seemed to fix on me, and they sparkled as it moved.

Mom opened her eyes and smiled sadly at me. "Your great-grandma Elissar was born in Egypt and spent her entire childhood there, so even after she moved to America and had your grandma Basima, she spoke her native tongue around the house.

"It was the first language your grandma Basima ever learned, and she still spoke it from time to time when I was growing up," Mom went on. "I never became fluent, but I carried her terms of endearment with me, like when I call you *qamari*, my moon."

Tears brimmed in her eyes, but she wiped them away. "In the end, when your grandma Basima no longer had her mind intact, she devolved into her childhood, and began speaking almost entirely in Arabic."

Mom got up and went back into the bedroom. I heard drawers opening and closing, and a few moments later my mom returned with an old picture in her hand. She sat back down in front of me, staring at the picture.

"I know you don't really remember your grandmother," Mom said. "She died when you were only a toddler, and because her mind had gone, she wasn't much fun to be around before that. But she did love you. She would've loved to have known you."

She set the picture down on the table and pushed it toward me. I recognized my mom right away, much younger but unmistakably her, and she was holding me on her lap. I was only about a year or two old with wild black hair. And the little old woman sitting beside my mom, her gray hair pulled back in a smooth bun.

"I don't remember much of what your grandma Basima used to say to me when I was a child, but one phrase does stand out, because of how often she yelled it at me when I got in her way or when she was having a particularly rough day with the spirits," Mom explained as I looked at the picture.

"*Idhhabee min honaa,*" Mom spoke clearly and slowly, letting her words sink in. "It means 'get out of here.'"

I tapped the picture in front of me, of the smiling old woman with my mother's eyes and wrinkled skin. "This is her? You think this is the woman from my dreams?"

"You tell me," Mom replied simply.

I stared down at it, trying to see the reanimated corpse from my nightmares in my grandma in the picture. Then I began to see bits of it—the cheekbones, the long fingers, even something in her smile.

"Why would she do that?" I asked, still looking down at the photograph. "Why would she come to me in such a horrific way and screaming at me in a language that I didn't understand?"

"She was trying to scare you," Mom explained. "She wanted to protect you, and she probably thought the best way to do it was to terrify you so much you'd run away and never look back."

Then Mom let out a heavy sigh. "She most likely tried to come to me first, but everything has been so . . . messy here. I can't get my thoughts straight, and the spirits come and go as they please."

I looked up at my mom. "But that means Grandma Basima knows things are bad here. If she went through all the trouble of contacting me, of opening my mind when it's always been closed, then that means things are *bad*."

"I know." Mom reached across the table and took my hand in hers. The black tattoos of vines wove up her arm, and they seemed to dance on her light brown skin as her arm flexed and she squeezed my hand tightly. "You should leave, *qamari*."

"We *all* have to leave," I insisted. "I know we need the money, but it's not worth getting hurt over, or maybe even dying for."

"You're not listening, Mara." She shook her head. "I *can't* leave. There isn't enough money for us all to get to Houston. Some of us have to stay so we can get paid, so we can pay for the gas to drive away."

The pain in her eyes and the grip of her hand told me she was telling the truth, that she would pack us up in an instant if she could.

Everything we had in the world was in this Winnebago, and it had been our home on wheels for the past five years. It may not have been much, but it was *everything* we had. We couldn't just leave it behind. Especially if we left before we got paid. We'd never be able to afford to replace it.

And everyone was in that same boat. All my friends and family—my mom, Gideon, Roxie, Luka, Hutch—they were all trapped in Caudry until they had enough cash to fuel up and escape.

"If you stay, I stay," I told my mom finally, and squeezed her hand back.

Mom opened her mouth, probably to offer up futile protests, but a knock rattled the metal screen door. I couldn't see who it was from where I was sitting, and Mom shouted for them to come in, rubbing her temple as she did.

Slowly, almost timidly, the door opened, and when I saw Gabe stepping inside my motorhome, I understood the anxiety on her face.

"I hope I'm not interrupting anything," he said with a sheepish smile.

40. truce

I told you I'd find you when I was ready," I said.

My mom had left to help Gideon, giving Gabe and me privacy that I wasn't sure I wanted. He stood in front of me with big hopeful eyes, so I stared down at his feet, at his expensive Nikes on the balding avocado carpet, and folded my arms over my chest.

"I know, but I heard that someone was hurt this morning," Gabe said, his voice tight with worry. "I wanted to make sure you were okay."

I softened a bit, allowing my arms to fall to my sides, and looked up at him. The devilish glint in his eyes and on his lips had fallen away, leaving only a beautiful boy with concern crinkling the corners of his eyes and creasing his forehead.

"I'm okay," I said. "Lots of people are leaving, and I'm trying to convince my mom to do the same."

"You're leaving today?"

"Maybe. I don't know." I shrugged. "But we'll be leaving as soon as we can."

He leaned back against the counter beside me, letting his broad shoulders slump forward. With his head bowed, his pompadour of rich chestnut hair wilted down.

"You weren't even going to say good-bye, were you?" he asked softly.

"I . . ." I let out a shaky breath and licked my lips. "I just didn't see the point."

He looked up sharply, his dark eyebrows arched and his lips twisted into a bitter smile. "You didn't see the point? How can you even say that?"

"I'm sorry I didn't tell you from the beginning that I was leaving, because you didn't know what I've known all along," I said. "That this will never mean anything, because I'll be gone before it can matter."

"If that's a lie that you need to tell yourself, then go right ahead, but don't you dare lie to me." He looked at me hard, then, with golden eyes blazing, and I flinched at the anger in his words. *"This* matters!"

He exhaled deeply, breathing out some of his anger. Then he straightened and moved closer to me, so close we were nearly touching.

"It's not the amount of time that makes something real. It's what happens in that time," he said solemnly. "Each moment is weighted against the next, and the moments I've spent with you have been more meaningful than almost all the ones I've had before it."

My heart swelled—I could actually feel it welling up inside me as it filled with all the many complicated and wonderful emotions I had for Gabe.

"I just don't want you to get hurt," I told him honestly.

He smirked. "I'm a grown man. I think I can decide for myself what pain I'm willing to endure."

"But this really doesn't change anything, Gabe." I shook my head. "I *will* be leaving. Maybe tonight, maybe tomorrow, but definitely very soon."

"All the more reason that I should be with you now, while I can," he persisted. "If you have to go, I'll be here to say good-bye. And if you stay, I'm here to help. But, either way, I want to be here, with you."

He reached out, brushing my damp hair back from my face, and he leaned in toward me. Just before his lips touched mine, he stopped.

"I won't kiss you if this isn't what you want," he said, his voice low and husky.

I put my hand over his and whispered, "I want you."

That was all the encouragement he needed, and his mouth was on mine, hot and passionate. His fingers tangled in my hair as he pulled me to him, and I wrapped my arms around him, loving the heat of his body against me.

The moment was shattered by the sound of applause, and we pulled away from each other to see what all the fuss was about.

With the AC on, we hadn't been able to hear anything going on outside of my Winnebago, but the loud clapping and cheerful hollering was loud enough to get in. Through the window over the kitchen sink, I saw what was left of the carnival crowding around Gideon.

Beside him, I could see only the curly blond top of her head, but I knew it had to be Della Jane. She was attempting to hold

Gideon's burly fist high up in the air, but since she was so short, it only went to about his head.

"What is my mom doing here?" Gabe asked, peering through the window beside me.

"I think she just made sure that the carnival will be open until Sunday," I said, and I'd never felt quite so conflicted about anything before.

Already grinning, Gabe turned to look at me. "That means you'll be staying until Sunday, right?"

"It looks that way." I tried to return his smile, but I couldn't shake my unease about staying at this particular campsite for another three nights.

"I should probably go thank my mom, then." Gabe took my hand and headed for the door.

In the few interactions I'd had with his mom, she'd been nothing but nice to me. So I couldn't explain the urge I had to dig my feet in and refuse to greet her, or the sour feeling that made my stomach sick.

So I let Gabe lead me out into the thick air and intense sunlight.

"We may have won this battle, but that doesn't mean that the war is over," Gideon was saying as we approached the semicircle of people around him and we were close enough that we could actually see Della Jane standing beside him. "There is still an animal on the loose, and we need to stay safe."

"The police have promised us that they'll have their best men on it," Della Jane interjected brightly. "So that should be taken care of very soon. Maybe even tonight."

As she looked out at the crowd, flashing her dazzling smile, her gaze finally landed on Gabe. And there it was again, the expression I'd caught when I saw her at Gabe's house. A split-second where her blue eyes went wide and horrified, and her smile faltered.

Then, as quickly as the look had appeared, it was gone, and Della Jane was all smiles again.

"As you all know, we are shorthanded," Gideon went on. "We need everyone to do what we can. If anyone wants to volunteer to participate in certain acts, let me know. I'll be in the big tent tonight, but I'll need an assistant since Roxie will be dancing."

I stepped up to run the museum, since Hutch was laid up, and Gideon began divvying up the workload to volunteers and allotting the tasks that nobody wanted. As things were being assigned, the crowd began to disperse so people could go to work.

The midway opened at eleven, but most of the sideshow acts didn't start until the afternoon, with shows in the big tents. The only thing that should've been open already was the museum, but it didn't pull in that much money so a couple hours closed up wouldn't bankrupt us.

Della Jane made her way toward us, walking barefoot on the grass with her baby blue pumps in her hand. She greeted us with the warmest of smiles, but her eyes seemed to linger too long on our entwined hands.

"If I'd known you were coming out here today, honey, we could've rode together," Della Jane joked.

As casually as I could muster, I slipped my hand from Gabe's. I ran it through my hair, not because it was getting in my face, but because I was looking for an excuse to let go of Gabe's hand. The look his mom gave me made me feel uncomfortable about the whole thing.

"I just wanted to see how Mara was holding up." He motioned to me, and his mom's eyes followed his hand, so her gaze landed on me.

"You must be happy about the big triumph today," Della Jane said. "I know I am just *thrilled* that you'll be around a few more days."

"Yeah, thank you for all your help." I forced a smile and ignored how tight her voice sounded when she said "thrilled."

"Did you drive your Mustang?" Della Jane asked, turning her attention back to her son. "If you walked, I could give you a ride back to town."

"Yeah, I drove." He motioned toward the bright red sports car parked at the edge of the campsite, standing out like a shiny sore thumb. Then he glanced around at the folks working overtime to set up for tonight. "And I was thinking that I would stay and pitch in. It looks like they need all the help they can get."

Della Jane frowned. "Your father was really hoping that you would help him at the restaurant tonight. Things have been busy, and you really haven't been helping him much this past week."

"If Dad's short-staffed, Selena can step up," Gabe suggested, with a bit of irritation in his voice.

"Selena didn't want to be a part of the business. *You're* the one that said you could handle the responsibility," Della Jane lectured.

Gabe grimaced and shoved his hands in his back pockets as he stared off at some point above her head. "No, I said I might as well have something to do since you keep insisting that I put off NYU for another year," he corrected her.

Della Jane sighed. "Family comes first."

"I'm taking tonight off to help Mara," Gabe replied with a finality that made his mom's shoulders sag. "The restaurant will be fine without me until Sunday."

Della Jane took a deep breath and crossed her arms over her chest, deciding on a whole new tactic to get her son to leave with her. "Gabriel, there is an animal on the loose. I just want you to be safe."

Something passed across Gabe's expression—something I couldn't quite read, but it was dark and shadowy, taking all the light from his eyes.

"If it's safe enough for them, it's safe enough for me," he said, meeting his mom's hard gaze with his own.

Since there didn't seem to be any room for her to argue, Della Jane only nodded. Her smile returned, though it wasn't nearly as cheerful as it had been moments ago. She kissed Gabe on the cheek and made him promise that he'd be safe.

As she walked away, she cast a look back at me over her shoulder, and it sent a chill down my spine. I'd never seen another person look at me that way, but it was a look I recognized immediately. It was the same look I'd seen in the abused tiger Mahilā's eyes whenever she saw someone she didn't trust—terrified, angry, and eerily primal.

41. the star

*S*tep right up to the greatest show on earth!" Gabe called out
to passersby.

From where I stood outside the Terrifying Curiosities &
Oddities of Past & Present museum, I had the perfect vantage
point to watch Gabe outside the big tent, trying to drum up
business for Gideon's magician act.

Gabe had taken one of Gideon's old top hats and placed it
carefully on his coiffed hair, and he'd gotten his hands on Luka's
devil sticks. He tossed the baton between two other sticks,
bouncing them off one another and pinwheeling it about.

After he did an especially impressive trick—tossing the baton in a spiral up through the air before nimbly catching it with
the sticks—the small audience around him began to applaud.
Gabe bowed, then immediately began upselling them on a ticket
to the show where he promised them that the real magic happened.

Roxie wandered over from the tent where she performed and

leaned on the trailer beside me. Most of the time, she'd hang out with me on her breaks between shows. She took a long drag from her cigarette on a break, and when she exhaled, she left a bright red ring of her lipstick on the butt of the cigarette.

Based on the black headband and fingerless lace gloves, I guessed that it was Madonna night. Roxie liked to mix up her dancing act with celebrity theme nights, usually using whatever clothes she had around, but she'd gone so far as to make a silver faux–chain mail costume to go as Aunty Entity from *Beyond Thunderdome*.

I leaned on the podium, turning my attention back to the spectacle that was Gabe instead of trying to attract my own customers. But, really, there was no need to even try. Gabe would've stolen any customers I tried to hook.

"He's like an old pro," Roxie commented.

"Yeah, he told me he did some juggling when he was younger, but I had no idea he'd be this good," I admitted.

"I don't know if I should be telling you this, but I like him," Roxie said, and I looked back over my shoulder at her. "Not, like, *like* him. But he's a good guy. And he's quite the showman."

"Why shouldn't you tell me that?" I asked.

Roxie shrugged a shoulder. "Because you don't wanna get attached."

"And you think your approval will cause me to get too attached?" I teased.

"Hey, a guy isn't worth his salt unless he's got Roxie's Stamp of Approval." She raised her fist and motioned like she was stamping it down on a paper. "Don't you forget it."

"I'll try not to," I replied with a laugh.

"So, that Della Jane chick is his mom?" Roxie asked. It would be impossible to keep that connection under wraps when everyone had seen the way Gabe interacted with her today.

My smile fell away and I turned back to watch Gabe. "Yeah, she's his mom."

"It's great that she's championing our cause or whatever, but . . ." Roxie trailed off. "It doesn't all seem strange to you? Her fervor about keeping us?"

"Everything about Caudry is strange. Why should she be any different?" I asked, but I was really just avoiding the same question I'd been asking myself.

"I would just keep my distance from her, if I were you." Roxie tossed her cigarette down and stomped it out in the gravel. "Anyway, I should get back to work."

I wanted to heed her advice, but I had no idea if that would be possible if I planned to continue seeing Gabe. And at the moment, I did really want to keep seeing him. The whole time I was working, I found it difficult to keep on task because I kept looking over at him.

Sometimes I'd catch him looking back at me. It was always right after I'd looked over, like he knew it somehow, and his eyes would catch mine, and he'd give me a sly smile, like he was privy to a joke that only the two of us shared.

After the last show of the night, Gabe came over and helped me close up the museum. The carnival had been busy, but it had been a quiet night. Uneventful, really, and that was nice after the last few days I'd had.

"Thanks for all your help tonight," I told Gabe as we walked back to the campsite from the carnival.

"No problem." He grinned down at me. "It was fun."

His hand slipped into mine, a simple gesture that felt so strangely normal and natural, like we were just a regular couple. It was a fantasy I let myself believe, falling into a comfortable silence as I imagined what my life would be like if we were just two ordinary teenagers. Date nights of movies and pizza. Promises of the future. Stolen kisses in the backseats of cars.

As Gideon said in the opening of his act, there is always something extraordinary in the ordinary.

With the campsite half deserted and everyone exhausted from doing double-duty, it was exceptionally quiet as we walked up to my trailer. I turned to face Gabe, preparing to say good night, since I had another long day ahead of me tomorrow, but the screen door to the Winnebago swung open behind me.

"Mara?" Mom asked, looking down at me with bleary eyes. Her dark tangles of hair fell free over her shoulders, and she pulled a violet shawl around her, despite the heat. The scent of incense and cloves—an added effect for her readings—hung on her like a cloud. "Good. You're safe and you're sound."

"Are you okay?" I asked as she stumbled down the rusted steps as she came outside. I reached out, grabbing her arm to steady her. "Where are you going?"

"I am fine, fine, fine." Mom waved me off, then she leaned and kissed me brusquely on the temple. "The night has been too long, and I'm staying at Gideon's so I don't take it out on you. I love you."

Rather abruptly, her haze seemed to vanish, and her gray eyes widened and flashed with intensity. She gripped my arms so tightly, I knew her fingers would leave red marks on my flesh. "Stay inside, *qamari*. Promise me you'll stay inside tonight."

"Sure, Mom." I nodded. "I promise."

Then her eyes locked onto Gabe. "You will protect her?" Her eyes narrowed, and Gabe stood unwavering under the force of her gaze. "There is a darkness within you, but there is strength, and there is goodness too. So you will protect her."

"Mom." I tried to keep my voice light and playful. "I don't need any protection."

"I won't let anything bad happen to Mara as long as I'm around," he told my mom firmly, ignoring my embarrassed protests.

"That's all I can ask." Mom seemed to relax then and finally let go of my arms. She touched my face gently and gave me a pained smile before telling me to be good, and then she rushed away, her shawl flowing behind her like a cape.

"I'm sorry about that," I said softly, watching my mother retreat into the sanctuary of Gideon's trailer, where he could soothe her pain and quiet the demons that tormented her. "She's a good mom, and she means well. She just has . . . spells."

That was the easiest way I could think to describe the episodes my mom experienced when the spirits had become too much for her and drained all her energy. And telling Gabe all about how my mom was a necromancer that conversed with the dead would break the illusion of normalcy I was fighting for.

"She loves you a lot," Gabe commented, but his voice sounded detached, and I looked up at his face and I could see that my mom had rattled him. Under the waning moon, his eyes were dark, and he took an uneasy breath.

"She does," I agreed, then decided to change the subject by motioning to the trailer behind me. "I have the place all to myself if you want to come in for a while."

With some effort, Gabe shook his head and cast off his distress, so when he looked down at me, his easy smile returned. "I did promise your mom that I would keep you safe, so as your official bodyguard, it is my duty to stay by your side all night long."

I laughed, but I took his hand again and led him inside my home.

42. the lovers

Have you always lived in this trailer?" Gabe asked.

"No, we've had this Winnebago for five years." I had my back to him as I adjusted the radio until I landed on Tears for Fears singing about being head over heels, and I turned back to face him.

He leaned back against the cracked counter with his arms out beside him, causing his white T-shirt to pull taut against his chest and biceps. He was looking around, appraising my home without any of the judgment or contempt I'd been afraid of.

Instead, there was this odd fascination playing in the burnt honey of his eyes. His hair had wilted from being under the top hat, so a few dark golden strands fell across his forehead, and I couldn't think of a time when I'd ever seen anyone sexier.

"Why do you look so amazed?" I asked, slowly walking over to him as music wafted out through the speakers around us.

He shrugged and offered me a sheepish smile. "I don't know. I'm just taking it all in."

"I know it's rundown, but I didn't think it was that *amazing*," I teased, and for once, I was just joking—not trying to cover up my insecurities.

With Gabe, I was beginning to realize that I didn't need to feel ashamed or embarrassed. Everything he saw about me, everything he learned, he just accepted. He never judged or shamed me. He just held his arms and heart open for me.

"No, no, it's not that," Gabe hurried to explain. "It's just . . . this is where you live. Where you fill your time and keep all your secrets. I just wanna take it all in, I guess."

"You're wondering how I fill my time?" I asked, stopping so I was mere inches from him. "Read books. Listen to music. Play cards. Kiss boys."

"Kiss boys?" Gabe asked with an arched eyebrow.

"Sometimes," I admitted with a sly smile.

"Like now?" He leaned down and kissed me softly, his lips barely brushing against mine. He wrapped an arm around my waist, pulling me closer to him and kissing me in that subdued way that only made me want him more.

I pressed my body against his, and he pulled back. I stared up expectantly at him, at the smile playing on his lips and the devilish glint in his eyes that I was falling for.

"You know what room I've really been dying to see?" he asked huskily. "Your bedroom."

"I have seen yours a few times, so it does only seem fair," I replied with a smile.

I took his hand, leading him back through the beaded curtain to my small room at the back of the Winnebago. For his part, Gabe did attempt to check it out—looking at all the books and scarves and jewelry and posters that covered the space.

But then I grabbed his hand, meaning to pull him to me, but the icy dagger twisted inside my chest, sending a freezing pain shooting through me.

"Mara?" Gabe asked, but before he could say more, I pulled him to me. I wouldn't let the cold stop me—not this time. I wanted to be with him, and I wouldn't let anything get in my way.

I kissed him as deeply as I could, hoping to melt the ice that ached inside my chest, and I pulled him back onto the bed with me.

Then his mouth was on mine, hungry and strong. My arms were around him, pressing into the firm muscles of his back, and I wrapped my legs around him. The ice in my chest still ached painfully, but I ignored it and focused solely on the way I felt as Gabe touched me.

His hands were slipping under my clothes. His fingers were bold and hot as they explored my body, running over the tender flesh of my belly before finding my breasts beneath my bra.

It was apparent that clothes were only getting in our way, and we parted long enough to strip them off. I barely took the time to appraise his body because I was so eager to feel him against me.

Then we were together again, and his mouth trailed down from my lips to my neck. His teeth scraped deliciously against my flesh as he moved down, sending pleasurable shivers through me. With his arms around me, I could feel his muscles as they barely held back from crushing me with their strength.

I wanted him—no, I *needed* him, needed to feel all of him. My body was aching for him.

I pulled away from him, and as I did, he gave me this wonderful helpless puppy look that belied the ferociousness of the hunger in his eyes and, for some reason, that made me like him so much more.

"One second," I promised him, and I leaned over to fumble through my nightstand drawer until I finally found a condom.

Relief washed over his face, and a few quick seconds later, it was on, and then his mouth was on mine. He kissed me for a moment, holding on to the last few seconds that we were separate, and then he slid inside me. A soft moan escaped his lips, and I closed my eyes.

The heat from him seemed to radiate all through me, and the ice that stabbed through my heart finally went away. It didn't just melt—it was as if Gabe set me ablaze from within, and all I could feel and think and be was him.

I dug my fingers into his back, and when he finished, he let out a low, guttural sound, reminding me of a soft growl.

He rolled onto his back, then pulled me into his arms. He kissed the top of my head, and I listened to the steady rhythm of his heart in his chest.

"I'm falling in love with you, Mara," he said softly.

"Me too," I whispered. In the delirium of the afterglow, I let myself really feel it—how much I cared for Gabe and how I wanted to spend all of forever with him if I could.

And then my mom's voice was echoing in my mind. *"There is a darkness within you, but there is strength, and there is goodness too,*" she'd told Gabe with the strange assertion as she'd eyed him up.

Lying in his arms against the firm contours of his body, I felt his undeniable strength. And I thought I could feel the goodness in him—in the gentleness of his touch as he stroked my hair and murmured how much he cared for me.

But soon the iciness in my chest began to take hold again, sending a painful shiver through me. I couldn't help but wonder about the darkness my mom had seen within him.

I'd known about it too, from the first moment I saw him. Deep down inside, I'd felt like I should be afraid of him, and despite all that, I'd never felt safer anywhere else than in his arms right now.

This couldn't last forever, no matter how desperately I wanted it to, so I just closed my eyes and tried to savor the feel of his arms around me and the sound of his heart beating.

But it only lasted a few moments before I heard Luka, screaming for dear life.

43. mend

Mara, what are you doing?" Gabe demanded, his words pinched with fear.

I'd leapt out of bed and grabbed my dress from where it lay rumpled on the floor, and now I struggled to pull it on over my head.

"Something happened to Luka," I told Gabe, and probably sensing that he wouldn't be able to stop me, he grabbed his jeans and hurried to get them on. "I have to help."

"Mara—" Gabe began, but I was already rushing toward the door. "Wait!"

I didn't want him coming with me—I didn't want him getting hurt or tangled up with whatever was happening around here. So instead of running out into the night, and possibly getting us both killed in a valiant but stupid attempt to protect Luka, I ran to the front of the Winnebago and looked out the windshield.

Roxie and Hutch were huddled in the doorway of Hutch and

Luka's trailer, and they appeared to have turned on every light, causing the warm yellow light to glow in the humidity around them.

They both stared off to their right, toward the sound of Luka's screams, so I followed their gaze. For a long second, I saw nothing, and then the outline of two figures appeared in the darkness, coming out from the swamp behind the campsite—one taller and burly, the other smaller and limping. Luka and Gideon.

"What the hell happened to him?" Gabe asked, his voice in my ear as he leaned over to peer out the window.

I glanced back at him, taken off guard by his presence and the fact that he could see anything. It was too dark where they were for me to see much of anything, other than their general shapes.

"I don't know," I replied, and opened the door. Since Gideon was here, and Luka appeared to be walking some, I decided it was safe enough for me to venture outside.

As they walked into the campsite, the light from the street-light finally hit them. Gideon had his shotgun over one shoulder and an arm around Luka, helping to keep him on his feet, and Luka was drenched in blood.

"Oh my god!" Roxie ran over and slipped her arm around his waist. "Are you okay?"

Roxie and Gideon led him over to the picnic table parked right up against his motorhome. He winced as they helped ease him down onto the bench. Roxie sat down beside him, while Gideon, Gabe, and I stood in a semicircle in front of Luka.

Up close, his injuries were still barely visible underneath his tattered, blood-soaked clothing, but I caught a glimpse of a few very nasty gashes. Luka held his arm across his stomach, and I suspected that he was helping to keep the organs inside until his body self-healed all the way.

"Do you need anything?" I asked.

"Just some towels to clean up," Luka said, brushing off injuries that looked like they would've been fatal on anyone else. "I think I'll be okay."

"I'll get some," Hutch piped up, eager to be doing something besides wringing his hands in the doorway of his own trailer. He was still recuperating from his own injuries, which was probably why he hadn't run out to lend a hand.

"Do you want me to call an ambulance or something?" Gabe asked in a faraway voice, and Luka looked up at him with a start.

"No, I'll be fine," Luka replied, and did his best to mask his pain. Like most everyone else in the camp, Luka tried to keep his extrasensory healing ability a secret from outsiders. It was easier than attempting to explain something that could not be explained.

"It's worse than it looks," Luka added with a weak smile, since Gabe didn't look convinced.

"What happened?" I asked, trying to detract from the fact that Luka looked like he belonged in a morgue or an ER at the very least.

But from where I was standing, I could already see the laceration across his chest starting to heal—the edges of the wound slowly moved toward each other, as if magnetized, and within moments the flesh would all be fused together as if it had never been torn apart.

I moved, trying to block Gabe's view in case he was looking, but his eyes were darting around everywhere, probably search-ing the campsite for signs of the creature that had attacked Luka.

"What the hell were you doing out here?" Gideon asked, like the world-weary parent he'd slowly become. "I told you all to stay in at night."

"Hutch was in the bathroom, and I really had to take a piss," Luka explained. "I only went out behind our trailer, and then that *thing*—attacked me."

Hutch returned just in time to hand Luka a stack of old tow-els and ask, "Was it a bear?"

"For the hundredth time, Hutch, there are no bears around here," Roxie reminded him, sounding more matter-of-fact than exasperated.

Luka shook his head as he pressed towels against his more egregious injuries. "I don't know what it was. I didn't really get a look at it. It was dark and it happened so fast. It grabbed me and dragged me out into the woods, and it was gonna kill me, until Gideon showed up with his shotgun and chased it off."

"What about you?" Roxie asked, looking up at Gideon with her wide blue eyes. "Do you still think it was a coyote?"

"No, it wasn't any animal that I've ever seen," Gideon said with a sigh.

"What about a werewolf?" Hutch suggested. "Or maybe a were-bear?"

Gideon shot an uneasy glance toward Gabe, who was still an outsider. He hadn't grown up in a world like we had, and to an outsider, we'd seem insane for entertaining the idea of a were-beast.

"Everyone should get inside," Gideon commanded, his

British accent coming out gruff. "Just because the animal is gone doesn't mean it won't come back."

"Luka, why don't we get you inside so you can rest and get cleaned up?" Roxie suggested.

I offered to help Luka inside, but Roxie had it under control. Luka had already begun healing enough that he didn't seem to be in as much pain, and it appeared easier for him to move. Of course, he had still lost a lot of blood, so he was weak and leaned on Roxie as she helped him up into his trailer.

"I should, um, I should actually get home," Gabe said, once Roxie and Hutch had gotten Luka inside his trailer. "My mom will be worried."

"Are you okay?" I reached out, touching his hand gently. He didn't pull away, but he didn't take my hand in his, either.

"Yeah, yeah . . ." Gabe said, but he wouldn't look at me. He just kept staring off into the darkness around us. "Blood just doesn't sit well with me."

"I'll walk you to your car."

He shook his head. "No, no, it's just over there." He pointed back to where his Mustang was parked at the edge of the campsite, right at the end of the streetlamp's reach. "I'll be fine. You can watch me from here. Stay here and stay safe."

I looked up at him uncertainly. "Okay?"

"Stay safe," he repeated, then he kissed me on the forehead.

He turned away without looking at me. I stayed outside, watching him until he got into his car and sped off.

Gideon was standing just outside his trailer, wiping the blood from his hands. Once Gabe was out of sight, Gideon cleared his throat loudly, which was his indirect way of summoning me.

"Are you okay?" I asked as I approached him.

"I'll be fine." He lifted his head, staring off at the empty spot where Gabe's car had been. "I didn't want to say anything while your . . . *friend* was here, but Hutch was wrong."

"Hutch is wrong a lot."

Gideon managed a weak smirk. "Be that as it may, I'm talking about his suggestion of werewolves. It's something I'd considered myself, but I've had a few run-ins with werewolves myself, and this is definitely no werewolf."

"How do you know?" I asked.

"Werewolves are powerful. They have substance." He held up his hands, trying to convey their heft. "Whatever attacked Luka, it was like chasing a nightmare. I could never really see it, even when it was right in front of me."

FRIDAY, MARCH 20, 1987

44. sanguine

O kay, so I got liver and beans," Roxie said, as she came into the trailer carrying a brown grocery bag. "I tried to get him bananas, but they didn't have any. Small-town grocery stores are lame."

I sat on the bench inside Luka and Hutch's trailer, the same way I had been all night since I'd talked to Gideon. Luka stayed up a bit, going into more detail about how he'd been certain that he would die and the creature was absolutely relentless as it tore at him. But eventually he'd passed out, and he'd been snoring softly in his bed at the back of the trailer ever since.

I slept some, tossing and turning fitfully on the bench, and once the sun finally poked its way through the curtains, Roxie got up, rousing from Seth's bunk in the back. Since Luka had lost a lot of blood, she went to the store to get foods to help him replenish. He could self-heal, but he couldn't replace things he'd lost—like a tooth he'd lost in a bar fight years ago.

"You're up early." Hutch yawned in his bed above the

driver's seat, and he leaned his head over so he could look down at us. "Did you guys sleep?"

"I slept some," I replied, suppressing my own yawn.

"It was a scary night," Roxie said as she made room in the small fridge for Luka's supplies. "It was hard to sleep after that."

"At least Luka's okay," Hutch said.

"Yeah, *Luka* is, but if it had been any one of us"—Roxie pointed to herself, me, and then Hutch—"we'd all be dead. We couldn't have survived that."

That realization had been keeping me up all night, along with the fact that Gabe and I shared something really meaningful before he'd gotten freaked out and run off. As Roxie had been quick to point out, seeing Luka like that was enough to scare away any rational person.

But it still felt odd and out of character. Gabe had seemed so . . . distant. He hadn't even really kissed me before he left, and it had only been a handful of minutes before that when he'd told me that he was falling in love with me.

Of course, none of that overshadowed the fact that there may very well be some kind of monster stalking our campsite. But I was learning the hard way that it was possible to be afraid for my life *and* nurse a broken heart.

"It's getting bolder." Roxie sat down on the bench across from me. "That *thing* is getting stronger and bolder. That's what I think."

After talking to Luka more last night, he'd confirmed what Gideon said—whatever it was that attacked him was impossible to really see or describe. So, we'd ruled out the possibility that it was an animal. Whatever it was had to be supernatural.

"How do you figure?" I asked.

"The attacks have been escalating in frequency and intensity," Roxie said. "So far, no one has been killed, but Seth and Luka are both lucky to be alive."

"Maybe it needs to feed to grow stronger," Hutch suggested. "Like a vampire or demon or something."

"It's not a vampire." Roxie shook her head. "When we were in Poughkeepsie last year, we met a vampire named Claudette. You could see her and describe her. She looked just like a normal person. And vampires trick you into letting you feed on them. They don't stalk campsites."

"Everything needs to eat to get stronger," I interjected. "I mean, Roxie just got food for Luka to help him get stronger."

"That's true," Roxie agreed. "It could just be a strange monster that woke up after a long hibernation, and it's really hungry." She paused before adding, "Or it could be a demon or something feasting on us because we have special powers."

I cast her a look across the table. "You really believe that?"

"I don't know." She shrugged. "But I can make fire just using my mind, and Luka can heal himself, and we were both targeted. Is it so crazy to think that there might be a creature that feeds on the supernatural?"

I leaned back, resting my head against the wall behind me, and sighed. "No. It's not."

"We need to kill it before it kills us," Roxie replied matter-of-factly.

"You think it's a demon, and you think we should kill it?" I asked with an arched eyebrow.

"Yeah. Doesn't your mom have all kinds of books on

demonology?" Roxie asked. "You should talk to her. She might know something."

"She's got some books," I admitted reluctantly.

My mom did have a few books on demonology and the occult, and when she was younger, I know she'd studied it more, so she may know something helpful. But she also hadn't really been herself since we'd gotten to Caudry. This place was making it hard for her to think straight.

Roxie leaned forward on the table, folding her hands in front of her. "Look, Mara, we have to do something. We're just sitting ducks here until nightfall. If we don't start becoming proactive, we'll be dead."

"I'll talk to her," I said.

"When?" Hutch asked from his perch above me.

"Now, I guess," I said, since it didn't seem like either of them would let up until I did. And it wasn't like just *talking* to my mom could really hurt anything.

"Make sure you ask her about demons," Hutch said as I started to get up.

"That is the plan," I muttered, glancing back at him.

"And also vampires, werewolves, warlocks, and anything else you can think of," he added.

"I think she's got it, Hutch," Roxie told him dryly.

When I left, Hutch was still adding suggestions of things I should bring up, which now included dragons and unicorns. Stepping out into the bright morning sun, the air already felt thick and suffocating. I took a deep breath and hurried over to Gideon's trailer.

Through the open windows, I heard my mom grunt loudly, followed by a loud banging sound.

"Lyanka, let me help you," Gideon's voice drifted warmly outside.

"I've got it," Mom insisted, sounding out of breath.

"Is everything okay?" I asked cautiously.

I leaned forward, peering in through the screen door. Gideon stood leaning against the counter, wearing a tank top and old jeans. In front of him, my mom was hunched over with her hair pulled up in a loose bun, and droplets of sweat stood out all over her tawny skin.

"Everything's fine." Mom straightened up, and I saw a large steamer trunk, one I recognized instantly. "It's here anyway, so I'm done."

"I would've helped you," Gideon persisted, but my mom waved him off.

"Come in, *qamari*." Mom turned her attention to me as she caught her breath. "Stop lurking outside like a robber."

I pushed in the screen door, my eyes still fixed on the trunk, and asked, "Is that . . . is that Grandma Basima's?"

"Yes, and before that it was your great-grandma Elissar's, and someday," she paused, exhaling deeply, "it will be yours."

The steamer trunk was battered and worn from age and travel. It was warped dark brown wood, held together with thick bands of iron.

"It's about time you see what's inside, don't you think?" Mom asked. From around her neck, she grabbed the skull key, taking it off for the first time that I'd ever seen.

45. armed

The key fit in the large lock on the front of the trunk, but evidently, it had not been opened in a while. Mom tried to turn it at first, to no avail, so Gideon took over and put his muscle into it. With an audible and angry click, the lock opened, and Gideon stepped back so my mom could open the trunk.

As Mom lifted the lid, I stood behind her and Gideon, steeling myself for whatever was inside. I half expected evil spirits to come swarming out and melt our faces off like in *Raiders of the Lost Ark.*

When no spirits came, I leaned forward and gasped in surprise. I'd spent much of my childhood fantasizing about what possibly could be hidden inside the trunk—everything from cursed candles to skeletons to actual monsters were suspected—but somehow, the small arsenal of weapons that it actually contained had never occurred to me.

The trunk was practically overflowing with weapons of every sort—jewel-encrusted swords, ancient daggers with wooden handles, crossbows with ornate designs, something that looked like an ice pick made out of ivory, and even a pistol.

"*Weapons?*" I asked, incredulous. "Why did Grandma have all this?"

"I told you," Mom said, giving me an odd look. "For battling the dark arts."

Gideon picked up the pistol carefully. "Why did your mother have a Luger?" he asked my mom.

He slid out the magazine, and when he cleared the chamber, a shiny silver bullet popped. After all this time one would've thought the silver would be tarnished and dirty, but it sat in the palm of Gideon's hand, shimmering like it was freshly polished.

"Different enemies require different weapons," Mom explained absently. She crouched down and began rummaging beneath all the weapons.

"And he'd best be careful." She cast a sidelong glance at Gideon. "That Luger belonged to one of Hitler's officers before he was decommissioned for hunting werewolves."

"Fortunately, being a Nazi isn't contagious," Gideon replied dryly, but he set the gun aside on the counter. "How did this come into your mother's possession?"

Mom waved him off. "Basima never told me how she came by most of these. She fought on the side of good more often than not, but she spent most of her time in the company of many unscrupulous characters."

I reached for a particularly ornate-looking dagger, and no sooner had my fingers brushed the cold steel than Mom slapped my hand, hard.

"Don't touch. Many of these weapons are cursed."

"Gideon got to touch them," I grumbled, rubbing my hand.

"Lyanka, we talked about this." Gideon's voice was soft and careful. "Mara is at an age where you must begin to show her how to use these things. And she should help us with this, because we'll need it."

Mom breathed deeply. "Be patient. I've spent all my life trying to protect her from this, and now I must ask her to join me."

"Join you in what?" I glanced between the two of them. "Why are you talking about me like I'm not here?"

"Here it is!" Mom exclaimed, ignoring me for the moment, and lifted out a large book that had been buried underneath the armaments.

It was a little bigger than a record, and three times as thick as anything Stephen King wrote. The cover appeared to be made of leather, stretched so taut it had cracked and been sewn together in several places so it looked like a patchwork Necronomicon.

"This grimoire has been in our family for generations," Mom explained, wiping the dust off the cover. She stood up and held the book to her chest with one arm, then reached out and took my hand. "Let's sit and talk."

I glanced over at Gideon, who offered me a half shrug, and then we both followed my mom over to the table. She dropped the book of magic onto the table with a loud thud, and I took the seat between her and Gideon.

"You know who I am," Mom said, still holding my hand. "I've spent my life talking to the spirits, communing with the dead and those that exist on another plane around us. You know the power that I have, the one that I believe you have."

I nodded numbly. "I know about your power, but I haven't really shown much of my own."

Mom smiled sadly at me, then looked to Gideon. "I discouraged you from getting in touch with your power, but that doesn't mean it's not there."

Gideon leaned toward me, resting his arms on the table. "And you know what I can do. That I'm a divining rod for others who have extra senses. I felt yours the day I met you, and it's been growing stronger as you've gotten older, the same way it did for your mother. You have the gift she has."

"Okay," I said, growing increasingly uneasy with the way they were talking to me like this. It felt like they were about to tell me they were splitting up or they had cancer or something.

"I thought that I could protect you from what became of Basima, and what's happened to me," Mom explained. "Of the darkness. Of the insanity."

She shook her head. "But there is greater darkness out there. There are dangers that will seek to hurt you because of who you are, because of the gifts you have, and if I don't teach you to protect yourself . . ." Mom trailed off, swallowing back her tears.

"The thing that's stalking us"—Gideon motioned to the swamp behind the camp—"it's not of this world. I felt it last night, when I barely stopped it from devouring Luka."

It was starting to feel like all the oxygen had been sucked from the room. The heat, the mustiness from the trunk, everything they were saying—it was all coming together into a heady concoction where I felt out of place and disconnected from everything around me.

Somehow, I managed to ask, "What is it?"

Gideon shook his head. "I'm not sure. I've never encountered anything like it before. It felt like . . ." He furrowed his brow, trying to form the words. "Like a black hole. It sucked in all the energy, becoming this indistinguishable darkness that's almost impossible to look at directly. But what I do know is that it's powerful, and it's *very* hungry."

I leaned back in the rickety kitchen chair, and it all hit me. I realized exactly what this weird meeting and trunk of magic weapons was about.

"You're going to try to kill it," I said. "And you want me to help."

"A creature like this doesn't just go away," Gideon elaborated. "We can't run from it, and even if we can, that only means that it will harm others. I've spent my entire adult life trying to protect those that society forgot or threw away." He shook his head. "I can't just leave this thing running loose to kill anything it wants."

"We have protections," Mom insisted. "There's the weapons, and this book is full of incantations to protect you and to ward off evil. I wouldn't let you join us if I thought you couldn't be kept safe."

"You don't have to talk me into it," I said. "This thing has been attacking my home and my family. I want to stop it just as much as you do. I'm in." I squeezed my mom's hand, trying to reassure her that I could handle this. "Just tell me what I need to do."

46. tenebris

As I tore the ticket of an older woman with a strong Southern drawl and two pudgy grandkids, I mumbled *vade retro me tenebris* under my breath.

The creature—demon/monster/whatever—didn't usually show itself until late at night, and Gideon was convinced it would be untraceable. The plan was to wait for the creature to find us, since it came to the campsite nearly every night. Once the carnival closed, we would prepare to fight back, so when the creature came, we would be ready.

The morning had been filled with preparations and lectures on weapons and memorizing incantations. But we still needed the money, so in the afternoon, we went to work. As Gideon frequently said, the show must go on, so on it went.

Mom had taught me incantations, and they were all in Latin, so I kept repeating them over and over to make sure I got them right when I needed them. The one she told me was the most powerful—*vade retro me tenebris*—meant "get behind me, darkness."

When I asked her why they were in Latin, she'd simply shrugged and said, "These spells are quite old, and when they were made, that's what they spoke. And since they work, there's no reason to change them."

The day had been long and hot, and it was hard to focus on anything. The biggest distraction—other than preparing to fight off a creature I didn't understand—was Gabe. Not his presence, but his absence.

I kept scouring the crowd, looking for him, but he never appeared. We hadn't had plans today, not officially, but we had seen each other nearly every day since I'd gotten to Caudry. And then last night, we'd shared something really special, before he'd left suddenly.

He'd told me that he was falling in love with me, and when I said, "Me too," I'd meant it. I felt more for Gabe than I had for anyone else, and I thought he really meant it too. I *felt* it in the tender way he touched me.

There had been other boys before Gabe, ones who said all the right words and promised a devotion that I didn't ask for, but only for the night. The next day, they'd be gone without a trace, and I'd never really minded. It was better that way.

But Gabe was different. I *believed* the words he'd told me. He wouldn't just end things that way. Just vanishing into the night never to be heard from again . . . would he?

The day was filled with too many important things to be done, so there was no time for me to go looking for him. When the carnival began to close for the night, I realized sadly that last night might very well have been the last time I ever saw him.

I didn't linger on that thought, though. There would be plenty of time for heartache in the future. Right now, I needed to focus and prepare for whatever the night had in store for us.

Mom hadn't done any readings today to help keep her strength up, and when I returned to camp, she was already setting things up. With incense burning in one hand and a mixture of herbs in the other, she walked around the campsite, doing a cleansing ritual to chase away darkness.

She smiled briefly at me but quickly returned to the task at hand, so I went over to join Hutch where he sat at the picnic table outside his camper. He had one of the swords I'd seen inside my mom's trunk, and he attempted to spin it, but his injured shoulder hampered his mobility, and the sword fell to the ground.

"You'll have to be more careful with that if you want to survive," Luka commented, leaning against the open doorway of his motorhome. His shirtless torso revealed no signs of scars, or any of the damage that had been inflicted on him last night.

"I'll be fine," Hutch mumbled as he scrambled to pick up the sword.

I sat down beside Hutch. "How is it going here?"

"Good. Your mom's been trying to get us ready," Hutch replied. "Roxie's over with Gideon, picking out a weapon."

"She wants to use her fire, but it's not reliable," Luka said.

"Your mom put salt around my camper." Hutch pointed to a line of white sprinkled in the grass.

It wasn't actually salt—it was a blend of many things, including ashes and ground gypsum, but I didn't bother explaining it to Hutch.

"She's trying to protect you, so the demon thing can't get inside and hurt you," I said.

"I told you it was a demon," Hutch said, sounding more excited about the prospect of a demon than he should.

"You also told me it was a bear," I corrected him.

"Maybe it's a bear demon," he said.

My mom had knelt down in the center of the campsite, with her palms flat on the grass in front of her, and her long halter dress pooled around her. The halter tied at the nape of her neck, showing off the dark ink of the sun and moon tattoos she had beside either shoulder blade.

"What is she doing now?" Hutch asked.

"She's saying an incantation," I said, straining to pick up the words she was whispering toward the earth, but I couldn't decipher them. "I think she's asking for other spirits and entities to help us."

"Other entities?" Hutch asked. "But isn't that like opening a door to more trouble? Don't we want *less* spirits around us?"

I shook my head. "Not exactly. My mom is friendly with the other side, and they will help her."

"*Boh je dobrý a diabol nie je až taký zlý k tým, ktorých má rád,*" Luka said, his words suddenly carrying a thick Slovak accent, so it sounded like *Boe he dough-bree, ah diablo knee he talk-sleek teom pret-eek ktoe mah-rot.*

"Did you just say a spell?" Hutch asked, narrowing his eyes at him. "Did you just put a spell on us?"

"No, it was something that my gramma used to say sometimes," Luka explained. "It means 'God is good, and the devil is not so bad to those he likes.'"

Mom stood, wiping her hands on her dress. Then she stretched her arms wide, pulling herself to the other side, and let out a deep breath. When she let her arms fall to her sides, she turned to face us.

"I think I've done all I can do," she said. "Now we must wait." Then she rested her eyes on me, gray and serious. "Mara, will you come with me for a moment?"

I followed my mom into our trailer, where one of her old Blue Öyster Cult records played softly. All the lights were on, as were all the lights in all the trailers. We wanted the campsite as bright as possible so we could see what was coming.

Once we were in the privacy of our home, Mom took my hands in hers. She bent down a little, so she was level with me. The lines around her eyes seemed more harsh than normal, and I wondered dourly how all this work she was doing was affecting her.

"Mara, *qamari*, I don't want to worry you, but I want you to know the truth," Mom said.

"That's a very scary way to start a conversation, Mom."

She clicked her tongue. "Mara, be serious. I need you to hear me now."

I swallowed hard, gulping back the fear I felt rising inside me, and I nodded. "Okay."

"Last night, Gideon gave me a pill to help me sleep, and it's the first time I've had dreams since we got here," Mom explained. "Basima had been trying to visit me, and my sleep was so deep, she was finally able to last night."

"She came to you in a dream?"

Mom nodded. "Yes. She told me that I can't shelter you any longer. That I must teach you to harness your power, or the monsters of this world will destroy you."

"How can I harness my power?" I shook my head. "I hardly have any, and I just talk to the dead. How will that help?"

"Oh, *qamari*." Mom smiled at me. "There are far more dead on this earth than there are alive. What do you think is more powerful?"

"How do I use it tonight, to fight this thing?" I asked.

"First, you must trust yourself." She put one hand on my stomach, pressing hard against the soft flesh beneath the fabric of my shirt. "Your intuition is potent, and you must listen to it."

"Okay," I said uncertainly.

"And then, you should use this." Mom stepped away from me and went over to pick up something hidden on the bench beside the dinette.

Carefully, she held up the antique crossbow I'd seen in the steamer trunk, along with a small, narrow satchel. She handed the bow to me, and it felt heavier than I expected, much heavier than the crossbow I'd used before with Seth.

The wood was rich blackwood with a purplish hue, with designs of winged monsters carved into it in intricate detail. The stock curved down, like the grip of a pistol, and my fingers brushed up against the trigger.

As soon as they did, I felt a jolt of cold surge through me. Only for a second, but it was enough to make my heart skip a beat.

"This was your great-grandma Elissar's," Mom explained,

running her fingers along the string. "She made it herself in 1922 to fight off the demons that were attacking her village. Her home, her family, her first husband, they were all slaughtered, but she survived, thanks to this, and she fled to America."

"And you think it still works?" I asked.

My mom nodded solemnly. "For you, it will work."

"How many bolts do we have?" I asked, looking down at the satchel in her hand. A few of them poked out of the bag, their silver pointed tips as unmistakable as the arrow for the crossbow.

"We only have six left, so you must use them wisely. You've trained with a crossbow before, so I know that you can handle this."

I held the crossbow up, looking through the sight—a small hole in a metal circle sitting atop the barrel. I'd fired a crossbow before, many times, and I'd been quite good, because screwing up meant that Luka could lose an eye that might not grow back.

Yet I couldn't help but feel like all this confidence in me might be misplaced. I didn't feel powerful or capable or even really understand what was being asked of me.

"Mara, I see the worry on your face." Mom gently took the crossbow from me and set it on the table, along with the bolts. "You can do these things, because you must."

She put her hands on my face, both in a gesture of comfort and to force me to look her in the eyes. "Something very bad is coming for us, and you must be strong to survive. You are strong, *qamari*, and you will not waver."

I swallowed hard, and the record began to skip, stuck on the line *don't fear the reaper*. My stomach turned sour, twisting bitterly inside me.

"What?" Mom asked, her eyes narrowing. "What do you feel?"

I shook my head. "I don't . . . I don't know."

"You sense it," she insisted, and I could feel the acidic churning of my stomach growing. She dropped her hands from my face and looked to the window. "It's here, isn't it?"

No sooner had she said that then I heard Gideon let out a battle cry.

47. demonology

I grabbed the satchel and dropped the strap across my chest, and then I picked up the crossbow. I didn't rush out—not yet because I didn't know what I'd be running into—so I stopped at the door to the Winnebago and looked out at the campsite.

Hutch stood on the steps of his own camper, brandishing a sword, while Luka attempted to pull him back inside. I couldn't see Gideon, not at first, but then Roxie lit up the sky with a fireball, burning white hot inside her hands.

For a split second, I saw it—the creature that had been stalking the camp. The fire seemed to warp around it, reminding me of a documentary I'd once seen about black holes. The light was pulled into it, and it was the bending that gave it its shape. The absence of light, like a shadow come alive—blurred edges and formless, but not.

It was like it had a cloak of nothingness camouflaging it.

I knew that it had substance. I had the seen the talons of its feet. I knew it was more than a shadow—it was something real that could be killed.

"I'll kill you, you bloody bastard!" Gideon roared, and he fired the cursed Luger at the demon shadow, but then it was on the move.

There was a blur of black in the darkness, and the trees of the swamp rustled and moved. Gideon ran after it, into the swamp, and I knew that if he went alone, we'd never see him again.

I threw open the camper door and ran out after him. My mom was screaming my name, and I suspected that she was giving chase, but I didn't slow. If I waited any longer, any signs of the creature—and Gideon—might be gone.

Into the forest I plunged, chasing after shadows in the dark. The moon was hidden behind clouds, giving me nothing to guide my path. The only thing I had was the twisting pain in my stomach—the pain seemed to intensify the closer I got, so I followed the hurt and ignored the branches scraping at my legs and arms, as if grabbing at me.

"Enough!" Gideon shouted, and his voice echoed through the trees, so I couldn't tell if he was a few feet to my left or twenty feet to my right, or maybe somewhere else entirely. "Leave us be! I will not let you hurt my people, not anymore!"

The gun went off three times, loud blasts shattering the night, and I put my hands over my ears. When I removed them, there was nothing. Even the wind through the trees had fallen silent.

Mara! a voice shouted, coming from within my head and

all around me. I turned to look for the source of the sound, and then I saw her.

Blossom. Her frizzy brown hair appeared nearly translucent, but I could still make out the spattering of freckles underneath her eyes.

You need to get out of here. Blossom's voice was in my head, but her mouth wasn't moving. She only stared at me with wide dark eyes. *If you want to live, you need to run. NOW.*

So I did. I burst forward, pushing back through the trees in the direction I thought was the camp, but I had no sense of anything. Being in a strange forest in the middle of the night was disorienting, but I had to keep running as fast as I could.

Behind me, the branches and trees crunched and snapped as the creature tore through them. I didn't scream—there was no one who could come to help me, and I didn't want my mom or Roxie rushing in after me and getting themselves killed. The only thing I could do was run faster.

Then the ground gave way beneath me. The tall grass and thick forest made it hard for me to see where I was going, and it was already too late when I felt my foot squelching down into the dense mud of the surrounding swamp.

I fell forward roughly and lost my grip on the crossbow. It slid out of my grasp, somewhere in the underbrush, and I didn't have time to search for it. I had to climb to higher ground, but the mud was swallowing my legs.

The creature was close enough that I could smell the sulfur on its breath. I could hear the beast behind me—it made a strange high-pitched guttural sound, like a demonic squeal of delight.

Grabbing a broken branch, I turned around to face the creature as it tore through the trees toward me. I brandished the branch like a weapon. If I was going down, I was going down swinging.

48. death

I couldn't see it, but I knew it was there, standing right in front of me. Its breath felt hot on my skin, and it would only be a few seconds before it tore into me.

But then the branches beside me started cracking. There was something else in the woods, charging toward us. Was there more than one demon?

A loud snarl erupted from the trees beside me, and I saw a flash of silver before it collided into the demon. The demonic shadow tried to engulf it, so the new creature almost disappeared, but it fought back hard, crashing into the swamp.

I had no idea what was going on, but I knew I had to escape while I had the chance. Grabbing the roots of a tree, I hoisted myself up out of the muck. The clouds had parted enough to allow the moon to shine through, and I saw the light glinting off the metal on my crossbow.

As the fight roared on behind me, I scrambled to grab my crossbow. Behind me, I heard heavy footsteps and ragged panting.

I whirled around, pointing the bow at whatever was chasing after me.

Instead of the darkness of the demon, it was a massive silver wolf, and it would've easily dwarfed a bear. Its fangs, exposed under the curl of its lip, could easily snap me in two. I took aim with my crossbow, right for its chest, but the wolf's expression softened and there was something in its eyes—dark golden brown and strangely familiar—that made me hesitate to pull the trigger.

Then the wolf lowered its head before turning and bounding away into the trees.

I lay on my back in the dirt for a second, catching my breath and trying to figure out what the hell was going on. But I didn't have much time for that; I had to get out of there before anything else tried to kill me.

I'd just gotten to my feet when a guy burst through the bushes. But it wasn't just any guy—it was Gabe, shirtless and barefoot. The only clothing he wore was a pair of jeans that looked like they'd gone through a shredder. His hair was mussed, his eyes were wild, and he was out of breath as he walked over to me.

"We have to go," Gabe commanded.

"Where did you come from, Gabe?" I asked in a trembling voice, but I already knew the answer and stepped back from him. "You were that wolf, weren't you?"

"We can talk about it later, but we have to get out of here now before that thing comes back."

"*Mara!*" That was my mom, screaming just outside the edge of the forest.

"Mara!" Gideon's voice followed right after hers, his accent lilting with panic.

The trees rustled behind us, and there was no more time to think or talk. Gabe grabbed my hand and pulled me along. His legs were longer and faster, and he nimbly leapt over a fallen tree before picking me up and lifting me over it.

We broke through the forest at the edge of camp and ran straight into Gideon, pointing his Luger right at Gabe.

"Don't shoot, it's Mara!" Mom yelled, and she practically pushed Gabe out of the way to wrap her arms around me. "Thank the heavens you're alive. I couldn't lose you, *qamari*. I love you more than the stars in the sky."

She let go of me long enough to grab my shoulders and give me one rough shake. "I gave you the crossbow and told you to harness your powers to protect yourself, not to kill yourself, Mara!"

"You shouldn't have followed me," Gideon said once my mom finished scolding me. He put his leathery hand on my shoulder. "I couldn't have lived with myself if you got hurt because of me."

"Did you protect her?" Mom asked, eyeing Gabe's shirtless torso. He had a few scratches on his chest, but they seemed superficial, so they were probably from branches clawing at him.

"I tried," he told her, but his eyes were on me, searching.

Everything happened so fast, and I couldn't think or catch my breath, and I just wanted a moment where the world didn't feel like it was falling away from me. I looked away from him, just for a moment, just to think, and I spotted Roxie. She was standing next to Luka's trailer, sobbing loudly, and Hutch had his arm around her.

That's when I noticed the tears in my mom's eyes, and the blood on Gideon's clothes. Dark, like the color of flaking rust, mixed with mud and leaves and a few strands of frizzy brown hair.

"What happened?" I asked.

Then I saw her. Luka was a few feet away from the campsite, crouched over her. Even from this distance, she looked like a rag doll that had been torn apart.

"Gideon found Blossom," Mom said gently, and rubbed my back. "She's dead."

"I know," I said.

I should've known it sooner. Blossom had been talking to me since she'd been gone—I'd heard her voice in my head quoting "The Spider and the Fly." And as I looked over at her body, my stomach twisting, I realized that she'd been the one who turned my stomach sour. She'd been trying to warn me of danger.

"I saw her in the forest," I said softly. "She told me to run."

Mom's breath caught in her throat as she stifled a sob. "She's watching out for you."

Behind me, I could hear Gideon asking Gabe where he'd come from and what he was doing out here. I wiped the tears from my eyes, knowing that I would cry plenty for Blossom soon, but right now, I had to find out what the hell was going on with Gabe.

"I need to talk to Gabe." I gave him a hard look. "Alone."

"We should all go back inside," Gideon said, but I'd already turned and started walking toward my trailer. Behind me

I heard Roxie crying, asking what they were going to do with Blossom, and Gideon promised that he'd keep her safe and they would decide what to do in the morning.

In the Winnebago, my mom's album was still playing, but I couldn't handle the sound so I flicked it off. I set my crossbow on the counter beside me, in case I needed it, and I poured myself a glass of water. I took a long drink with my back to Gabe, but I could feel his eyes on me, the way I always felt his eyes when they were on me.

I took a deep breath and turned back to face him. He stood before me, looking more scared than I'd ever seen him before.

"What are you?" I asked finally.

49. confession

Well, um . . ." He lowered his eyes and cleared his throat. "People would call me a werewolf."

My heart dropped from my chest, and I closed my eyes, letting his words sink in. Since I'd grown up around people with all kinds of different supernatural abilities, I wasn't as shocked as perhaps the average person would've been.

I also knew that I was still keeping my secret from him—that I was a necromancer, and that most of my friends had extra-sensory powers of their own—and I was probably keeping it for the same reason he had. The shame and lack of understanding that came from telling a "normal" person.

But considering my friends and family were being attacked by a creature that we didn't understand, his confession carried a more terrifying weight with it.

"It's not like the movies, though," Gabe rushed to explain. "When I change into a wolf, I don't just turn into an animal. I'm still in control of myself. I can even control when I change. It's harder when there's a full moon, but I'm still in control."

"A full moon?" I opened my eyes. "There was a full moon the beginning of this week."

"I know, like I said, I'm still in control," Gabe insisted, and took a step toward me. "I'm always in control of myself."

"How does it work, then?" I asked. "If the moon doesn't make you change, why do you change?"

"I don't know." He shrugged. "It's just something I do from time to time. Like, my body craves it, and if I don't run off some built-up wolf energy every now and then, it does get harder to handle. But I do it. I usually just run through the trees for a while, and then I come home."

"How long have you been a werewolf?" I asked.

"Technically, all my life," he explained. "But I didn't start actually changing until I was twelve."

"You were born a werewolf?" I cocked my head. "Does that mean your family are too?"

"You remember when I told you about the Brawley legacy?" Gabe asked with a crooked smile. "It's not just the house and the money. We're werewolves. My mom, my sister, my uncle Beau, my grandpa, we're all wolves."

I tilted my head back and stared up at the ceiling. "Oh, hell, there's a whole pack of you."

"It's not like that." Gabe reached out, trying to touch my arm. "We're not *bad*."

I looked back at him, into his beautiful golden eyes, and now I understood exactly what I felt when I met him. I'd sensed that I should be afraid of him, and I could never understand why.

And still, even though I knew exactly who and what he was now, I couldn't make myself be afraid of him. In his eyes, I saw the same guy that I'd been falling for, the guy who made my heart race when he held my hand, the guy who cared for me without judgment and without conditions.

But I couldn't just pretend like everything was fine. We couldn't just go back to the way things were, not when I still didn't know who or what was hunting us.

"So you're saying that you have no idea who killed my friend Blossom?" I pointed toward the window, to where I'd seen her body before we came into the trailer. "That you didn't have anything to do with it?"

"*No!*" Gabe insisted emphatically. "I'm sorry for your loss and everything, but I don't even know who Blossom is, and I've never killed anybody."

"What about your family? Could they have done that?" I asked.

He shook his head. "No, I don't think so. And whatever that was that I fought in the woods, I don't know what it was, but it wasn't like any other werewolf I've ever met. It was . . . darkness. I could feel it pulling me in, like it was sucking out my soul through my skin."

He shivered visibly then, and I wanted to comfort him, but I didn't know how. I wasn't sure if I should touch him, or throw him out. Everything felt so off it was hard to know what to think.

"Why didn't you come see me today?" I asked.

"After what happened to Luka last night, I was afraid that my family was somehow involved," Gabe explained. "My mom and sister both insisted they didn't have anything to do with it, but I came out tonight to see for sure. I had to make sure that I was safe for you before I came around again."

"I was afraid you'd changed your mind about me."

"No, Mara." He stepped closer to me and put his hand on my face, cradling it. "I'll never change my mind about you."

I looked up into his eyes, and I wanted to kiss him so badly then, as badly as I've ever wanted to, but the moment felt wrong. *Everything* felt wrong tonight. I lowered my eyes, so he moved back from me.

"I just need some time to think," I said. "The past twenty-four hours have been maddening, and I haven't slept much."

"No, of course. This has to be so much for you to take in." He took a step back toward the door. "I'll leave you alone, then."

"Thank you."

He paused before he left. "I'll see you tomorrow, though?"

I nodded. "I think I would like that."

He offered me a small smile before leaving. As soon as he was gone, I started crying, and I wasn't even completely sure why. Blossom's death, the faded adrenaline, the monster lurking in the words, his status as a werewolf. It was all too much.

I went back to my room and collapsed on my bed. A few minutes later, I heard the front door creak open, and footsteps quietly padded toward me. I could smell the incense on her clothes, so I knew it was my mom before she said anything.

She climbed into bed beside me, wrapping her arms around me and holding me close like she had when I was a little girl.

"I love you, *qamari*," she whispered.

"I love you, Mom," I said between sniffles.

"Is there anything I can help with?"

"I don't know." I wiped at my eyes. "Everything is just too much."

"Don't worry about it now." She stroked my hair. "Get some sleep, and we will find a way to sort this all out in the morning. Everything always looks better in the light of day."

50. the sun

My mom was wrong.

When I woke up, the sunlight stung my eyes. My entire body ached like I'd been through a train wreck, and it took all my effort to pull myself out of bed. Mom was still sleeping, but she'd moved over to her own bed sometime in the night.

I went into the kitchen to brew myself a pot of coffee and to attempt to come up with a plan about what to do next. It wasn't even seven in the morning yet, and through the window above the sink, I saw Roxie sitting at the picnic table smoking a cigarette.

I poured two cups of coffee—one for me and one for her—and opened the door to the Winnebago and nearly tripped over Gabe. He was curled up on the ground, using a packing blanket for covers, and he sat up with a start when I almost stepped on him.

"Your boyfriend spent the night sleeping outside your

door," Roxie commented dryly. "I haven't decided if that's romantic or creepy yet." She flicked her ashes. "Maybe both."

"Sorry," Gabe said as he clambered to his feet. "I just wanted to make sure you were safe. I thought if the thing decided to come back, I wanted to be here."

"Gabe!" I gasped. "You could've gotten yourself killed!"

"I'm okay," he insisted with a subtle curve at the edge of his lips.

Last night, he'd been subdued and apologetic, but he seemed more relaxed now, probably in relief that we'd survived and I didn't hate him. The glimmer had returned to his eyes, and there was a grace to his long limbs as he brushed away the grass stuck to his bare skin.

I set one of my cups of coffee on the step so I could help him, my fingers brushing against his abs, and I was surprised by how warm his skin felt after spending the night sleeping in the grass. I think I'd read somewhere that werewolves ran hot, and that explained the constant fiery temperature of his flesh.

When I went to pick a blade of grass from his chest just above his heart, Gabe put his hand over mine and gently held it in place. His heart pounded quickly beneath the palm of my hand, beating the same way it had when we laid together the night before last.

It was a quiet but powerful reminder that Gabe was still Gabe.

"But since you're okay, I should probably get home and put some clothes on," he said, with a light teasing in his voice.

"I suppose that you probably should," I agreed half-heartedly. When he spoke again, all joking had disappeared. "I was thinking that you should come over and talk to my parents. They know more about all of . . . my legacy, especially my mom, and she might have some insight about what's happening here."

"Sure." I nodded, ignoring how uneasy the thought of talking to his mom about all of this made me feel.

"You wanna come over around eleven?" he suggested, and I nodded again. "Good. I'll see you soon, then."

He let go of my hand, then briefly but wonderfully pressed his lips to mine. He walked off, presumably toward his car parked in the fairground parking lot, and offered Roxie an awkward wave as he did.

I grabbed the coffee and went over to where Roxie was stubbing out her cigarette. The hood of her sweatshirt was pulled up, but her bright blond hair poked out around the edges. Based on the neon color of the sweatshirt, I guessed that she'd borrowed it from Hutch. Her eyes were red from crying, and her cheeks were uncharacteristically puffy.

"How are you holding up?" I asked as I handed her a mug.

"Oh, I've had better mornings." She sipped her coffee and took a deep breath. "I think I always knew Blossom wasn't coming back."

"Really?" I asked in surprise. "You seemed the most convinced that everything was fine."

Whenever I mentioned the possibility that Blossom might be missing, Roxie was always quick to come up with a reasonable explanation about where Blossom might be.

"Denial is how I cope. If I just deny everything, it can't hurt me, right?" She laughed darkly. "I don't know. I just couldn't face the thought of losing somebody else I cared about."

I rubbed her back, and Roxie leaned over, resting her head on my shoulder before saying, "I think we're gonna cremate her. Blossom told me and Carrie once that if she ever died, she wanted her ashes spread over a field of flowers. So that's what I think we're gonna do."

"So is Gideon planning to call the police?" I asked.

"No," Roxie said. "We know how she died, and we don't want to deal with the assholes that live here. They'd probably just take her body and send it back to her stupid hippie drug-addict parents, assuming they even found them, and Blossom *hated* her parents. She wouldn't want to go back to them."

She sniffled, then went on, "We were thinking we'd have, like, a ceremony or something tomorrow before we left."

"I think Blossom would like that," I said.

Roxie sat up a little and peered at me from under her hood. "Did I hear you correctly last night? Blossom's been talking to you?"

"Yeah, she has. I didn't realize it at first, but I think she's just been trying to watch out for us," I explained.

"Does she sound okay? Like, do you think she's happy?" Roxie asked.

"I mean, it's hard to tell when she's just telling me to run for my life," I admitted. "But I saw her last night, in the woods, and she looked okay. She looked like Blossom. My mom can probably help you talk to her, if you want."

Roxie nodded and wiped her nose with the back of her sleeve. "I think I'd like that."

"Do you know what Gideon has planned for today?" I asked.

"I don't know." Roxie shook her head. "But we only have to

stay here one more night, and then we get paid and we can get out of here for good. If we can just keep that thing at bay for one more night, we're golden."

"Only one more night," I murmured, and I'd never been so happy and so sad to leave a place.

51. cursed

The cast-iron wolf head glared out at me from the bloodred door, and I stayed frozen on the porch outside of the Brawley mansion. A warm breeze blew by, ruffling my dress and making the long branches of the willows dance and groan.

When I reached Gabe's house, my grandma Basima had returned to scream inside my head, *idhhabee min honaa.* Her voice sent an ice-cold chill all the way through me. I didn't know what to do, but I knew I didn't want her yelling at me or scaring me or freezing me out anymore.

"It's okay, Grandma Basima," I whispered. "I know Gabe's a werewolf, and I can handle it."

No, Mara, idhhabee min honaa. Her voice sounded like it was right in my ear.

I closed my eyes, trying to will her away, but I saw enough from my mom dealing with spirits to know that they didn't just go away because you wanted them to.

"Please, Grandma," I said quietly. "You have to let me handle this on my own."

He is more dangerous than you know! Basima shouted in English this time, and the words echoed painfully through my skull.

The front door creaked open, and I rushed to compose myself so I didn't look like a crazy person. But based on the confused look Gabe was giving me, it hadn't worked.

"Were you just talking to someone?" he asked, glancing around the empty porch.

I shook my head. "Nope. It's just me."

He cocked his head when he looked back at me. "You know I have super hearing, right? It's a werewolf thing." He motioned to his ears. "So I heard you saying something."

I took a deep breath and decided it was time for us to get all the secrets out in the open. He'd told me he was a werewolf, so he couldn't react that badly if he found out that I was a necromancer.

"I was just talking to my grandma," I explained, causing Gabe to look around again. "She's dead." His head snapped back toward me and his eyes widened. "I'm a necromancer, and so is my mom."

For a moment, he said nothing. He just stared at me with his jaw slightly open.

"My parents are out having brunch with the mayor and the sheriff, so why don't you come inside and we can talk about this all before they get home?" He stepped back and opened the door wider.

He led me into his living room, where we sat together on the bright red sofa, and I proceeded to tell him everything I knew about necromancy, and although my abilities were only just manifesting, I had a sense of what they would be because of my mom's experiences.

Gabe took it all well, nodding and asking a few questions. So I decided to plunge on ahead and tell him that I wasn't the only one who had special powers, and that really got his eyes to widen.

"This is all so crazy." He leaned back on the sofa and stared off into space. "I've always suspected that we couldn't be the only ones. I mean, if werewolves are real, then that means that there's probably all kinds of other things out there. But I've just never met any."

"It's hard to bring up in conversation," I agreed. "People don't always react well to things they don't understand, and you never know who to trust."

"Yeah, exactly." Gabe nodded. "My mom used to tell me horror stories about our ancestors being hunted and murdered."

"It's hard to find people that accept you when you're like us," I agreed.

Gabe had been staring off, but he looked at me then. He moved closer so his knee pressed against mine, and took my hand in his. His eyes met mine, burning with something more powerful than lust.

"I don't want you to go tomorrow," he said, with the earnestness in his words verging on pleading.

"Gabe—"

"I've never met anyone like you or had a connection with

anyone the way I do with you," he said, interrupting my protests. "I don't want to lose you."

I shook my head, forcing myself to ignore the pain in my heart. "It's not just that my family, my friends, my whole life is leaving tomorrow. But there's a monster here trying to *kill* me. I can't stay."

"What if the monster goes away?" Gabe asked.

"How?" I asked. "We don't even know what it is or what it wants, let alone how to stop it or make it go away."

"When I was a wolf, I was able to chase it off," Gabe said hurriedly. "Maybe my mom and Selena can help, or maybe they'll know something that I don't. I don't know. But we can't live here with that monster either."

I hesitated before saying, "Even if that's true, even if you can stop it—and that's a *really* big 'if'—I don't know."

"I don't want to force you or anything," he said. "I just want you to consider staying with me longer."

"I'll consider it but . . . I can't make any promises. You're asking me to give up the only life I've known, you know?"

"I do." Gabe lowered his eyes. "I'm sorry. I don't mean to be pressuring you like this. There's too much going on, and who knows what the night will bring."

We might not even survive the night, I thought, but I didn't say it aloud. It only made everything more confusing and terrifying.

On another day, in another place, I would've been thrilled by the prospect of setting up in a real house with a real life with someone who I was crazy about.

But that was before I realized that I was a necromancer, like my mom and my grandma before her, and I knew the insanity and dangers that went along with it. Not to mention the darkness that seemed to envelope Caudry.

As much as I cared about Gabe, I knew I could never make this place my home.

I stood up, suddenly feeling like I needed space to breathe and think.

"Are you okay?" Gabe asked, getting to his feet more slowly. "I didn't mean to upset you."

"No, I'm fine. I just . . . needed to move," I explained lamely.

I began wandering through the expanse of the living room, admiring the artwork in bold primary colors clashing against the frosted wallpaper and gold fireplace.

The mantel of the fireplace seemed to serve as the place for more personal photos. A picture of Selena in a cap and gown, Gabe as a toddler with a puppy, the two kids with their dad in front of one of his restaurants.

But the one that really grabbed my attention was an eight by ten of Della Jane—younger, with her curls as wild as ever and a flower in her hair. Her head was thrown back a little with a smile so wide, she had to be caught mid-laugh.

Beside her stood a shirtless man with a peace symbol painted on his chest. His hair was disheveled with a slight curl to it. He was taller than Della Jane, and his arm was looped around her shoulders, squeezing her close to him.

But it was his smile that caught me. He had the exact same smile as Gabe.

Behind them was a crowd, though they were too blurred to be distinguishable. A banner hung from a tree, the fabric rippled and slouching, but between the wrinkles, I could just make out the words:

Equinox Festival
1974

"That's my uncle Beau," Gabe explained, coming up behind me.

"You look like him."

"Yeah, I get that a lot, mostly from my mom," Gabe said, then there was a long pause before he added, "He killed himself."

"What?" I asked, making sure I heard him right.

"Last summer, he drowned in the lake," he explained. "Only way to kill a werewolf is with a silver bullet, but when we're in human form, we're just as vulnerable as anyone else."

I didn't know what to say, so Gabe went on. "They officially ruled it as an accident, out of respect for Beau and my family. But he killed himself. He filled his pockets with rocks and walked out into Lake Tristeaux."

"I'm sorry." I touched his arm. "Do you know why he did it?"

He shrugged emptily. "If Mom has any suspicions, she won't tell me. I thought it was because of the curse."

"What do you mean?"

"That he just got sick of living and dealing with the curse," Gabe elaborated. "My mom lucked out with my dad, because he's been so supportive, but Uncle Beau wasn't as fortunate. His fiancée left him when she found out. He tried to fill his life with parties and friends after that, but it wasn't the same."

"Loneliness is a curse itself," I said.

"Yeah," Gabe agreed, but furrowed his brow, like he was thinking something. "But lately I've been wondering if there's more to it than that."

"What do you mean?"

Instead of answering, Gabe tilted his head and looked toward the door. "Wait."

"What?" I asked.

But then I heard it—the front door opening, followed by Della Jane's heels clicking on the floor. Gabe reached down, taking my hand in his, and led me toward the entry, toward his family, and I felt the ice in my chest growing.

"Those mimosas were strong," Selena was saying.

"You had *three*," Della Jane chastised her, but then she saw me with Gabe.

That panicked primal look flashed in her eyes, but she managed a smile, while Selena and Julian gave much more genuine-looking grins.

"So that's why you couldn't make brunch this morning," his dad teased cordially in his thick accent.

"We need to talk to you," Gabe said, and the gravity in his voice made the smiles fall away from everyone's faces. "We need you to tell us everything you know about werewolves."

52. legacy

Gabriel Bardou Alvarado!" Della Jane gasped. Her blue eyes widened, flashing with anger. "How dare you divulge a secret that isn't yours to share?"

"Mom, listen—" Gabe moved forward, shielding me from his mother's wrath, even though so far, it did seem to be entirely directed at him.

"No, you know better, Gabe!" she snapped.

"Della," Julian said calmly, putting his large hand on his wife's shoulder. "The cat's already out of the bag, so to speak, and anger won't fix anything."

Della Jane took a deep breath. "I suppose you're right."

"It's so unfair that Gabe gets to tell his girlfriend, and I can't tell Logan anything," Selena said. Her lips were stained with bright pink lipstick, and she stuck them out in a childish pout.

"Selena, honey, Logan is an idiot and an asshole, that's why you can't tell him," Della Jane told her daughter coolly. "Now, why don't you get us all something to drink? I think we'll all head out to the veranda and have a conversation."

Without saying anything more, Della Jane took off the blazer she wore over her flowered sundress and slipped out of her pastel stilettos. She turned and walked down the hall toward the back of the house.

Julian gave us both an uneasy smile before following her. Gabe squeezed my hand—for his comfort or mine, I'm not sure—and then he led me through his house to the covered porch in the impeccably groomed garden. Bushes and greenery created mazes within their yard, and a large statue of a wolf sat in the center of it all.

Several weeping willows filled the sprawling backyard, their sinewy branches all reaching toward the pillars that surrounded the veranda. Spanish moss hung from the branches and a small gazebo to the back of the yard, giving it all an otherworldly feel.

The sun had hidden behind gray skies, and a soft mist made the air hazy, though it did nothing to alleviate the heat. A ceiling fan whirred lazily above us, and a muggy breeze blew through the open porch.

Like in the house, the patio furniture was very art deco. Boxy shapes of solid black and bright white with chrome accents. I sat on the small, firm sofa with Gabe, across from his parents, with a glass coffee table between us.

No one said anything, not until Selena brought several glasses of Pepsi. She set them on the table before perching on the elegant white bannister that ran around the veranda, and though

Della Jane asked her daughter to get refreshments, she made no move toward them.

"You should've talked to me first, before telling anyone," Della Jane said finally.

"I had no choice," Gabe said. "I hadn't meant to tell Mara, but I already told you about the monster that has been attacking her and everyone else in the carnival. I was trying to find out what it was when the monster nearly killed her, and I transformed to protect her."

Della Jane appeared unmoved, playing absently with her dangling earrings. "That may be how you felt, but revealing the curse doesn't just affect you. You put your whole family in danger."

"Mara's no danger," Gabe insisted. "She has her own secrets, like ours."

"I'm a necromancer," I said.

While Selena reacted noticeably—her eyes widened and she mouthed the word *wow*—and even Julian raised his eyebrows, Della Jane didn't react at all. It was almost as if this wasn't news to her at all.

Then I remembered the invitation for us to come to Caudry in the first place had actually come from Della Jane, through Leonid Murphy. Between his sketchy history and his recent suicide, I wondered what he'd told Della Jane about us that had made her so excited to invite us here.

My stomach began to sour—the painful acid that seemed to accompany danger, like the monster in the woods. Della Jane's eyes settled on me—her blue eyes as hard and cold as ice—and

I realized that she knew. Leonid must've told her exactly what we really were in the carnival.

But that didn't explain why she'd invited us here, or what that had to do with the monster in the woods, or why she was afraid of anyone finding out they were werewolves.

"Mara?" Selena asked, and by the expectant look on her face, I guessed that she'd been asking me something.

"A necromancer means she can talk to the dead," Gabe answered for me.

"I'm sure the dead have all sorts of interesting things to say," Della Jane commented, her warm Southern drawl doing nothing to soften the venom in her voice. "But I thought you came here to talk about us and our little family secret."

Gabe leaned forward, resting his elbows on his knees. "I just feel like what's happening out in the woods with that thing—it has to be related."

"Why on earth does it *have* to be related?" his mom asked. "Maybe it is a dog or just an honest-to-goodness coyote."

"No, I saw it. It's . . ." Gabe's forehead crinkled as he tried to find the words to describe it. "It's like a wolf made out of a black hole and mixed with a dragon and the devil."

Della Jane offered up a shrug of her narrow shoulders. "That doesn't sound like a werewolf at all."

"Yeah," Selena agreed. "The only three wolves we know around here are me, you, and Mom, and you know that none of us would ever do that."

"I know it's not you guys, and I'm not even saying it's a werewolf," Gabe explained. "When I was fighting it, I felt like it was draining my energy from me. But not in a human sort of way, like it was taking my *powers*. And with everyone in the carnival having extraordinary abilities, I'm worried it might be hunting them because of their powers."

"Gabe, don't you think if I heard of something like that I would've told you about it?" Della Jane asked. Her tone had a sense of reasonability and civility to it, but there was a harsh undercurrent of patronization. "Warned you to stay away from it?"

"But you have been warning him to stay away from the carnival, haven't you?" Selena asked, turning her inquisitive gaze on her mother.

"That's just because I didn't want him getting too attached to a girl who's leaving, but I can see that's already too late," Della Jane explained with a sigh.

"So you haven't heard anything at all? Uncle Beau never said anything?" Gabe pressed.

Della Jane held up her finger toward him and snapped, "Don't bring your uncle Beau into this nonsense."

"But it hasn't even been a year since he killed himself and now—" Gabe began.

"He did not kill himself. It was an accident," Della Jane insisted.

"—is the time you used to come back for his parties," he went on, ignoring his mother's protests. "He always had his big parties in March, and you'd come to visit him, and leave me and Selena at home, because you said they were no place for kids."

"They weren't any place for kids," Julian interjected. "They weren't even a good place for adults."

Throughout the exchange so far, Gabe's father hadn't said

anything really. He'd mostly rubbed his chin and stared off into the yard, as if he wanted to stay out of all of this as much as possible.

"Your uncle has nothing to do with this, so just leave it alone," Della Jane warned him.

"But Mom, why can't we just talk about this?" Gabe asked, growing exasperated. "What if you know something and you don't even realize it?"

"You're worried about your girlfriend?" Della Jane attempted a new approach and softened her voice. "How about this? She can stay with us tonight. I can make up one of the guest rooms and then you won't have anything to worry about. We've never been attacked here, and we have three wolves to protect her if anything comes."

Gabe turned to look back at me, placing his hand on my knee exposed below the hem of my dress. "I know that doesn't fix anything, but it would keep you safe."

"I . . ." I faltered. Everyone's eyes were on me now, and I struggled to choose my words carefully. "I appreciate the offer, but I can't leave behind my family and friends. Unless they can all stay here, I can't."

Della Jane held up her hands, like there was nothing more she could do. "I'm sorry, Gabe, but I can't extend that offer to a group of traveling strangers." Then, abruptly, she stood up. "And now I've said all that I can. This week has been long, and I think I'm going to lie down."

She offered me the thinnest of smiles before turning and walking back in the house. The screen door slammed behind her, making me jump.

"Dad, can you talk to her?" Gabe implored him. "She knows the curse better than anyone."

Julian leaned forward, taking an otherwise untouched glass of soda from the table. "I think you need to let this one alone, Gabe, and it's best if you ask your friend to leave."

53. crossed

Gabe offered to give me a ride home, after apologizing profusely for his mom, but I insisted on walking. I needed time to clear my head and make sense of it all. But the long walk didn't help much. I arrived back at my Winnebago with clothes and hair dampened by the mist, and just as confused as ever.

We didn't even bother opening up the sideshow part of the carnival. Doug Bennet stuck around, running a few games and rides on the midway, but even he'd lost a good chunk of his workers. Nobody wanted to work around here with an unknown creature stalking us.

Most of the sideshow had left, except for those who literally didn't have a cent to their name. Gideon worked on arming them, while my mom spent the afternoon with her head buried in books, trying to find incantations to protect us.

I'd gotten out her book of demonology and sat on the bench across the table from her, hoping to see if I could figure out what exactly this monster was. Mom hadn't been able to find anything useful, so she'd resorted to her old deck of tarot cards for answers.

She flipped over a few cards, staring down at them furtively, and without looking up, she asked, "What is his secret?"

"What?" I tried to look at her cards, but she'd already begun scooping them up and shuffling them again.

"Gabriel. He's hiding something. You know what it is?"

I closed the book and set it down on the table, buying myself some time before I decided to answer truthfully. "Yes. He's a werewolf."

Mom inhaled through her nose, then tossed her head from side to side, thinking. "Werewolves can be good people, but they make dangerous suitors. Their passion isn't always easily controlled."

"You've known werewolves before?" I asked.

She nodded. "Your grandma dated one briefly. He was prone to fits of violence, but he was also a drunk, so . . ."

I leaned back, resting my head on the back of the couch. Through the front windshield, I could see that the sun had already set behind the woods. The sky had begun to darken, shifting from pale purples to navy.

Night would be here soon, and then the creature would come, and we still had no idea how to stop it.

"Here, *qamari*, let me do a reading for you," Mom said suddenly, pulling me from my thoughts.

"Do you think we really have time for that?" I asked. "I mean, we only have a couple hours to figure out how to stop the creature."

"*That* is why I'm doing the reading," Mom corrected me,

and handed me the deck of cards. "Shuffle the deck while you think of your question."

As I shuffled the deck, I realized I had too many questions to ask. How do we stop the monster? What is Gabe's mom hiding? Should I stay with Gabe?

"Cut the deck," Mom commanded, so I did as I was told. She had me cut the deck three times, taking a card each time I did, and I laid them out in a three-card spread. My mom set the deck of cards aside and began flipping my cards over.

The first card she turned showed a nude couple in a passionate embrace underneath a large shining sun—the Lovers.

The next card revealed a woman sitting on a throne, draped in fabric of red and gold. The background blazed behind her, as if it was on fire, and she held an ornate scepter in her hand. The card was upside down to me, so it was the Queen of Wands in reverse.

The final card flipped showed a woman wearing a gown that looked as if it was made of the night sky. She was blindfolded, and in one hand she held the scales, and in the other she held a sword—Justice.

"What are the cards telling you?" Mom asked.

"You want me to read them for myself?"

She nodded. "I would like you to try, *qamari*."

I took a deep breath and began, "The Lovers in my past shows the struggle between two choices, the pull between one path and the other. The Queen of Wands in my present shows something cruel and malicious is standing in my way. And Justice in my future means it will all be resolved soon."

"Do you have any sense of how it will be resolved?" Mom asked.

Then, as clear as a bell, I heard Basima in my ear, saying, *Your aim must be true!*

My eyes immediately went to the crossbow, still sitting on the counter in the kitchen where I had left it. Its dark wood seemed to glimmer in the dim light of our trailer, and I went over to pick it up, wanting to feel the weight of it in my hands.

"Where did you say that came from?" I asked. "My great-grandma made it, right?"

"I don't know all the details, only what Basima told me, but yes, your great-grandma Elissar made that sixty-five years ago," Mom explained. "Her first husband was a soothsayer with great power to read the future, and before they were even married, he told her to begin making that weapon.

"Then, one night, a demon attacked her village," Mom went on. "Her husband and her family were killed, but thanks to that crossbow, your grandma managed to save herself."

I had left the bolts in their satchel and hung them off the bench, and my mom reached over and picked them up. She pulled out the bolt, twisting its cold metal in her hands.

"Basima claimed that these were forged from the sword of Henricus Institor, who prolifically hunted demons and witches in the fifteenth century, and then they were dipped into the venom of the black mamba that had been cursed by Elissar herself," Mom expounded.

"So Elissar was very powerful?" I asked.

"Basima thought she was," Mom clarified.

"So . . ." I held up the crossbow. "If this has killed demons before, do you think it could kill one tonight?"

My mom's eyes were hopeful, but her lips were pursed in an uncertain line. There really would be only one way to find out.

A knock at the door interrupted my thoughts, and I set the crossbow down to answer it, though I already knew who it was.

Gabe stood outside, his hands in the pockets of his jeans. His fitted New Order T-shirt pulled taut over his broad shoulders, and his chestnut hair was slicked back.

"I know you told me that you have to be here tonight, with your family and friends," Gabe said. "I understand that, but I want to be here with you. If you're fighting tonight, I want to fight beside you."

54. omen

If you're gonna be here, then we're putting you to work" was my mom's response to Gabe's offer, and she meant it.

First she sent us with with herbs and powder to put circles around everything that needed to be protected. As we walked around the campsite, Gabe slipped his hand in mine, and I realized what a strange thing it was that, at this point in my life, preparing for a monster attack could double as a date.

"I hope you don't mind that I'm here," Gabe said quietly. We were at the edge of the campsite, with the crescent moon lighting the sky above us, as I carefully sprinkled the white powder of ashes and gypsum.

"I don't *mind.*" I cinched up the pouch of powder so I could give Gabe my full attention. "I just don't want you getting hurt."

"I don't want you getting hurt, either," Gabe replied with a smile. "That's part of the reason why I came here."

"What's the other reason?"

"Well, if this is your last night in Caudry, I want to spend it with you." He bent down, kissing me gently on the mouth.

"Mara!" Mom yelled from the other side of camp, destroying the moment. "Take Gabriel to Gideon's trailer and get a weapon!"

"There isn't time for kissing now," I said. "But when this is all over, we'll finish this."

When we got in the trailer, Gideon was poring over the grimoire, trying to find something that my mom may have missed. Hutch sat beside him, polishing his sword, and offering up propositions about how to handle demons and monsters. Most of them seemed as if they were based on something he'd seen in movies or read in comic books.

Gideon barely glanced up when Gabe and I came in, and he motioned at the open trunk and told us to have at it. I knelt beside the trunk first, carefully pulling out various weaponry and handing it to Gabe for further inspection.

He took a sword from me, and the blade barely touched his skin before I heard a loud sizzle. Gabe winced and dropped the sword back into the box. A red line had been seared across his hand.

"Are you okay?" I asked.

"I'm fine." Gabe rubbed his hand, then shrugged it off. "It must've been made of silver."

"So you're a werewolf?" Hutch asked casually from where he sat at the table.

Gideon looked up long enough to offer an apologetic grimace. "Lyanka came and told us while you were doing the protection rituals."

I mouthed the word *sorry*, but Gabe just shrugged it off. I hadn't told everyone—my mom had, apparently—but in the end, it didn't really matter. We all had secrets here.

"Yeah, I'm a werewolf," Gabe replied.

Hutch cocked his head. "How do I know it wasn't you that attacked me?"

"The thing that attacked you, did it look like a big silver wolf?" Gabe asked.

Hutch seemed to think about it for a moment, then shook his head. "No."

"Well, then it wasn't me. I look like a wolf."

"He does," I agreed. "I've seen him."

Gideon lifted his head suddenly, staring off at nothing, and I was about to ask him what was wrong but then I saw the change. His normally sky-blue eyes began to darken, changing to an indigo so dark it was nearly black.

"What's happening to him?" Gabe asked.

"He's having a vision," I whispered, and put my hand on Gabe's arm.

"Do you want me to get your mom?" Hutch offered, looking at Gideon warily.

"Just give him a minute," I said.

It only lasted a few seconds, with Hutch, Gabe, and me all watching him with bated breath. Gideon remained stoic, as if in a trance, and then the color in his eyes began to fade. He breathed in deeply, and his whole body relaxed.

"What'd you see?" Hutch asked.

"It's hard to explain." Gideon blinked several times, as if clearing his vision. "But it's coming for us, and it's very hungry."

As soon as the words left his mouth, a howl echoed outside. I'd heard dogs howl before, but this was different. It sounded more like a force of nature, like a crack of thunder.

"Oh shit," Gabe groaned. "My mom is here."

55. the queen of wands

When I followed Gabe outside, his mother was standing in the center of the campsite.

Everyone had come out to see what the commotion was about—my mom stood in front of our trailer, pulling her shawl more tightly around her; Roxie and Luka sat on the table outside Luka's trailer; and Gideon and Hutch followed Gabe and me outside, staying a few feet behind us as we approached Della Jane.

Barefoot and without any jewelry, she appeared strangely subdued as the wind blew through her blond curls. Despite her small stature, tonight she gave off an aura of something much more powerful.

"Gabe, you need to come home."

He shook his head. "No. I'm staying here to fight with them. If you're worried about me, you can stay and help."

"This isn't a discussion. You are coming home with me right

now, Gabe," Della Jane commanded, and her voice twisted with a guttural growl.

"You can't just drag me out—" Gabe began, but I saw the look in her eyes, the one I'd seen at their house this morning.

"You know," I told Della Jane, interrupting Gabe. "You know what's going on here."

Her eyes flicked over to me, only for a second. "I know it's not safe for my son."

"No, Mara's right," Gabe realized. "You know exactly what's going on here, and I won't leave until you tell us."

"This isn't how I wanted to tell you," Della Jane admitted before taking a deep breath. "Before we moved back here, I told you that we needed to come to take care of the Brawley legacy. You thought I just meant the curse and the house, but it's much more than that. We're the keepers of the Kirpka."

Gabe shook his head, not understanding. "The Kirpka?"

"The Kirpka are demons," Della Jane explained. "Every thirteen years, a Kirpka will rise from the Nukoabok Swamp to feed, growing more powerful on the days leading up to the vernal equinox."

"What do they eat?" Gabe asked, but I already knew the answer.

Roxie had actually been the first to figure it out, that whatever was stalking the campsite wasn't just seeking out a meaty snack to munch on. They wanted to feast on our flesh and our powers.

"They feed on the paranormal beings that coexist with humans," Della Jane said, attempting to gloss over the fact that the demons wanted to eat *us*. "The Kirpka help maintain a balance on the earth, so humans aren't overpowered by those with superior abilities."

"Holy shit." Gabe put a hand to his mouth and took a step back from his mother. "You brought the carnival here to feed them."

Della Jane tried to step toward him, but he moved back in revulsion. For a moment, she let her hand hang in the air, but as she let it fall to her side, she looked utterly heartbroken.

"It's not like that, Gabe," Della Jane pleaded with her son. "They exist whether we help them or not, but now we have some say, some control, so they don't hurt us."

"We're paranormal too!" He motioned between himself and his mom. "How can you possibly be working for them?"

"God is good, but the devil is not so bad to those he likes," I whispered, repeating the line I'd heard from Luka.

"I'm not working for them!" Della Jane insisted.

"You *feed* them innocent people!" Gabe countered with a low growl.

"No, Gabe, you're twisting it. This is our legacy, to protect our family—"

"That's what all the parties were about with Uncle Beau, weren't they?" Gabe cut her off, his lip curling back in disgust. "He was traveling all over looking for people like us. And those big parties he had, that's when he sacrificed them to the Kirpka?"

"We don't sacrifice them," Della Jane tried again. "It's the Kirpka that—"

"You bring them here like lambs to the slaughter in exchange for your safety!" Gabe shouted. "How is that anything other than a sacrificial offering?"

367

"Gabe, you don't understand," Della Jane said, trying to explain. "This isn't how I wanted to tell you. It wasn't supposed to be like this. Beau was supposed to help explain to you and teach you, so you could take over for him. But then last year he said he couldn't handle it anymore, and I tried to reason with him."

"And he killed himself because he grew a conscience," Gabe realized.

Gideon cleared his throat. He'd been standing beside us, but now he came up closer, trying to catch Della Jane's attention.

"This is all well and good, and you can sort out your family dynamics later," Gideon said. "Right now I need to know what we can do to stop them."

Della Jane rubbed her temple. "You're not listening to me. The Kirpka cannot be stopped! That's why we made this pact with them centuries ago."

"She's lying," Selena said, appearing from the shadows at the edge of camp. She walked toward us, barefoot in a sundress, with her black hair flowing wildly.

"Selena!" Della Jane gasped. "What are you doing here?"

Selena glared at her mother. "Dad told me what's really going on and about the Kirpka."

"He doesn't know what he's talking about." Della Jane tried futilely to reason with her. "You shouldn't be here."

Selena continued walking toward us, giving her mother a wide berth until she stood beside Gabe.

"He told me that the Kirpka accepted the deal because were-wolves are hard to kill and they don't like fighting us," Selena explained. "So I'm here to help Gabe and Mara."

Then I felt it. My stomach soured, creating a painful burning pit inside me, and a gust of wind came up—strong and cold. Even the campers began to tremble. The powder I had so carefully sprinkled around the campsite filled the air, and when the moonlight hit it, it sparkled like glitter.

I shook my head. "It's too late. The Kirpka is coming."

56. vortex

I bolted across the campsite and practically dove into my Winnebago. I grabbed the crossbow off the counter, but when I went for the satchel, I accidentally knocked it to the ground, sending the arrows flying to the floor.

As I scrambled around to gather them, the screen door slammed shut behind me.

"Mara," my mom said breathlessly. "You should leave."

"No, I can't," I said as I crawled under the table to grab the last of the arrows, and it was everything I could do to keep from throwing up. It felt like I'd been punched in the stomach.

"You can go with Gabe in his car and drive far, far away from here," Mom pleaded with me.

I shook my head. "No, Mom, I can't, because it's too late. It's already *here*." I put the bolts back into the satchel and dropped it over my shoulder.

She grabbed my shoulders, forcing me to face her and see the terror in her eyes. "Remember the incantations I taught you. They will save you, *qamari*."

Roxie started shrieking, so I had no time to say anything more. I grabbed the crossbow and dashed outside.

A strange darkness seemed to have descended over the campsite. It felt as if nothing existed outside of this circle. The streetlamp had gone out, and the bulbs in the Christmas lights that had been strung around camp popped. The wind raged on, not strong enough to blow us away, but leaves and debris flew around. Campers rattled, and it sounded as if the earth had begun to hum.

It was like we were being sucked into a vortex of darkness.

"It's here!" Roxie shouted from her perch with Luka outside his trailer, but at first, I couldn't see anything.

In the very center of the campsite, Gideon, Gabe, Hutch, Della Jane, and Selena had formed a loose circle, their eyes darting around the ever-growing shadows. Out of the corner of my eye, I would see it for a second, but then it would be gone again.

I didn't really see the Kirpka, not until it grabbed Selena and she let out a bloodcurdling scream.

57. monstrous

As the Kirpka tore into Selena's flesh, I truly saw it for the first time.

It had four legs, but it used two as arms as it grabbed onto Selena. The limbs were slender and covered in inky black scales, and the long fingers ended in hooked talons. The body appeared to be covered in daggerlike fur, resembling the quills of an angry porcupine. The demon's head was massive, with an elongated snout filled with rows of razor-sharp teeth.

Even from where I stood, I could smell the sulfur radiating off the creature. But it was its eyes that made my blood run cold.

It had four eyes across its face, and they were like portals to another world. They weren't black, but rather devoid of color. They sucked out all the light and life, and when I looked the demon directly in its eyes—only for a split second—I could see the underworld inside them.

Della Jane screamed and her human voice transmorphed

into the bay of a wolf. She jumped, and as she did, her flesh began tearing away as silver-and-bronze fur pushed out through it. Her body stretched, her dress tore off, and her golden curls shifted into pointed ears.

By the time she landed, she was on all fours—a massive, snarling wolf.

She charged at the Kirpka, and as soon as she collided with it, the demon seemed to dematerialize. While it had been attacking Selena, its form had appeared real and permanent, but it was on the move again, so it'd returned to its blurred shadowy form.

As Della Jane tangled with it, it was as if she was pulled into the darkness—her own fur becoming a mixture of darkness and shadow. Hutch picked up Selena, carrying her toward Luka's trailer, where she could be out of harm's way.

Della Jane cried out in pain, and within seconds, Gabe had shifted from human to wolf—fur ripping apart his clothing.

The two of them against the demon seemed promising at first. But it was hard to see exactly what was happening—tufts of fur flew up into the air, snarls echoed through everything, and the shadow of the demon hid them.

Then the Kirpka threw Della Jane across the campsite, sending her flying into Roxie's damaged Airstream where she collapsed onto the ground. Blood soaked her bronze fur, and she let out a plaintive whimper.

If two werewolves couldn't handle it, I didn't know how Gabe could on his own.

Gideon must've had the same train of thought I did, because he took aim at the swirling mass of fur and darkness that was fighting at the edge of camp. That's when I realized he was pointing the Luger full of silver bullets.

"Gideon, no!" I shouted, and dove at him, but I reached him a second after the gunshot cracked through the air.

Gabe yelped and fell to the ground.

58. the devil

The Kirpka began circling the campsite again, trying to draw us into the center where it would be easier to pick us off.

The shadow hit Hutch first, but it spit him out just as quickly—probably realizing that Hutch had no supernatural powers. He flew through the air and landed in front of my Winnebago, moaning and bleeding, and my mom immediately rushed to his side.

We couldn't let the Kirpka keep going at us, or we'd all be dead soon.

"Roxie, light it up!" I shouted. I stood in the dead center of the camp, holding my crossbow up and waiting to take aim.

Roxie's powers hadn't been working well since we'd gotten to Caudry, and her first attempt at a fireball was only a plaintive little puff of fire. But as the Kirpka took a turn charging at her, she tried again, and this time a huge fireball burst from her hands.

The demon snarled and jumped back from it, but for a split second, the creature was fully visible. I fired a bolt at it, but it leapt out of the way and my arrow landed in the dirt.

Hurriedly, I reloaded the crossbow, and Roxie's bright blue burst of fire revealed the demon in the shadows. I shot at it again, but it was too fast. My hands were trembling, and I didn't know if I could aim and shoot fast enough to hit the demon.

It was circling closer to me, so when Roxie sent a fireball toward it, the heat from the flames blew my hair back. When it went dark again, it attacked me.

I couldn't see it—I only felt the razor-sharp talons burning in my side as it threw me to the ground. I rolled onto my back, ignoring the pain as best I could. My nose was filled with the creature's pungent sulfurous scent, and the whole world went quiet.

It was just me and the demon standing over me, with its eyes trying to suck in all my energy. I could literally feel the life being pulled from me, like a darkness seeping through my skin. Drool dripped down from its teeth, landing on my skin like scalding water.

The crossbow felt like ice in my hands, and I lifted it up.

As I said *"Vade retro me tenebris,"* I heard Basima's voice with mine, speaking through me. The demon snarled, and I aimed the crossbow between its eyes and pulled the trigger.

The sound it made when the arrow struck was like a thousand screams erupting at once. Like every soul it had ever eaten crying out in pain.

I clamped my hands over my ears, certain that my eardrums would explode.

Bright white light began shining from the creature, through its eyes and the gaps between its scales. But the light kept growing, until it was completely engulfed in it.

The Kirpka let out one last angry howl before exploding into pitch-black ashes that rained down on us.

59. cleanse

My ears were still ringing from the Kirpka's death cries, and I glanced around the camp, trying to make sure everyone was okay, but then my eyes landed on Gabe.

He'd returned to his human form, lying on his side, and I crawled toward him, ignoring the burning pain from the Kirpka's claws. He looked peaceful and still, with bloodied wounds marking up his bare skin, but it was the gash with burnt edges on his temple that scared me.

"Gabe?" I whispered thickly, and his flesh felt unusually cold as I touched his arm. *"Gabe?"*

Then slowly, his eyes fluttered open, dark golden and confused.

"You're alive," I gasped in relief, and without thinking, I kissed him quickly and roughly on the mouth.

"Is it over, then?" Gabe asked.

I nodded. "I think so."

He sat up, wincing as he did, and touched at a particularly

nasty-looking wound on his temple. It was a long bloody cut across his head, leaving a thin bald line in his hair, but flesh around it had turned purplish and it had blisters as if it was burned.

"Did somebody shoot at me with a silver bullet?" he asked, touching the wound gently. "At least it just grazed me, or I might be dead."

"Selena!" Della Jane wailed, breaking through our moment.

I looked back to see Della Jane kneeling over her daughter's bloody body. My mom had wrapped a shawl around Della Jane, covering her naked body, but she was too busy sobbing to notice.

"Oh no," Gabe whispered. He tried to stand up, but his legs gave out from under him. "Can you get some clothes, and help me over to my sister?"

I did as I was told—rushing over to borrow a pair of jeans and an old T-shirt from Gideon. When he saw my own injuries, Gideon insisted on helping Gabe. After I brought the clothes to Gabe and he changed as quickly as his pain would allow, Gideon helped him to his feet.

"I can handle it from here," Gabe said, letting go of Gideon and hobbling across the grass to where his mother knelt sobbing.

"My baby, my poor baby," Della Jane cried, brushing Selena's hair back from her face. "Wake up."

"Mom," Gabe said gently, and put his hand on her shoulder. "She's gone."

Della Jane recoiled from his touch. "And that's your fault! None of this would've happened if you hadn't gotten involved with these people!"

Gabe stepped back as if he'd been slapped.

"I did what I had to do, so I could keep you all safe!" Della Jane stared up at him with tears streaming down her face. "Why did you have to ruin it?"

"You made a deal with the devil, and you didn't think you'd get hurt?" he asked, sounding as if he was fighting back his own tears.

"And this is all for nothing," Della Jane went on in a trembling falsetto. "What if others come? What will I do then?"

60. the world

The red-and-white flashing lights broke up what little semblance of peace had fallen, as morning descended on the camp.

All of us were battered and sore, though our wounds had been tended to. Most of the mess and the aftermath of the battle against the Kirpka had been cleaned up. Gabe had eventually gathered his mom and his sister, deciding they could come up with a better explanation for her death away from here.

We'd gone about packing up and getting ready to leave. Hutch and I hadn't been much help, since we were both nursing serious injuries. Mom kept whispering incantations under her breath as she dressed my wound, insisting that I needed the help of the afterlife.

I had been helping where I could, pulling up stakes outside the campers, when the black-and-white police car rolled to a stop in the center of the camp. It was nearly a minute before Deputy Bob Gendry finally hauled himself out, holding a thick manila envelope. He surveyed the campsite through his aviators and grimaced as Gideon walked toward him.

"What seems to be the problem today?" Gideon asked.

"Well, I'm here on behalf of the town of Caudry." Bob cleared his throat, and it sounded like it pained him to be cordial to us. "You were promised a salary for your 'work' "—he paused to do air quotes—"so I'm here to deliver your fee."

He held the envelope out toward Gideon. Gideon eyed him for a moment, unsure if this was a trick, but since it didn't seem to be one, he took it. Then the deputy took off his sunglasses, so we could see the disgust in his eyes.

"I don't know what the hell happened between you and the Alvarados, and I don't care," Deputy Bob said. "I'm certain the tragedy that's befallen young Miss Selena had something to do with you, but since Della Jane has the sheriff in her back pocket and she's insisting that we let you go, well, then that's what I have to do."

"We'll be out of here just as soon as we're finished loading up," Gideon assured him.

"I have a message from Della Jane, though," Bob continued. "She said that if you ever step back into Caudry again, she will take care of you herself. And though she didn't ask me to, I will be happy to help her."

Gideon nodded once, but didn't say anything more, because there was nothing to say. Once the deputy had gotten into his car, Gideon went back to loading up the trailers.

Hutch and Roxie were putting the finishing touches on Roxie's trailer—which basically meant duct-taping anything that was coming loose. She'd have to drive slow, but it'd be doable.

We finished packing up quicker than we ever had before, and Gideon gathered everyone to go over the plan—where we'd stop for gas, how we'd divvy up the money, where we were meeting up.

But since my mom was driving, and I knew we'd just follow Gideon there, I didn't really need to listen. I walked away from them to the edge of the camp, staring out toward the road.

"I don't think he's coming," Roxie said, pulling me from my thoughts. She stood beside me and lit a cigarette. "You can't really blame him, either. He lost his sister, and his whole life is in shambles."

"I know. But I was hoping I would see him one last time."

"Mara?" my mom called from behind me. "We should get going."

I was just about to turn back when I saw it. A shiny red dot barreling down the road toward us. My heart caught in my throat as Gabe drove his Mustang right up into our campsite.

The T-top was down, so the wind had ruffled his chestnut hair. He'd barely parked the car before he leapt out, jumping over the driver's-side door, but he took slow, deliberate steps over to me.

"I was afraid I wouldn't get to say good-bye," I said around the lump in my throat.

"Actually, I didn't come here to say good-bye." He took my hand in his, and his eyes were soft and hopeful. "I wanted to know if I can come with you."

I was too startled to say anything for a moment, but I finally managed to get out a meek "What?"

"I know it's sudden, and if you guys don't have room—"

"We always have room," I replied quickly, reciting Gideon's motto. "But what about your family? Your life?"

He looked down at the ground. "I don't have a life here, and my family is . . ." He chewed the inside of his cheek for a moment. "My family's been doing some pretty despicable things for a long time, and I want to put as much distance between me and them as I can."

"What if you change your mind?" I asked.

He laughed darkly. "I don't think I will, but if I do, there's plenty of roads that lead back here, and plenty of phones to call home."

"Are you sure you wanna do this?" I asked, barely able to hide the excitement in my voice.

"I've never been more certain of anything," he replied.

Still holding his hand, I led him back to where my mom and Gideon were talking outside the Winnebago.

"Gabe wants to come with us," I said, and neither of them looked surprised.

Gideon nodded once. "We've always got room, but we should get moving. I wanna get out of this place as soon as we can."

"You can ride with him, if you want," Mom offered. "And we'll discuss sleeping arrangements when we get to Houston."

That was all the encouragement we needed, and we hurried back to his car. The Mustang drove faster than the motorhomes, so we sped on ahead. It wasn't until we were on the long bridge that led out of Caudry, over Lake Tristeaux, that the ice in my chest finally dissolved completely, and I relaxed into the seat.

Gabe looked over at me, grinning, and that glint of something devilish and dangerous sparkled in his eye, and I knew he'd be up for anything. We could follow each other to the ends of the earth and back.